THE **TANTALUS** LETTERS

A NOVEL

LAURA OTIS

THE TANTALUS LETTERS
A NOVEL

iUniverse books may be ordered through booksellers or by contacting:

iUniverse
1663 Liberty Drive
Bloomington, IN 47403
www.iuniverse.com
844-349-9409

ISBN: 978-1-6632-0209-3 (sc)
ISBN: 978-1-6632-0208-6 (e)

Library of Congress Control Number: 2020914772

Print information available on the last page.

iUniverse rev. date: 08/31/2020

PART I
WINTER

No neuron is more than five to ten synapses
away from any other neuron.

—M. P. Stryker

Josh left for Israel today. "I'm taking them to Israel," he said. I wonder how his wife would put it: "He's taking us to Israel"? I picture them on the plane, in the night, after many hours, the kids finally quiet, the dull roar of the air, the chill, that blue felt thing they call a blanket. He falls asleep against her shoulder, all that outrageous brown frizz crushed against her neck. As his thoughts scatter in the darkness, does he think of me? I doubt it. He should be out of reach for at least a month.

Funny, it shouldn't matter where he is, New York, Tel Aviv, or cruising at 33,000 feet. I can only talk to him in cyberspace. It's as if there are three levels with this guy. First, real life, dressed, face-to-face, the most distant, everywhere people watching. We can talk but say nothing, and we don't dare risk a look.

The second level, the intermediary one, is email. Even with this one, there are servers and hackers and I don't know what all who can supposedly read the stuff, so it's not safe. We have to write to each other in code, he says. So I send in-jokes, metaphors, French, recurring images, loose references, until it's all like a dream. What he sends, I couldn't say whether it's code or a testosterone screen, but if it's passion, it's the most muted passion I've ever seen. Email magnifies my passion in translation, like a sprayer on a hose. On his hose, it's a heavy foot that slows the flow to a trickle. Out of the email valve I pour enough words to keep me sane, all the words that bubble up like lava when I rerun the images of level 3. Since the last time I saw him, it would be most accurate to say that the images run me. They're in control, like a virus. They use my life to spread themselves.

Level 3 is bed. Can I say that one is the most real? It drives the other two, gives them their reason for being. It's never more than a few hours, like some time window that opens between parallel universes, briefly, only briefly. I've never known anything like it, that window.

The first time I saw Josh was during a talk I gave on *Tess of the d'Urbervilles* and female desire. I was saying how Hardy keeps dwelling on her mouth, when I looked up and saw him studying me intently. He wasn't just looking. His eyes seemed to be focused on my own mouth, analyzing the way it formed words until I got so self-conscious, I could hardly talk. I felt myself blushing, burning under that laser gaze. When the session ended, I waited for him to introduce himself and was surprised when he didn't. He stood over in a corner with a whole bunch of people, and they doubled over laughing at something he said. He seemed to know everyone in the room except for me.

Then, as I was talking to one of the other panelists, I felt a hand on my shoulder, and I tensed. Somehow he had snuck up behind me. I don't know how, because I thought I was watching him the whole time. "Hi, I'm Josh," he said, and he asked me to go to lunch with him. We talked for two hours, fast, excited talk, books and theory and New York, one tangent after another. He never mentioned a wife or kids in all that time, although I did see the ring on his finger. "Lee Ann," he said, "that's too much name for a woman your size, you got a one-word body."

I blushed. I never blush. I don't know what it is with this guy that he can make me blush like that. Never fails either. He said that he would call me Leo because I looked like a hungry cat. "Leo," he said, "would you come up to my room with me now, would you do that?" He was looking at me with that penetrating stare, direct, intense, but full of laughter. I had known him for two hours. "Would you do that, Leo?" I realized I was trembling all over, but especially in my lips. This had never happened to me before. I mean, guys have come on to me, but not point-blank like this. This was chutzpah the like of which I'd never seen, and I loved him for it. His eyes hadn't left my lips, as though they were hoping to catch my answer in the process of formation. I thought of *Gone with the Wind*, of Scarlett in mourning at the bazaar. Rhett Butler bids a hundred dollars in gold to dance with her, and Dr. Meade says, "She will not consider it, sir." Then, ringing out across the great hall of colored hoopskirts, comes Scarlett's voice: "Oh, yes ah will!" That line has become my motto in life, and that's what I told him, oh, yes ah will.

Actually, that's not what I said. What came out of my mouth was "Let's go." We tried not to run down the corridor. When the elevator doors slid closed, he said "C'meah" and, without waiting for me to obey, pulled me right up against him. It was pure, aggressive concupiscence, his tongue sliding neatly, startlingly into my mouth. "Wow," he breathed when the warning ding of the elevator forced him to push me away. That was the first time, a lost afternoon of violent interpenetration. We've done it every year since, four years, same meeting, same machinations, same time window opening between two universes that explode when they come into contact. Josh's hands are always so confident, as though they have a right to be on me, as though they belong on my thighs, where he says he's been imagining them all year. It's the thought of him fantasizing about me all day that turns me on. But that isn't the best part of it. I open my mouth to speak, and he's saying what I was going to say. Everything he tells me about him, it's as if I already know it, and he knows everything about me. I've never felt so close to anyone. When we're lying next to each other, we are wide, wide open, and he tells me everything he feels. His hair is so much softer than it looks, sweet, springy brown stuff.

God, I wish I were that neck he could fall asleep against. That's my dream, to fall asleep next to him and wake up with him. I never have: he kicked me out as usual this year when the fear set in and the time window slammed shut. I don't blame him. He was probably thinking about his kids. That leaves email—or it did until now. So I subject you to my images, if you can take it. If you talk about someone when he's not there, is it a kind of revenge? How is the lab? Is there a winter solstice in California?

19:22, 17 DECEMBER 1996
FROM: REBECCA FASS
TO: LEE ANN DOWNING

I KNOW WHAT YOU MEAN ABOUT THE LEVELS. I SHOULD BE lecturing you to stop thinking about men, especially unavailable men twice removed, but I would only achieve new levels of hypocrisy. I'm in this lab 15 hours a day now, getting ready for this conference in Chicago. But on the oscilloscope screen and the computer screen and even in the kitties' cage in the animal room floats Owen, and I'm running out of strategies to make him go away. The thought of his four-year-old daughter will usually get his face off the screen for a few minutes, long enough for me to write a good caption. Basic fear is pretty good too, fear of screwing up or not finishing this talk on time. Best is someone asking me for help, or better, needing it without asking for it.

I'm worried about Marcia. She's been living with our chair, Killington, and he's reached his average half-life for a relationship, six months. (God, I hope you're wrong about all the people who can read this stuff.) The guy dumped his wife five years ago, and since then he's been going through 23-year-old grad students and lab techs with the glee of a four-year-old smashing sandcastles.

Now it's my grad student. She's been depressed lately, and she's been wearing these really sexy clothes to the lab. I hope she doesn't lose it when he dumps her. I'll tell her what my advisor told me, that men will come and go, but nobody can take your PhD away from you. And to think that they neuter these poor kitties. Last night I got another one of those calls. You can always tell them because there's a silence at first, as if the guy is deciding whether to go through with it, realizing he's going to have to talk to a real person. They start slowly, and you have to humor them because it could always be a legitimate call. This guy last night said, "Uh, hello, is this Dr. Fass?" and I said yes, it was me. But once he knew he had me, he didn't waste time. "You torturer, you criminal, you fucking Nazi," he hissed. "We know what you're doing to those poor cats, sticking needles in their brains! You'll burn in hell, you Nazi bitch! God sees what you're doing!" I hung up at that point. I always wait too long to hang up. I'm so fascinated by the way they think, I can't resist listening even when it hurts so much. They're sick, of course, but you can't help wondering. Maybe I really am as evil as they say. You have to keep an open mind, keep looking at yourself and what you're doing. I wish they wouldn't call me a Nazi, though. I hate when they call me a Nazi.

So having condemned lechery, I wrestle with my own—mud wrestling would be more like it. Chicago is Owen's town, and in three weeks I might jump from level 2 to level 1 and/or 3 like an excited electron achieving a new quantum state. You forgot a level, and I don't know how to classify it: the phone.

Let's see: with level 1, real life, you get vision and hearing, that's pretty good, but no touching and no freedom. With email you get nothing, basically, although the freedom is unlimited. With bed you get it all, the whole system shorts out, and then you get a year of guilt and electrical repairs. I can almost hear Scotty now: "She can't take it, Captain!" But when did Kirk ever pull out because Scotty said she couldn't take it?

Oh, yeah, so anyway, what do we do with the phone? I press 11 digits right now, and I could be talking to Owen, a real voice in real time. The phone should give you the freedom of level 2 and the intimacy of level 3, without touching. But somehow phones are against the rules. I know when I'm in Chicago, my hand is going to be running over those buttons, my prefrontal cortex sending loud, angry signals to the motor centers not to push hard enough to turn my brain's private messages into public electronic ones. Calling Owen would be a violation. His wife lives with him, and his adorable little kid. I can't call him without calling them, no matter what kind of signals I want to send. Do you ever think about the phone? Ever think of calling Josh? Oh—Tony and Marcia are calling me—they're in an interesting cell. Gotta go.

23:30, 17 DECEMBER 1996
FROM: REBECCA FASS
TO: OWEN BAUER

MY GRAD STUDENTS WERE IN THE MOST AMAZING CELL TONIGHT. I think I told you how it works. The kitty's unconscious, eyes open, seeing but not knowing he's seeing. We listen to his visual cortex, sort of like the KGB bugging his brain. It's so crude. Basically, we're sticking a needle into this beautiful, sensitive, exquisitely tuned cell and eavesdropping, deciding in our blundering way what turns it on. We can listen because the electrode is hooked to a speaker—sounds like popcorn when the cell gets real excited, one pop per spike. We turn puffs of ions into sound.

Tonight, we found this neuron that only fires when a bar of light moves diagonally across the screen. Tony kept moving the bar and getting nothing, back and forth, back and forth, and then he set the cell off by accident when he put the flashlight down. After that we tried all sorts of things, circles, spirals, backwards, forwards, but the neuron liked only diagonal sweeps. Why would a cell do that? It's enough to make you believe in God.

Then the neuron died. I could see the potential creeping up from −80 mV, all the bad positive ions seeping in. We were ripping the membrane with our pushy electrode, and we killed the cell. A lot of times I feel worse about the cells than I do about the cats. It seems like we can either know a cell and kill it, or let it do its thing and know nothing. I'm a knower, of course, but I hate trashing things. Tonight, I feel like some kind of rapist or serial killer of the mind. What if God is a neuron in the occipital cortex?

Watching that cell die on my oscilloscope screen reminded me of my own mortality. My cells have been keeping the good ions in and the bad ions out for 35 years now, and the moments I've felt most alive have been the ones I've spent with you. I mean no disrespect to Trish, and now to Jeannie. But it seems like such a waste to have these feelings and do nothing with them. I want to see you. Four years ago, in Germany, we bonded, and I knew why I was alive. I would want to be alive anyway, to figure out how the brain works, but that time with you was different from any kind of living I've known before or since.

I'm going to be in Chicago in three weeks, to give a talk at a conference. How do you feel about getting together? We could just have lunch or something. I miss you. It's strange to miss someone you never see, but the memories persist, and part of my mind demands confirmation. My brain wants to compare its images to reality and be assured they came from reality to begin with. What do you say?

18:03, 18 DECEMBER 1996
FROM: OWEN BAUER
TO: REBECCA FASS

OF COURSE I WANT TO SEE YOU. FUNNY, THIS TIME OF YEAR HAS been making me think of Germany too, pitch-dark at eight in the morning, dark again by four, gray in between. I remember you at the Christmas Market, in the dark, trying to figure out which wooden animal to buy. Watching Jeannie grow shows me the distance I've come since then, the way the water grows between your ship and the dock you've left. I still can't believe that I helped make her. She's so smart now, talking for herself, thinking for herself.

It's good to come home to her because work sucks. The damned accelerator is down again, and everyone's pointing fingers at everyone else. Our department head, Rhonda, mainly points at me, and it's going to be a while before I can get any experiments done. Why does this woman hate my guts? Just looking at my face seems to drive her crazy. In the meantime, I'm on the phone, lobbying, ordering, fighting for the chance to do something useful.

Trish is depressed. She gets this way sometimes. Right now, she has a pretty good reason. Her mother back in New Jersey is getting stranger and stranger, and it looks like she's going to need someone to care for her full-time. The other day a friend of her mother's called us because they were out shopping and her mother suddenly started crying because she thought the dog was dead. "We've been out here for three days," she said, "and he hasn't had any food or water." She needs to go to one of these Oliver Sacks guys. You must know more about this than I do. Trish has a sister not too far away, but she and her mother were never on good terms, and someone has to take responsibility. Her father's dead. I want to help her, but it's one of these cases of paralysis where everyone has to agonize for a while before anyone can do anything. I'm trying to be as supportive as I can. Trish may be in New Jersey with Jeannie when you're in Chicago. The temptation is going to be strong. I haven't done this for four years, and I don't want to risk hurting Jeannie. I can't imagine life without her anymore. But I do want to see you. When will you get here? Where will you be staying? Let me know, and I'll see what I can figure out.

11:22, 22 DECEMBER 1996
FROM: JOSH GOLDEN
TO: LEE ANN DOWNING
SUBJECT: THE KEY TO ALL MYTHOLOGIES

HELLO, DARLIN.

Here the sun blasts away, spent the morning at the beach with the kids, writing the cell book in my head. Thinking about *Middlemarch* by the Dead Sea is something to which only Casaubon could relate. Hope I'm not him.

This is the right way to think about cells, contexts and connections. This whole place is a palimpsest, endlessly rewritten, everyone fighting to erase a piece and rewrite it again.

So many people to see, but vacation can't keep me from my favorite drug. Five days out, and here I am in cyberspace. My computer summoned me like a witch doctor calling his zombie.

So I thought I'd wish you a Happy New Year and assuage your New York fears. This ain't the Bronx, darlin, they won't blow us up. Here the streets are safe and the borders are murder.

Looking forward to future contacts, to try in your luscious lock my Key to All Mythologies.

18:30, 23 DECEMBER 1996
FROM: LEE ANN DOWNING
TO: REBECCA FASS

YOUR CHAIR SOUNDS LIKE THE EVIL KING IN THE *TALES OF ONE Thousand and One Nights.* Is it possible he'll run out of women? Maybe to halt his devastation of the female population, we could get Marcia to tell him stories. Would he listen to stories? If we could just keep him with one woman, he would stop smashing the egos of all the female grad students and endangering the future of science. Why does anyone want him anyway? Have you considered saltpeter in his coffee?

Josh is shameless. Finally he writes me something—well, more than suggestive, from Israel no less, with his wife and kids close at hand. But who am I kidding? I totally loved it. You know, I don't even know his wife's name. He always just refers to her as "my wife." I hate when they do that, like "my golf club" or something. There are some things he'll never tell me.

Everywhere I turn, the air is full of whirling words: maturity, sacrifice, character, responsibility. The words and the laws seem so alien to the feelings they're supposed to control. I remember laughing with Josh in bed, holding out our arms one next to the other. His was strong and brown, mine thin and white. They lay so beautifully next to each other, like one hill outlined fuzzily behind another. And then the words: adultery, lechery, harlotry, whore. Yes, I've been reading *The Crucible* again. The words and the images don't go together. It's like some dumb censor put in charge of monitoring art he can't understand.

I ask myself all the time how I got to be such a sleazy whore. Because the truth is that, wife or no wife, I want Josh so badly, it's like physical pain. If I had another crack at level 3, I wouldn't hesitate. 10 years ago, in grad school, I didn't know anyone who was married. If you liked someone, you got to know him better, and if he liked you back, you went straight to level 3. There was no need for level 2 back then, because there were no wives. You could say just about anything you wanted, anywhere, anytime. What have I been doing for the past 10 years? Finishing a thesis, getting a job, writing books, writing articles, reading articles, flying around, giving talks, grading papers, getting tenure. I've always worked at least 60 hours a week. There have been guys, but I've left them without hesitation when they've gotten in the way of my work. Suddenly everyone seems to be married, but the attractions are the same as they were 10 years ago. Except now if you proceed, it's a crime for which they would stone you to death in Kabul. Hence the emergence of level 2.

I remember a time when I was so miserable I wanted to kill myself because no guy wanted me. The truth is, though, I've never been happy living with a guy. At night they dump piles of change on the dresser, and they shed hairs all over the bathroom that are a pain to clean. At some point, they start telling you what a lousy human being you are. You never get enough work done, and within a few months, you feel as though you're not alive. It's like you're trapped in a phone booth watching life happen all around you.

My work makes me feel alive, what I've got spread out on my desk today: *Les Liaisons dangereuses*, Michel Serres, a French dictionary, Nietzsche, a German dictionary, and the latest lingerie catalogue. This last works wonders to keep you from eating or picking at your face while you read. I know that I would hate a husband and child for coming between me and my work. I've always felt best about myself when I'm alone.

Still, the lust is hardwired in. Josh turns me on the way the books turn me on, pure chutzpah, pure intelligence, pure force of words. I wonder what it's like to be his wife. I hate the thought of the sacrifices she's had to make—the work she can't do, the hairs she's had to clean up, the degrading slavery of caring for two children, the times he must have turned on her and yelled about all the things wrong with her. She's had to endure all this, and I just steal some of the good stuff and run. Hurting a wife is like kicking a POW shackled in a prison camp. Yet I can't seem to stop myself. That moment of laughing in the dark, of studying the curves of my arm against his, followed—I didn't tell you this part—by his lips descending to kiss my arm, it's just more real. It would be worth anything to live another moment like that, and I know that if I can, I will.

Don't feel bad about wanting to see Owen. I think this is what we're here on earth to do. I wonder if Killington rationalizes his conquests the same way.

20:21, 30 DECEMBER 1996
FROM: REBECCA FASS
TO: OWEN BAUER

I'M GOING TO BE AT THE WINSTON HOTEL, WHERE THAT ICY green canal crosses Michigan Ave. It scares me to walk over that see-through bridge, but I'm dying to see you. If you still have misgivings, feel free to call this off. I don't want anyone to get hurt by this. I would love to see you, but only if we can do it without causing harm.

12:43, 6 JANUARY 1997
FROM: OWEN BAUER
TO: REBECCA FASS

I AM TORN. TRISH AND JEANNIE WILL BE IN NEW JERSEY, AND she needs me while she watches her mother's mind undo itself. I find it intriguing that the first thing she's lost is the sense of time. Is this something so new, fragile, artificial in us, that it's the first thing to go? Jeannie already understands the difference between three hours and three days. Was it maybe just that her mother used the wrong word and wanted to say "a long time," and "three days" seemed about right?

At any rate, they'll be gone, and it's all too easy. The anticipation has me bathing in memories of you—always so matter-of-fact, even with your ankles on my shoulders. Why did you always cry when—but I can't write this. Two days, and I'll be living it. I shouldn't be. I'm a lousy actor and a lousy liar, and you can't know what it's like to have this happening in your head and not be able to talk about it with a person who's part of you. Trish suspects nothing. I've been talking extra hard about work, all of Rhonda's cracks about funding and productivity. If they don't renew my fellowship, I'm out of a job, living off Trish and hating myself, and renewal depends on Rhonda's recommendation. We're close to having the system up again, and if we succeed, I'll have to work day and night. That's what I told Trish anyway, shifting the balance in favor of her taking Jeannie. It's true—but that's not what I'll be doing.

God, I want to see you. Part of me has been in suspended animation, and it just woke up again. When will you be free?

19:06, 7 JANUARY 1997
FROM: REBECCA FASS
TO: OWEN BAUER

IT'S HARD TO KNOW ABOUT TIMING. THERE ARE MILLIONS OF talks I have to go to and a million people I have to see—not just the competition, but people to talk to about postdocs for Tony and Marcia, who will probably finish in a year or two. I also want a new postdoc, someone to do anatomy when Dawn gets a job. Networking—you know—that's what these meetings are for, and all these people are depending on me. Reinforcing synaptic connections could mean anything from breakfast at 7 to drinks at 11, so I'll have to reinforce mine with you in between. I'm concerned about causing pain by doing this. Are you sure you still want to see me? Feel free to change your mind. My dendrites are tingling, but we can keep it at any level you want. It's your life—you make the call.

22:03, 9 JANUARY 1997
FROM: REBECCA FASS
TO: LEE ANN DOWNING

WELL, THE SLIDES ARE FINALLY DONE, THE TIMING ON THE TALK is 9 minutes 47 seconds, and I'm ready to go. The images that worried me, Dawn's electron micrographs, are gorgeous. You can see everything there is to see when one cortical cell meets another. Dawn is an enigma, quiet, self-possessed, always delivers. She seems tormented by something but won't say what. I know she's politically active, so maybe it has something to do with that. Dawn and Tony have been great this week. Marcia is, well, preoccupied. I'm going to have to do something about this when I get back. It's been a marathon. We all crashed in the lounge for a few hours last night, or this morning I should say, didn't bother to go home at all.

When I go to meetings like this, but more when I write grants, I realize how responsible I am for everyone. If I screw up, if I can't keep the money coming in and the lab going, we're all out on the street. Is this what it feels like to be a mother? Something tells me this is more what it feels like to be a father. I wouldn't know. My own took off with some gorgeous babe when I was young. But you've heard all this before.

Aside from the fact that I have to convince everyone in neuroscience I am seeing synaptic connections form in a blindfolded kitty, the main thing on my mind is Owen. He wants to see me, and Trish and Jeannie will be away. Am I low enough to do this? Sleep with the husband of some poor woman trying to deal with her demented mother? I wonder what her mother's synaptic connections look like. I wonder what mine look like.

What has this woman done to deserve this? When you pit biology against morality, biology always wins. I can't resist the idea of touching Owen again. It's been, let's see, about two years since I've been with a man, and that was a few nights preceded by the other two years since Owen. It's either this or the Orgasmatron. Other men—when I emerge from the lab like a locust, to mate— are like the shadows of puppets in a cave, and Owen is the sun. Once you've seen the sun, that's pretty much it. I wonder how Plato would work the Orgasmatron into his philosophy. I need some sleep. I can't believe I'm going to do this, remembering what my own mother went through. There's no way to justify it. But if he'll do it, I will.

Through all this, I keep thinking of Tony's cell. It fired just for diagonal sweeps. Why? Why would we need a cell that does that? What I'd really like to do is stay here in the lab and look for more of them. Thanks for being there. I'll let you know in a week what happened.

17:22, 14 JANUARY 1997
FROM: LEE ANN DOWNING
TO: JOSH GOLDEN
SUBJECT: FLYING

YO, YOU BACK YET? I NEED TO KNOW IF YOU DO DREAMS. EARLY this morning, I was flying, feeling the most incredible sensation of lift. I must have been coming in from Europe, because I took off over the ocean, and I know I was heading for New York. I flew into a mist swirling so thick I had no more sense of space. Not only could I not tell whether I was headed west, I had no idea whether I was veering up or down into gray waves. But I shot out of the mist at sunrise to find New York shining before me. I touched the Twin Towers as I flew between them, cool, smooth glass against each palm. I almost crashed into the Empire State Building, and I rocketed straight down along the face of it.

As I headed out over Long Island, it became harder to stay airborne, and I had to land several times. I could always rise again, flapping as hard as I could. It was all a matter of faith. Finally, night was falling, and I was getting cold, and I had lost the ability to fly. I asked a man where I was, and he said Belle Meade, and I thought, "Oh, good, that's not far." He said, "I saw you eyeing those golf carts. You can sleep in one of them if you want." I was thinking about it seriously when I woke up.

So, when you're here, shake off the dust and apply your Key to this dream. What does it mean, boss?

11:30, 15 JANUARY 1997
FROM: JOSH GOLDEN
TO: LEE ANN DOWNING
SUBJECT: BACK

YEAH, I DO DREAMS, BUT I CHARGE FOR THEM.
I flew in—you're gonna love this—yesterday morning. Maybe I passed you.

You're built for flying, a hundred pounds of matter threatening to change into energy at any moment, and at least 10% of it is hair.

New Jersey is a bad joke after Israel, a simulacrum, everything a copy.

Coming out of the sun into that mist of yours, I can't orient myself. No fixed point anywhere. Why don't kids have this problem? Just called their friends and ran off.

I sat down at the computer and found you circling, waiting for a sign from the control tower to come in for a landing.

How've ya been? You found any nice young gentlemen to satisfy those appetites of yours?

C'mon, Leo, you know what flying means.

Stay out of golf carts, though. Golf is highly overrated as a transcendental activity offering access to the world of perfect forms. But sleeping in golf carts could be a great way to meet a nice doctuh. I'll have to alert my female relatives to this strategy. Should I also alert the doctors?

18:26, 15 JANUARY 1997
FROM: LEE ANN DOWNING
TO: REBECCA FASS

JOSH IS PISSING ME OFF. HE'S LIKE A PUSH-ME-PULL-YOU, THE WAY he turns me on and tells me to find someone else at the same time. He hits the memory key and the body key, and my system goes crazy the way it does when you hit shift and control at the same time. And then he says to go away and find a nice doctor. What goes on in his head? What does he want? Thank God he's back, at least. The only thing he could do that would really hurt me would be to stop writing.

Our semester is about to start at last, thank God. I hate vacations. I'll be teaching a new course, Sex and Death: Shakespeare, Laclos, Stendhal, Nietzsche, Hardy, and Mann. I can't wait. I get so many ideas from the students, and they love the books so much. Then there's my 19th-century course, and composition, but the Sex and Death class makes life worthwhile. How was the conference? I'm glad you're back too.

19:42, 15 JANUARY 1997
FROM: REBECCA FASS
TO: LEE ANN DOWNING

THE CONFERENCE WAS INTENSE. MARIN'S GROUP AT THE National Institute of Health is doing almost the same experiments we are but getting different results, so there were some tense moments when I had to compare our protocols without giving too much away. There's a guy there named Jacobsen who I think may want to do a postdoc with me, and he's good, so I have to keep him interested.

Underneath all this was the impending meeting with Owen, which turned into a whole night and morning—beautiful and terrible now that it's over. So, racked with guilt, I feel I'm in the right position to size up Josh. The human brain has an astonishing capacity to think two contradictory thoughts at the same time. He wants to have wild, uncontrolled, everlasting, screaming, bestial sex with you. And he wants to be a virtuous, responsible, reliable, respectable father and overall good guy. He wants eternal youth. He wants the power that comes with age. Ever add vectors? When two forces act on a point mass in different directions, the resultant force is the sum of the two component forces. How does it feel to be a point mass? Is it flattering or destructive to have all that energy focused on you? What forces are you exerting on him? You're just about the least passive person I ever met. Sex and Death sounds great. I had forgotten what it was like. Sex, I mean.

19:14, 16 JANUARY 1997
FROM: REBECCA FASS
TO: LEE ANN DOWNING

WELL, I FINALLY DID IT—CONFRONTED MARCIA ABOUT Killington. It was excruciating because he's my boss, and I'm her boss, and I had to reach out to her while maintaining a certain distance. If I do anything to alienate him, he could make our lives hell, and how could I know that, in her condition, she wouldn't tell everyone if I let her know how badly I want to do a John Wayne Bobbitt on him?

Marcia showed up at 10, in spandex, her face all puffy and her eyes as red as a laboratory rat's. She sat at her desk with her face in her hands, so I decided it was time to do something. I called her into my office and told her I was worried about her and wanted to help. The poor girl was terrified I was firing her, and she started

Laura Otis

crying and swore she would work harder, really she would. I lost it then and told her that I knew what the trouble was, and I thought she was wonderful and wanted to keep her here.

Then it came out. He had done it at breakfast, I think the same morning I was soaping Owen's back in the shower. He's been seeing Bonnie, this new grad student from Gordon's lab who started here in September. "Don't hold on to this," he told Marcia, along with some stuff about flow and turbulence and particles and fusion. I think he meant "Don't hold on to me."

Once she got going, Marcia had some interesting things to say about men. "I think what they want," she said, "is to fuck women and then kill us when they're done so that we can't ever bother them again." The force of this thought scared me, and I tried to disagree. What about men who marry, I asked, don't they want to stay with a woman? "Oh, they're exactly the same," she said. "Don't you see? It's just a front. They go out after a few years and start fucking and dumping women same as ever, only now they have the perfect excuse: 'I'm married.' If you protest, you're Alex Forrest from *Fatal Attraction* and you want to boil their fucking rabbit."

There she had me. It was so hard not to blurt out that I had just been with one of these, and not seeing him when I woke up this morning was agony.

"Men are viruses," she said. "I mean, think about it. What's a sperm? DNA in a protein coat, with no means of reproducing itself except with help from a cell. It latches on to the egg, shoots in its DNA, places an order, and we cook a baby—which gets his name when it comes out."

I won Marcia back when I got her to laugh. Given the fucking-and-dumping scenario, I told her, Killington at least deserved points for consistency for having dumped his wife first. So we laughed together, her with her bright red eyes and me with the images in my head that I couldn't let out. I fed her the line about how men will come and go, but no one can take your PhD away from you, but it didn't work as well as I'd hoped—planned lines never do.

I also told her I didn't think all men were bad and that there was still hope. I wanted to hold up Tony as an example. He's been going out with this nice Asian woman from Berg's lab forever, and he seems to treat her well. But this struck me as bad politics, like telling your kid how good her brother is. God, running a lab really is like being a mother. Anyway, Marcia didn't believe me. I told her to stop wearing spandex to the lab because it was making me feel fat. "Now, go get in a cell," I ordered. "Get me one of those diagonal ones." I can't say she's cured, but it helped break the tension.

What I want to know is, is she right? I believe Owen is a good person. He may dump me, but it will be to save his family, not because he's tired of me. Maybe I'm just reassuring myself. What do you think?

What about Josh? I can't believe half the human species is bad. Thinking that would be like hating life itself. Biology runs us and drives us, and monogamy isn't natural. So what should we do about it? Probably we're defining "good" and "bad" all wrong. I'm sure this is what Killington thinks, and Owen too. Being away from him now is like physical pain, as is my knowledge that in yielding to biology, I may have hurt a woman and a little girl. I'm no better than Killington. If I do a John Wayne Bobbitt on him, someone should do a North African job on me.

17:49, 17 JANUARY 1997
FROM: LEE ANN DOWNING
TO: REBECCA FASS

Go, Marcia! I mean, all power to her! She's right, of course, but she's giving only one side. How old is she, 23, 24? Is she going to tell me she's never dumped anybody? She's right; she just needs to cross out "men" and write "people." Who doesn't want to have wild sex with someone but not have to deal with his/her moods, mess, interference, and offspring?

She's got Josh down, all right. He's all male, testosterone out the wazoo. What turns me on with him is the wrestling. He always wants to be in control. He'll entice me in with some flattery or libidinal dare, then push me away, waving his wife and kids like a virtual hero waving a crucifix at a vampire. I write with the knowledge that he can pull the plug at any time and walk away absolutely in the right.

Five years older, and he thinks he's my father—the male thing: you tell him how you feel; he tells you what to do—always ready with helpful advice. I think his heart is good, like Owen's, the way all our hearts are good. He just hates the part of himself, sometimes, that wants to get it on with me, and that translates into hating me. So we do it with words, steal each other's phrases and turn them around, grapple with each other in an exquisite lingual battle of pleasure and pain.

As you get older, people force these roles on you. Josh is a good dad as far as I can tell, does all the things dads are supposed to do: protect, provide, make the call, settle the fights, totally reliable. But this is never enough, and people have to live for themselves too. I see these exhausted people schlepping after their kids—women with faded faces, women who've chopped off their hair and gained 30 pounds—slaves, people without identities. The dads seem no happier, big-bellied, lecturing, teaching, often angry, the women listening vacantly, the kids screaming, bloodsucking monsters draining the life out of their creators.

I refuse to kill myself this way. You can either marry and have kids, or live, and I'm going to live. My friends who've gotten married and had kids, it's as if they've died, or no, it's like invasion of the body snatchers. The people I know are being turned into zombies one by one, their souls displaced and their bodies occupied by aliens who think only of diapers and apple juice. Sometimes I feel like I'm the only one left, with no one to talk to and an army of zombies after me, operated by aliens via remote control.

Yet life is rigged so that if you don't pair up and make babies, it's impossible to find love or even talk to anyone. To have human contact without becoming a zombie, you have to steal intimacy from some poor slave who has already sacrificed her soul to get it. I'm a libidinal gypsy bandit who violates virtually. Cyberspace, level 2, is a valve that lets you bond without violating in fact. As far as Josh is concerned, to recover his virtue, all he has to do is turn me off, and as long as he knows this, he's okay. Josh and I need each other. He's a slave who wants to live a little, and I'm an outlaw who wants to bond temporarily. Who's worse? Neither you nor Killington deserves to be cut. You can't cut the lust out of a person. Lust is what we are. And Marcia is right anyway. How would you define life?

18:01, 17 JANUARY 1997
FROM: LEE ANN DOWNING
TO: JOSH GOLDEN

How would you define life?

23:30, 17 JANUARY 1997
FROM: JOSH GOLDEN
TO: LEE ANN DOWNING
SUBJECT: LIFE

LIFE IS AN ANTHILL SEEPING OUT OF A CRACK IN THE CURB, seething with black crawling things, and a kid kicking it.

Life is all you can eat.

Life is sucking the meat out of a shrimp's tail.

Life is a grease spot that won't come out.

Life is breathing through a shower of black hair in your face.

Life is our dog howling at the fire siren.

Life is kicking.

Life is what kicks back.

19:26, 20 JANUARY 1997
FROM: REBECCA FASS
TO: LEE ANN DOWNING

LIFE IS WRITING TO YOU AND EATING THIS TURKEY SANDWICH while Tony and Marcia set up tonight's kitty. Life is what will happen if I get this grant proposal out in a month. Life is wishing this sandwich tasted like a turkey. Life is the turkey. Life was waking up and realizing Owen was next to me. Life was waking up this morning and knowing he wasn't. Life is wanting more. Life is the cell that fires only for diagonal sweeps.

19:37, 20 JANUARY 1997
FROM: REBECCA FASS
TO: OWEN BAUER

WHAT IS LIFE?

12:37, 21 JANUARY 1997
FROM: OWEN BAUER
TO: REBECCA FASS

FUNNY YOU SHOULD ASK ME THIS. WHO AM I TO JUDGE? I JUST live it.

Trish called to tell me her mother woke her up at 3:30 a.m. and burst into her room fully dressed but with all her clothes on backwards, crying, "I don't know where I am!" It scared Jeannie half to death. Trish had to explain that Grandma is sick and that very old people sometimes don't know what time it is. She's good that way. I don't know what I would have said.

Trish and Jeannie should be back in a day or two. The mother has been officially checked out by a social worker who has to rate her mental fitness. She's on the waiting list for a bunch of homes, and they've found a nurse to watch her. The accelerator is up, and I'm working day and night. I'm trying as hard as I can not to think, but I want you anyway.

19:11, 21 JANUARY 1997
FROM: REBECCA FASS
TO: OWEN BAUER

I HAD NO IDEA I WOULD MISS YOU THIS MUCH. EVERYTHING IN my mind has been rerouted so that all the pathways go through you. I did something the other day I've been putting off for a long time—talked to my student Marcia about getting it together. She's been the most dedicated, hardest-working person you can imagine, but unfortunately, she's been living with our chair, and he's dumped her for this year's model. It's left her devastated, and she hasn't been good for much in a while. I've been determined to pull her out of the nosedive she's in before she crashes and burns. So I did my best.

Through the whole talk, all I could think of was you. I wondered how different I was from my boss, who just sleeps with women when he wants, then leaves them when he wants, without regard for their feelings, or social roles, or politics, or anything. Is he just honest? Are we all like him, just can't admit it? What do you think?

I have to go now, but I will lie down with you in my mind as I have been doing these past few nights and will be doing for many nights to come.

13:13, 22 JANUARY 1997
FROM: OWEN BAUER
TO: REBECCA FASS

I THINK WE ARE LIKE YOUR BOSS, WITHIN LIMITS. THESE LIMITS hit me today when I picked up Trish and Jeannie at the airport. Jeannie was jumping all around, so happy to see me. What hurts the worst is their not knowing. Until now the only thing I've had to keep from Trish is Germany, and that was different somehow, because I went there for a long time, but this time you came here. Why should that make a difference? I can't tell you.

I'm terrified she's going to read my mind, or at least the signs that show what my mind is doing. I've been keeping away as much as possible, feeling safer here in my underground tunnel, less capable of being read. All the face time is scoring points with Rhonda, who feels more powerful if she thinks you're working 16 hours a day because you're afraid of her.

And of course, I think of you all the time. If I were a cartoon, the bubble coming out of my head would have just one thing in it: you all slippery and laughing in the shower, with soap all over you.

All my love,
Owen

9:32, 24 JANUARY 1997
FROM: OWEN BAUER
TO: REBECCA FASS

I'VE TURNED INTO MAXWELL'S DEMON NOW. IT'S LIKE THERE'S A barrier between me and Trish with a tiny window in it, and I sit there perversely falsifying the natural flow of particles. Anything that would normally cost me energy to talk about—work—I let through, and all the particles that would normally get through— lust, misery, all the images that strike me through the day—I occlude. They whiz and bang and ping off the walls of my closed, frustrated brain.

I don't know how much longer I can keep doing this. Trish has asked me many times what's the matter, and I tell her work, Rhonda, fear of losing my job, but she doesn't buy it. She may be a nurse, but she's a better scientist than I am: she knows about controls. Work and Rhonda have been closing in on me for a long time, but I've never shut down like this before. I think I may have to tell her, just tell her and get it over with, for us to have any kind of life together. This is harder than I ever imagined it could be.

18:13, 24 JANUARY 1997
FROM: LEE ANN DOWNING
TO: JOSH GOLDEN

SO YOU WANT TO SINK YOUR TEETH INTO LIFE BEFORE IT KICKS you to death. Am I right?

22:06, 24 JANUARY 1997
FROM: JOSH GOLDEN
TO: LEE ANN DOWNING

YOU'RE RIGHT AS ALWAYS, BABE. I WANNA EAT IT.
And you, darlin, what do you want to do with it?

12:14, 25 JANUARY 1997
FROM: LEE ANN DOWNING
TO: JOSH GOLDEN

I WANT TO READ IT. I WANT TO WRITE IT. I WANT TO INSCRIBE IT with the tip of my pen and the tip of my tongue.

21:30, 26 JANUARY 1997
FROM: JOSH GOLDEN
TO: LEE ANN DOWNING
SUBJECT: TIPS

YOU CAN INSCRIBE ME ANYTIME, DARLIN. YOU CAN WRITE ALL over me.

Your words are a rousing flamenco clatter that makes my middle-aged heart dance.

You remind me of my kids, way too smart for me and inexhaustible.

Give a man a break and go apply all your tips to that book of yours.

7:56, 27 JANUARY 1997
FROM: REBECCA FASS
TO: LEE ANN DOWNING

I'M AFRAID OWEN IS GOING TO TELL TRISH EVERYTHING. IF HE does and destroys their life together, especially that poor little kid's life, it will be my fault. I feel ashamed now, and so depressed. Even that guy Jacobsen's formal request to do a postdoc in my lab couldn't snap me out of it. I can't blame Owen, because I can't know what it's like to come home to someone every day and not talk to her about the monster in your head. I worry about him too. What will happen to him if she leaves him and takes the kid? There's this little old lady in my head who keeps telling me I should have thought of this before the door to my hotel room clicked shut behind us. I still have the nerve to miss him, even now.

19:00, 27 JANUARY 1997
FROM: LEE ANN DOWNING
TO: REBECCA FASS

I DON'T FUCKING BELIEVE HE'S GOING TO TELL HER. I MEAN, what goes on in his head? If you want to talk guilt distribution, I'd say it falls a little more on the guy who indulged his libido despite his wife and kid and is going to make himself feel better with a Chernobyl catharsis. God, why do they even have to exist? If only we could reproduce by parthenogenesis.

Today was a particularly bad day to ask for my opinion, since Josh has suddenly lowered his paternal screen and is waving that cross at me again: back, back, dangerous, monstrous woman! I don't know why I write to him. I'm addicted to it, I guess. Today I want to kick him in his patriarchal—but no, no, I still like him, maybe even love him, in spite of everything. It always hurts so much when he says, "Back!" I even look like a vampire, pale, thin, white skin, black hair, always hungry, and he makes me feel like a monster. Sometimes I feel like I'm a flea on the surface of his life and he's going to squash me.

You have to hand it to him, though. He's frighteningly smart when it comes to having it all, so much smarter and ultimately kinder than your sensitive physicist. He's a genius at keeping things on a certain level, and in the process, he saves not just his own ass but also his wife's and my feelings. If someone ever broke in and read our email, s/he would see a never-ending series of invitations and libidinal jabs on my part, countered by the most adroit and kindhearted deflections on his. I am the aggressor.

Josh would never tell. If it came down to it, he would deny everything and cut me off before I knew what hit me. What no one will see is him pulling me against him, with an insistent strength that surprised me, and saying, "C'meah." He made sure there were no witnesses.

But of the two of them, Owen is the bigger prick. I wish Josh could talk to him and set him straight. Tell the idiot to keep his mouth shut!

22:14, 27 JANUARY 1997
FROM: REBECCA FASS
TO: OWEN BAUER

DON'T DO IT. I MEAN IT. I FEEL TERRIBLE FOR HAVING DONE this to you, and I want to help any way I can. I'm here. Talk to me. Maybe you can let all the fast particles out the back door. I can't know what you're going through, because I've never been married, but I'm sure it would be a disaster to tell. Maybe this state won't last, and the particles will lose energy with time. If we were wrong, it won't help to spill everything all over the place. We can just try as hard as we can not to do it again.

Talk to me, talk to anybody, but not to her. Hang on. I was old enough to see what my mother went through, and I can see what Marcia's going through now. For a woman, no matter how much else she has going for her, it makes her feel erased as a person when her guy wants someone else. You can stop the pain now before it hurts anyone but us. Don't tell her, don't do it!

12:46, 28 JANUARY 1997
FROM: OWEN BAUER
TO: REBECCA FASS

OKAY, YOU'VE CONVINCED ME FOR NOW. I'M GOING TO HOLD OUT. I feel like some kind of pathetic dike holding back a flood. Work just picked up, luckily, and I take it as an omen. Trish has gone into a retaliation withdrawal of her own, angry that I won't open up to her. I see hope. Maybe if I reach out and try to bring her back, she'll forget that I started it, and we can meet in the middle.

Listen, I wanted to ask you about something that I've been wondering about for a long time. You're always talking about being "in" a cell, especially lately since you found this diagonal kind. In physics "in" makes no sense. There's no atom or particle to be "in," just possibilities that something might be in a given space at a given time, and just about anything you find can be smashed up into something smaller. That isn't even it. There ISN'T anything; there isn't any "thing," just very fast associations. You can't be "in" anything, because not only is there no "in," there's no "thing" to be in. I think "in" is a biological idea. Keeping things out that want to get in means staying alive.

What does it feel like to be in a cell? I feel as though you've gotten into me, and I can't decide whether it's a biological "in" or one of these split-second associations. I always turn theoretical when work picks up. Maybe all those particles whizzing around in circles create a field in my brain. Let me know. I'm curious about this one.

19:27, 28 JANUARY 1997
FROM: REBECCA FASS
TO: OWEN BAUER

THANK GOD! I MEAN, THANK YOU FOR HOLDING OUT. I FEEL responsible for putting you through this. It's easy for me. I can just walk away. It sure must be different when you have to come home to someone. Please let me help if I can.

That's a hard question, how it feels being in a cell. What I feel is guilt, but that can't be all I feel, or why would I do it? The first time I ever saw anyone get a cell, I wanted to do that for the rest of my life. It was the smallness, partly—the thrill of being in one cell, one unit of consciousness—but you have a point about the physics. The same thing happens when you get bigger as when you get smaller. Is consciousness the units, or what happens when they talk to each other?

So probably the answer is that I'm an eavesdropping pervert who likes to poke herself into things. But I do feel guilty about it. I don't know. I should ask Marcia. I think she's in a cell now. Or do you want Tony? Do you want a male or a female perspective, or doesn't it matter? What does it feel like to be inside a woman?

19:48, 28 JANUARY 1997
FROM: REBECCA FASS
TO: LEE ANN DOWNING

HE'S NOT GOING TO TELL, AT LEAST NOT NOW, THANK GOD. He really had me scared. I mean, I did this; it is my fault, and I have to face the consequences, but that poor woman and that poor little kid! Owen asked me a weird question. He wanted to know what it's like to be inside a cell. So I asked him what it's like to be inside a woman, and suddenly I had this terrible urge.

What do you say we experiment on the guys? It figures I would come up with this, considering that my whole life is one big experiment, but the question intrigues me. Suppose you ask Josh the same thing, and we compare what we get. This whole desire to penetrate and, as Marcia put it, implant the viral DNA seems so foreign. And yet he has a point; this is kind of what I do. I feel as if I've been exposed. You say Josh is testosterone-poisoned, so I'd like to hear what he has to say. Why would anyone want to ram himself inside us?

9:09, 29 JANUARY 1997
FROM: LEE ANN DOWNING
TO: REBECCA FASS

You're a genius. No wonder you get grants. This is the greatest idea you've ever had. I'm going to ask him tonight. Of course we should experiment. What else are they good for?

9:23, 29 JANUARY 1997
FROM: LEE ANN DOWNING
TO: JOSH GOLDEN
SUBJECT: A PENETRATING QUESTION

Hey, guy. I have a question. Research for my Sex and Death class, which starts Monday. What does it feel like to be inside of a woman? I feel a need to understand the male perspective. Do you remember in *Born Innocent,* when all the lesbians rape this poor girl with a broom handle? Probably you've figured this out by now, but no woman has ever had an urge to do anything remotely like that. We're just not into sticking things into people—well, okay, every now and then a pin, but not on a regular basis. So please help me if you can. Do you think I could get a grant to investigate this?

12:38, 29 JANUARY 1997
FROM: JOSH GOLDEN
TO: LEE ANN DOWNING
SUBJECT: A PENETRATING ANSWER

You are my favorite vice, Leo. I swear, someday you're gonna make some guys very happy. It'll take more than one of us to handle you, 'cause you are outa control.

So, all right, you know when you're peeling an orange, how it feels? There always comes the moment when the peel is off, and you pull the plug off one end, and you slip the stringy white thing out, and there's this empty, beckoning hollow. Suddenly you have this irresistible urge to stick your thumb straight into it. So you do, and it pushes back, all this moist, firm flesh around your thumb, hugging and pressing, and you feel it all around you, sucking, clinging, alive. That's it. It's the impulse to stick in your thumb, because it's your orange, and you peeled it, and you've earned the right to be there.

You don't want to do this with every orange, of course. Sometimes you just want to run your fingertips over the surface and feel the color. Sometimes you want to smell it, oh, so delicate, through the peel, and roll its coolness over your face. Every orange makes you want it in a different way. To stick your thumb straight into that fullness—that you do only with the few who demand it.

Have I answered your question? How does it feel to the orange?

P.S. If you get a grant for this, I'm droppin a dime and callin Congress.

P.P.S. What goes on in this Sex and Death class?

17:03, 29 JANUARY 1997
FROM: LEE ANN DOWNING
TO: REBECCA FASS

AGENT L, CALLING HEADQUARTERS. HE SAYS IT'S LIKE STICKING your thumb into an orange, but now he wants me to say how it feels to the orange. I hadn't counted on this. He's experimenting back on me. What should I tell him?

19:57, 29 JANUARY 1997
FROM: REBECCA FASS
TO: LEE ANN DOWNING

Gee, when did I become the Kremlin? I guess this is what you get for experimenting on people. Interesting data, though! I like this guy.

I know exactly what Josh means. I do that all the time. It's the most fun part of eating oranges—except that after your thumb goes in, you usually pull the sections apart, which would confirm Marcia's theory: fuck 'em and kill 'em (fuck 'em and eat 'em?). I need to ask Marcia.

What Owen asked me is the question I need to answer on this grant proposal, on which I've been working 16 hours a day and will be for the next few weeks: Why do I want to stick electrodes into cells? I can't use the orange, although Josh has expressed the first reason I can relate to. Owen is taking his time as usual, letting the particles whiz around for a while before he responds.

You're on your own, speaking for the orange. I authorize you to tell the truth. I wonder if we could communicate to them what it feels like to have someone inside you—or even more challenging, what it feels like to *want* it. I wonder if a man could ever understand this. Maybe a gay one. Let's try it. See if Josh gets it. I like this guy. If anyone could understand it, it would be him.

19:45, 30 JANUARY 1997
FROM: LEE ANN DOWNING
TO: JOSH GOLDEN
SUBJECT: INSIDE

You're talking to a guy, and he says what you're thinking before the words reach your lips, and he fills you with laughter.

His eyes are so dark, almost black, and his intelligence beams out of them, right through your peel, scanning the fissures of your sections. The energy dances over that white lacy net just under your peel. The current sparks at the plug, which is one focus, then spirals around in your globe, down from the surface toward the deeper circle in your innermost core.

In the end you never know whether he peeled you or you peeled yourself, but there you are, the hollow leading down to infinity, waiting to be filled. To be that hollow is a great loneliness, a great ache. There is a yearning, a drawing feeling in every cell, the way you long to put food in your mouth when you're hungry. It's comforting but more than that, when you finally get filled. You know you're alive, and you hang on, and you push back to show that yes, you're alive, yes, you want it, yes, more, please more, and you so, so love to be taking it into you.

It's not about penetration. It's not even about phagocytosis, that slow undulation of a hungry amoeba surrounding its food. When it happens, there isn't any inside anymore; there isn't any outside. Scotty has shut down the shields, and the hull has dissolved. The whole universe has dissolved into sweet, warm juice.

That's how it feels to the orange.

Sex and Death: that would be Shakespeare, Laclos, Stendhal, Nietzsche, Hardy, and Mann, my main men. I'll consult you periodically for expert advice.

Do you ever go into the city? Can I see you sometime? I miss you.

We started *Romeo and Juliet* today. Sleep dwell upon thine eyes, peace in thy breast. Would I were sleep and peace, so sweet to rest.

13:33, 3 FEBRUARY 1997
FROM: OWEN BAUER
TO: REBECCA FASS

You ask hard questions, and with a sudden unexpected run of accelerator time (Dave got sick and bequeathed his to me) and another tense period at home, I haven't been able to think about "inside." Not even in moments that could be considered research, but I won't talk about them.

Trish's mom has taken to shitting in random places around the house, and the nurse quit. We need to upgrade to one who is shit-tolerant, and Trish will have to go back to New Jersey. She's upset, of course. She's come out of withdrawal and is doing everything she can to make me talk before she goes. She's in catharsis mode, wants to get all the pain settled and done with before she takes off.

I have headed down into the tunnel, determined to create a smashup so big and so spectacular that I'll finally see my top quark. It's not that different from a bunch of kids getting together and making their Tonka trucks go as fast as they can and smashing them into each other to see what will happen—just costs a lot more money. Don't tell the Department of Energy or the National Science Foundation.

I can tell you identify with the cell you're poking, and today I feel like one of my particles, cycling at top speed, headed for a collision, waiting to see what I'll break into. Someone else is working the controls. Maybe we experiment to reassure ourselves we're not the cells or the particles. Like you, I want to know what's going to happen, and I'm arrogant enough to want to see it.

To be inside a woman? That should be as biological as you can get, but strangely, it feels more like physics. The idea of inside and outside no longer applies. It's like the failure of classical mechanics.

The approximations are reasonable until you're moving at the speed of light, you're with a certain woman, and you feel her skin against yours. Then there's no way to define spaces. It's the most comforting, the most reassuring feeling in the world. It's seeing your top quark. It's knowing that every good thought you ever had about life is true. It's a challenge. It shakes up your mind, because you've never thought that if all the good ideas are right, then what are you supposed to do?

All my love,
Owen

17:06, 3 FEBRUARY 1997
FROM: LEE ANN DOWNING
TO: REBECCA FASS

WELL, I TOLD HIM, OR TRIED TO, IN ORANGE-SPEAK. TO ME IT'S spirals and tendrils, these little vines growing out from the tips of your breasts and the outermost point of your pleasure center, growing and twisting, turning inward, twirling around inside of you, all the way back to your kidneys. Once the vines are in place, they become a net that conducts energy over the surface of your body. Sometimes a word or an image will supply more voltage than the nerve net can handle, and it sparks, the arcs jumping from one primary focus to another.

I might have done better when I translated this sparking into orange-speak. Is that how it feels to you? A few things are essential to nourish the vines: dark eyes, a wicked intelligence, and an even more wicked command of words. Then the tendrils poke out their little green shoots, and if he breathes on them, they grow. How does wanting feel to you? Lift your bleary eyes from your grant application and tell me. What did Owen say?

20:11, 3 FEBRUARY 1997
FROM: REBECCA FASS
TO: LEE ANN DOWNING

I CONCLUDE THAT IF THIS IS THE MINDSET OF MEN IN 1997, THE human species is in trouble. Well, maybe not, as long as they want to keep fornicating. First we get oranges, and now quarks. No more classical mechanics, no more boundaries, just time, space—and top quarks. I wish I could compare Josh's and Owen's thoughts to whatever Killington told Marcia. God, if only we could ask him! Now there's a data point I'd like to see.

Me? I don't want men anymore, just Owen. I know what you mean about the vines, but I find it easier to relate to Josh and his orange. I love plunging my finger into a piece of fruit and feeling it resist. Does this mean I'm gay, or just human?

I'm worried about Owen. I still think he may tell.

What do you think is a good title for a grant proposal on why we have to find out how manipulating the visual environment of cats affects the connections their cortical cells make?

9:23, 4 FEBRUARY 1997
FROM: LEE ANN DOWNING
TO: REBECCA FASS

HOW ABOUT "WHAT YOU SEE IS WHAT YOU GET"?

11:16, 4 FEBRUARY 1997
FROM: JOSH GOLDEN
TO: LEE ANN DOWNING
SUBJECT: JUICE

WAS THAT YOU OR THE ORANGE TALKIN, THAT LAST?

You know what happens when you reach for a hologram, darlin, we can only play orange juice on the Holodeck.

I know where you're comin from, and you know I love hearin you.

I hate to think of you alone. Aren't there any lucky, lucky fellas out there smart enough to see through your peel? Please think about it.

You are so beautiful, Leo, and you deserve such happiness.

21:29, 4 FEBRUARY 1997
FROM: LEE ANN DOWNING
TO: JOSH GOLDEN
SUBJECT: NIGHT

THERE'S A CALLIGRAPHIC STROKE ON MY SCREEN TONIGHT, A naked streak in the dust where I touched the screen. I ran my fingers over the words, trying to feel their author. I forgot … I am so, so tired tonight, and I can't be that voice you love to hear. I read myself into oblivion today, trying to send so many ideas into the tunnel that there would be no room for any emerging. But tonight, my fingers spoke for me instead. I know the limits of this level of communication, and I know what I can't say.

Alone? I would feel alone with someone who's not— No one connects here; no one appeals. I want only to fall asleep in warm, brown arms and forget myself in liquid ocean night. To breathe as one, the last whisper lost in darkness, nestled together on a marshmallow bobbing off into the black. Oh, if only, if only, if only!

11:03, 5 FEBRUARY 1997
FROM: JOSH GOLDEN
TO: LEE ANN DOWNING
SUBJECT: BACK TALK

OH, LEO.

Don't break my heart.

You know I can't.

Maybe you shouldn't write to me.

Just be that voice out there,

Be that voice to me again,

And I'll scratch your back with back talk.

Just talk, Leo.

Talk about your class, your book,

Your ragin mind,

But no Night.

17:20, 5 FEBRUARY 1997
FROM: LEE ANN DOWNING
TO: JOSH GOLDEN
SUBJECT: NON SEQUITURS

YOU GOT IT. I'LL TALK ANY TALK, BE ANY VOICE, AS LONG AS YOU'LL hear me.

There's this guy in my Sex and Death class who is going to be a problem. He has his hand up to talk all the time, but nothing he says ever has anything to do with what's happening in the discussion. He throws in things at random, like a guy shoveling coal onto a heap, one shovelful as good as another, all contributing equally to a pile called Participation. He's like noise. I can tell the other students want to swat him, and I might, except that I find him fascinating. Can anyone really be that stupid? Or is he seeing something we don't see? God forbid he should write email.

21:36, 5 FEBRUARY 1997
FROM: JOSH GOLDEN
TO: LEE ANN DOWNING
SUBJECT: NON SEQUITURS

WOULDN'T KNOW ABOUT NON SEQUITURS.

Everything I say is meaningful, purposeful, lucid, and constructive.

The Stalwart Shoveler could be a misunderstood genius.

Keep studying him and let me know.

Good on class, now give me book talk.

17:00, 6 FEBRUARY 1997
FROM: LEE ANN DOWNING
TO: REBECCA FASS

How are you? How are the cells, and how is the physics situation?

Josh wants me to tell him about my book, and I can't. After I turned my thesis into the first book, my mind went blank for a while, but in the past few weeks something has happened, and I know what I want to say in book #2. If I had the guts, I'd call it *Boiling the Rabbit*. *The Crucible*, *Liaisons dangereuses*, *Fatal Attraction*, they're so much alike. The words sink into your flesh like arrows, especially Arthur Miller's: harlotry, lechery, where my beasts are bedded.

I want to write a book about representations of female desire and female rage. Marcia has it down: in real life, both men and women sleep with married people who have kids, but for some reason, it's the single women who are depicted as monsters, the desecrators of the family. Valmont does quite a number on the Tourvels, but it isn't the same as Alex and that rabbit or little what's-her-name starting the witch hunt. I have to figure out what the difference is, and when I teach *Liaisons* this semester, I'm going to find out. Do they think we have more imagination or something? Or that we'll actually do what they want to do, kill their wives?

It's keenest in Miller, with that powerhouse language. I guess this is how you turn out if your father's a professor and your mother's a pianist: an angry reader with a hyperacute ear. I know the mindset, and I know the words that compose it: self-control, self-sacrifice, self-denial, always "self" with that hyphen linking it to something heavy to drag around like a freight train. Never a happy little-engine-that-could self, puffing along uncoupled.

Why can't self just hook up to a freight car for a while, pull it around, and then let it go? Self is a whore unless it pulls a train for life, and everyone thinks that if it won't pull, it will ram other trains and derail them.

How am I supposed to talk to Josh about this? One sentence, and he'll scream to Scotty to raise the shields. I don't see any way to make this funny, and if I show him even the tiniest tip, he's so smart that he'll get it all. The person I'd really like to talk to is Marcia. She'll know what I'm talking about. Do you think I could talk to her?

21:27, 6 FEBRUARY 1997
FROM: REBECCA FASS
TO: LEE ANN DOWNING

THE CELLS ARE GOOD. PHYSICS IS NOT. I HAVEN'T HEARD FROM Owen in a few days, and I'm worried. It could mean he got another run of accelerator time, but I'm still not sure whether he's going to tell her. Without me as his safety valve, he might blow up and spew his guilt at her instead. I don't think I feel female rage the same way you do. I don't rage. I work.

The concept of your book makes sense to me, just not the trains. We need trains to pull the carrots we grow out here to you and Josh in New York, and if the little engine that could decides in Kansas City that it's sick of hauling carrots, you and Josh get vitamin A deficiency. Wasn't the little engine that could a hero because it pulled a heavy load of toys? I thought the little engine won a prize for self-control, self-sacrifice, and self-denial.

I can see why you would compare a woman to an engine. I think I may be pulling this lab. You need an analogy where the engine can uncouple without hurting anyone. But that's the idea, isn't it? An uncoupled female engine is supposedly more dangerous than an uncoupled guy. Is the guy the freight car full of carrots? The logic is not working here. I can see the idea: the free woman is pure destruction, but the free guy is a likable scoundrel out for a good time. They cried when little Danceny shish-kebabed Valmont, but they cheered when Beth Gallagher blew Alex Forrest away.

How can you talk to Marcia? What do I say? "Oh, I've been discussing your love life with my friend from college, and she wants to study you for her book on female rage?" Can't you study one of your own students? This is my lab we're talking about here, my grad student. She's barely hanging on, and if she knows I talk about her, she might lose it. Let me know what you make up to tell Josh. This should be good.

18:33, 7 FEBRUARY 1997
FROM: LEE ANN DOWNING
TO: JOSH GOLDEN
SUBJECT: BOOK TALK

I WANT TO WRITE A BOOK ABOUT WANTING—REPRESENTATIONS of how men and women want, and the myths we dredge up to depict them. It's just been conceived, and the cells are only starting to divide. I know only Valmont and Merteuil, Tantalus and Calypso, Narcissus and—and that's about it. Dido, maybe. There aren't too many stories about women wanting men. Why?

18:49, 7 FEBRUARY 1997
FROM: LEE ANN DOWNING
TO: REBECCA FASS

SUPPOSE YOU TELL HER I'M WRITING THIS BOOK, AND I WANT TO talk to women age 21–25, and I need to talk to some in the sciences since I only know grad students in literature. I bet she'd buy that. I won't let on that I know anything. Given my correspondence with Josh, I should already be up for an Academy Award. With men, you have to do a Moll Flanders and keep something in reserve. It's the wanting you have to hold back: if he ever finds out how badly you want him, it's over. You let him know you want level 3, and you lose level 2. So you express the wanting in code, like in a dream, and you get to keep on dreaming. I'm sure I can do the same with Marcia. Trust me, I'm an expert.

14:33, 8 FEBRUARY 1997
FROM: JOSH GOLDEN
TO: LEE ANN DOWNING
SUBJECT: BOOK TALK

SOUNDS GOOD, LEO.
   If anybody knows female desire, it's you.
   Be glad to help you on the male end. I'm always wanting.
   How about Tristan, Lancelot, David, Samson, and all those biblical guys?
   How about *Fatal Attraction*?

16:59, 8 FEBRUARY 1997
FROM: LEE ANN DOWNING
TO: REBECCA FASS

SHIT! HE KNEW! THIS GUY IS A MIND READER, I SWEAR. ALL I said was I wanted to study myths of male and female desire, and he comes up with *Fatal Attraction*. Does this mean I don't get to talk to Marcia?

9:15, 10 FEBRUARY 1997
FROM: OWEN BAUER
TO: REBECCA FASS

I TOLD HER. NOT JUST ABOUT WHAT HAPPENED A MONTH AGO, but about Germany as well. I am so sorry, Becky. In the end I just couldn't stop myself. Now it may all be over. I love you both. I have to try to save my family.

12:15, 10 FEBRUARY 1997
FROM: REBECCA FASS
TO: LEE ANN DOWNING

IF EVER THERE WERE FEMALE RAGE, IT'S EVERYWHERE TODAY, a great big flask of 10-molar sulfuric acid that shattered on the floor and somebody's got to clean up—first the glass and then the acid, which has dissolved most of the tiles.

He told her. I can't escape the thought that if I hadn't done anything, he'd have had nothing to tell, so we're equally to blame. That poor little kid. Are they going to scream at each other in front of her? He just sent me a couple of lines, a sort of virtual grenade, and now nothing. All I can do is wait and imagine what's happening in Chicago. I wonder if I'll ever get to talk to him again.

Well, I am guilty as charged, and I'm getting what I deserve. It's Trish who didn't deserve this. The glass and acid are rightfully hers. Want to interview her?

If you want Marcia, you got her. She's doing a cat tonight, and I'm going to work with her. I don't want to go home. I'll speak with her and see if she wants to talk to you. My guess is she will. If only I could talk to her about Owen.

18:58, 10 FEBRUARY 1997
FROM: LEE ANN DOWNING
TO: REBECCA FASS

THE SPINELESS, SHAMELESS SON OF A BITCH! I CAN'T BELIEVE HE did that. How could he? Don't let this destroy you. I still think it's his fault. These sensitive pricks, they share their feelings like Mount Vesuvius shared its feelings with Pompeii. Don't be too hard on yourself. He's not worth it. God, am I glad that I'm in love with a patriarchal control freak. These testosterone types lust like crazy, but they don't melt down.

22:32, 10 FEBRUARY 1997
FROM: REBECCA FASS
TO: LEE ANN DOWNING

LEO, YOU ARE BEING UNFAIR. IF OWEN IS DRECK, I'M DRECK. We're all the same dreck, made of the same stuff. That's what my mother called my father when she knew he was off covering some story every day and some woman every night, and then later when we almost got thrown out of our apartment because he wouldn't send us any money. Now I get to be dreck too. I wonder if it's dominant, the dreck gene?

You don't know Owen. I don't think either one of us can imagine what it's like to have lived with someone for years and shared every thought, even a child that's half him and half her, and suddenly not be able to talk to her. There's something beautiful about the way they live that I'm not sure I'll ever be able to feel with anyone, that merging. You need to be able to merge to raise a child, and if he's wrecked their bond, we should at least give him credit for trying. You don't know how wonderful he is, how deeply he can feel, not just for him but for everyone else. What kills me is that something so beautiful could turn into something so hideous and destructive.

Why do we have to live imprisoned in cells? All the hate in the world, and two people express their love for each other, and it's a crime. *Beziehung*, connection, that's German for relationship, *Ich habe eine Beziehung gemacht*, I've made a connection. Life is connections, thought is connections, everything is connections. Why do we have to live cut off from each other when we can think and grow and love and touch and open a whole new pathway for consciousness to flow through?

You know, at that conference, Owen and I talked almost all night. He told me about particles and his boss from hell and his daughter's mind, and I talked about Marcia and the cats and what it feels like to hear the cells firing and listen to those voices in the night calling me a Nazi. It was dark, and I couldn't see him anymore, only feel his legs against mine and his hand on my arm. Mostly I remember his voice in the darkness, his voice responding to mine.

It finally happened at dawn, when we had welded the connection with our voices, and our bodies followed in a sort of dream. We slept a couple of hours, I think. When we laughed and maneuvered in the shower, I've never felt so relaxed in my life. I've never lived any moment that was so real. And then he was gone.

Why does that bonding have to be bad? He's not going to leave his wife and kid and never send them any money. He lives for them. He just made another connection, one that doesn't have to detract from his life with them. Neurons can make hundreds of connections. You always call yourself a whore, which I think is insane. I don't feel like a whore, although I'm sure she calls me that. What a joke, me a whore, a woman who wears size nine Nikes and has sex once every two years. No, me, I'm the Nazi bitch who sticks needles into cats' brains to find out how they work.

I feel sorry for Trish, but most of all for him. I don't think it's weak to tell things. I didn't want him to, and I tried to stop him, but if I'd cared enough, I wouldn't have set him up for this kind of torture in the first place. I can't judge him for not being able to withstand what I don't know if I could withstand myself.

Marcia and I stayed up all night with the cat. I guess I felt a shadow of what Owen must have felt, trying to hold back. I lost count of the cells we listened to. Marcia was the one taking it all down. I listened to the crashes of ions going in and out, in and out. We found two diagonal cells, far apart. I'm still not seeing any pattern in where they lie. Maybe there isn't supposed to be one.

Marcia is eager to talk to you, not just to cathart about Killington, but about everything. If only I could be a grad student again and talk. If only I could talk to Owen. What in God's name is going on in Chicago?

10:01, 11 FEBRUARY 1997
FROM: OWEN BAUER
TO: REBECCA FASS

SHE DOESN'T KNOW THAT I WRITE TO YOU. THAT'S WHY I CAN still write. I want to be fair to both of you, and it seems wrong to cut you off. As you know, my primary loyalty is to my family, if I can save it after what I've done. But you matter to me too. You must be hurting, and you must be wanting to know what's happening.

Trish is as devastated as a human being can get, and it's my fault. She's going back to New Jersey, and she's taking Jeannie, but she's promised me she's coming home. Some things are too personal to tell you, and I can't.

We're trying our best to keep this from Jeannie, but she's too smart and knew instantly that something awful was happening. Stories, songs, videos, dinosaurs, she pushes them away and wants the truth. I get the feeling she settled down with *Pocahontas* last night just because she felt sorry for us.

Something maybe I can ask—Trish wanted to know all about you: your work, what we did when we were together, and that big one, what you look like. I'm trying to tell her as little as possible, but the demon is dead. I'm not a selective valve or a window anymore, just a gaping hole between two chambers. I wonder if this is what it feels like to be dead: information flows into you and out of you, free flow, no selection. How much can I tell her? Do you care? I guarantee you, she's not the type to send a letter bomb.

I am thinking of you, and I want you to know how sorry I am that I let this happen. I'll keep writing to you as long as I can, but if I let her know I do, she may make me promise to stop. I would do anything now. I have never seen a person hurt so much. She hit me, Becky. I wasn't going to tell you this. She hit me again and again, mostly in the face, and I just stood there and cried.

12:37, 11 FEBRUARY 1997
FROM: MARCIA PINTO
TO: LEE ANN DOWNING

HI. HOW ARE YOU? I THINK IT'S GREAT THAT YOU'RE STILL friends with Becky after all this time. You knew her in college? Hardly anyone here talks to anyone who's not a scientist. Can you tell me more about your book? She says it's about single women and the way books and movies portray them, and you wanted to hear the perspective of women in science. Go for it! Ask me anything. Just don't ask me to shut up. I have a LOT to say right now.

17:30, 11 FEBRUARY 1997
FROM: LEE ANN DOWNING
TO: REBECCA FASS

I LIKE MARCIA. SHE HASN'T EVEN GOTTEN STARTED YET, BUT I suspect she may uncover whole new levels of female rage.

I'm sorry if I offended you about Owen. I just disagree. I'll hold back on the four-letter words, but I think you can find a worthier idol to worship.

You're not a Nazi or a bitch or a whore (I agree that this one is pretty funny—I can't see you in a merry widow). You're just a person, and Trish is no better than you are. It's like we have this complex: we think that married women and mothers must be holy, and the rest of us are bitches and whores.

When I think of Josh's wife, there's just a blank. She's a normal woman, like us, and if I were married to him, she would do the same thing to me. You're only a Nazi if you get out the calipers and measure his head and tell him he's racially inferior, and you're only a bitch if you call her up and tell her that her husband likes your breasts better than hers, and you're only a whore if he gives you a couple hundred bucks.

Just get the proposal out and keep doing the cats. I'll let you know what I hear when I tap into Marcia. What's going on with Owen?

16:56, 11 FEBRUARY 1997
FROM: REBECCA FASS
TO: LEE ANN DOWNING

It's horrible, horrible. She hit him. I may not be able to write to him anymore. I don't think she hit him in front of the kid, but the kid knows what's going on. I can picture her there trying to pretend she's watching *Pocahontas* and wondering why Mommy hates Daddy's guts all of a sudden and what she did to make it happen. I used to be that kid. I was staring at Bullwinkle; that's the only difference. What in hell is wrong with my neurons? Why can't they learn anything?

She's got the kid in New Jersey, and anytime now she's going to start telling her what a jerk her father is, and the kid will start feeling as if she doesn't have a father anymore. I worry about Owen alone too. I worry he won't eat, and he won't go to work. He's not like us. He needs people around him to keep him functioning. This morning he sounded like he was in pretty bad shape. If she finds out he writes to me, she could cut us off. I wish I could do something to get him through this.

Marcia isn't doing well either. Since the pep talk, she's been working like crazy, but the way she dresses, if she were standing on a street corner, they'd be stopping and asking how much. She must work out a lot, because she has the most beautiful body: long waist, straight spine, lovely breasts, hard butt, no thighs at all, and she makes sure the whole department can see her. The guys must be half out of their minds, but they stay away. I think she's been marked as "neurotic": someone who cries, gets angry, and worst of all, talks when you dump her, so they look at her as a luscious, poisoned fruit. In the lab she's trustworthy, someone who sees everything and wants to describe it. Be careful with her. She means a lot to me.

20:25, 11 FEBRUARY 1997
FROM: LEE ANN DOWNING
TO: REBECCA FASS

I'LL TREAT MARCIA BETTER THAN THE GUYS DO; DON'T WORRY. I would keep writing to Owen to make sure he's okay. Don't feel guilty about writing. I think email has immunity, and it can't be a violation. Probably your messages are helping him.

This is actually what I wanted to ask about tonight. Valentine's Day is coming, and I'm dying to write Josh something soft and sweet. I want to break the rules for once, really make him remember, make him writhe and twist in bed at night the way I do. I'm not sure how far I can push it, though. If he gets mad, which he always does if he senses an intrusion, the least he would do is cut me off. I mean, shit, he could have me busted for sexual harassment or something. He's scary when he gets mad. All that intelligence crystallizes into formal, ice-cold, articulate phrases that slam down in front of you like a spiked portcullis. If his gate falls on you when you're fleeing his castle, it will pierce you and crush you to death.

But then, if he lets my message through, and lets the heat of the words flow though him, and says mmm ... It's a gamble—no, not a gamble, a carefully crafted, irrational feat that will demand every shred of my skill. I don't know what Josh feels for me, but for one night I want him to feel for me what I feel for him: this terrible, lustful, mystical, murderous longing. It's as if desire wants to reproduce itself, and it pushes me to write the words that will do it. What do you think? Should I go for it?

17:44, 11 FEBRUARY 1997
FROM: REBECCA FASS
TO: LEE ANN DOWNING

SOUNDS RISKY. WHY DON'T YOU RUN IT BY ME FIRST?

22:30, 11 FEBRUARY 1997
FROM: LEE ANN DOWNING
TO: REBECCA FASS

OKAY. HERE'S WHAT I'D LIKE TO SEND HIM. READ IT WITH HIS eyes.

Valentine's Day in New York

It's eight in the morning, dazzling bright for February, and I'm walking down to buy a week's worth of bagels. The baker fishes them out of the vat, gooshy and steaming, and shovels them from the oven, burning hot. On the walk home, the bagels warm my ribs right through my down jacket. I watch an old Chinese man walking his two granddaughters to the bus stop, and I am so, so happy to be walking down this sunny street, because I am going to see you today.

Waiting for the train, I sing "Hot Stuff," happy, brazen woman-wanting. Usually I sing my moods before I know I have them. The train comes scouring up, and even its roaring yellow snout seems to be smiling. My black boots crack up Fifth Avenue until I see you beside the lion, and I break into a run. You spread your arms wide, and they lock around me, and you catch me up and spin me around. I swing my legs up and spread them wide in a great big jitterbug V for victory. They wrap around you and lock behind you. When you are done kissing me, you say, God, Leo, I sure am glad to see you; we've waited way too long to do this.

You keep your hands on me all day. I love your hands: warm, firm, confident, knowing. They know what they want to touch, and they touch it, without any shame or hesitation.

At the museum I lean back against you and look up at the Picasso paintings. I say it must hurt to be cut in pieces like that, a breast off to the left, a nose over on the side. But you say, no, he knows what he's doing, he's not showing the way it is. That may not be the way you see it, but that's the way you think it. You can think fast, like the frames of a movie, but no matter how hard you try, you only think of one part at a time. I don't know, I say, but could you please feel me to make sure all my parts are in the right place?

We talk, talk, talk about the paintings, our students, our books, ourselves, and people from our high schools we haven't seen in 20 years. We fall silent only in the hushed circle of water lilies, holding each other in the apricot shimmer.

In the street the wind blows every way at once, and my hair swirls up so I can't see or breathe. You pull my hair away from my face, and suddenly you pull me against you and kiss me, your tongue hotly alive in my mouth. The people on Fifth Avenue curse and elbow their way around us. A few tourists hoot, and one guy yells, "Hey, BUDDY, do 'er at home, will ya, yer blockin' the friggin' sidewalk!" We have to stop kissing because we're laughing too hard.

Around us, every window glitters with red and silver foil. The street is a tunnel of roses and chocolate hearts. Leo, you say, I'm starvin', and we look around for a coffee shop. You ask me what I want to eat, and I say, nothing, I'm too happy. You frown and say, that's no good, Leo, you gotta eat, so I order a fat-free, sugar-free cranberry orange muffin, and you get a roast beef sandwich. We break the muffin into little pieces, and you feed it to me, bite by bite. Then you say, I know what you need, Leo, and you disappear for a few minutes. When you come back, you have a baby red heart from the labyrinthine drug store next door. There are only four pieces of chocolate in it, and you tell me, here, this is for us. You pick one, and you hold it to my lips, and I bite into it, gently, softly, slowly, so that my lips close over your finger and thumb, and you say, oh … Then I feed you your piece, and you say, mmm, and kiss my fingers, and when the chocolate is gone, you say, c'mon, Leo, let's go for a walk.

Out on the street, my hair is everywhere, and you say, this is gettin' outa hand, Leo, we gotta do somethin' about this. You buy me a red satin scrunchie from a booth on a corner, and it does the job.

We walk into the park, and we look for places that people haven't found. Finally we spy a lone spot between some trees and cold, hard rocks. I'm freezing, I say, and you say, c'meah, I'll warm you up. You're always warming me; you never get cold. I press as close to you as I can, and you fold yourself around me and push me back against the rocks. I run my lips all over your neck, and I dig my hands into your springy brown hair. Leo, you whisper, I want you so bad, I want to be inside of you. I say, I wish you could be, and you push against me as hard as you can, as if you really were inside. We stop moving and hold each other as tight as we can, until I have to say, stop, I can't breathe, these rocks are hurting my back. Something is making you want to stop too, but you won't tell me what it is.

The sunlight is fading, and the gray is coming. On Fifth Avenue, people are starting to shiver and hurry. We pat our lion as we pass him, and we stop for one more cup of coffee. Tomorrow I teach *Liaisons* and *Robinson Crusoe*, and you teach *Moll Flanders* and *Hard Times*. We are holding hands as we're washed down the gullet into Penn Station, and you say, "You first."

You walk down with me to my train, and as we wait for the doors to open, you pull me against you. You say, "You know I can't do this, Leo, but you know the truth. I think you're so wonderful," and I say, "No, you're wonderful, I like you so much." The bell rings shrilly, and the doors open, and you say, "You be good, Leo, take care of yourself," and you push me into the car. I wave to you, my big red satin scrunchie on my wrist, and you wave and turn to go. I am drained and empty, thinking of nothing, and so very proud that I didn't cry until after you were gone.

What do you think? Can I send him this?

9:41, 12 FEBRUARY 1997
FROM: REBECCA FASS
TO: LEE ANN DOWNING

ARE YOU OUT OF YOUR MIND? YOU CAN'T SEND HIM THIS. JOSH'S reaction aside, you could lose your job. Didn't you say people can read this stuff? If you want to live dangerously, do, but don't risk your job. I mean, come on.

Then there's him. I don't know how to say this, but this is girls' stuff. Guys don't get turned on by this kind of stuff. They throw up on their keyboards after they've hit "delete" 15 times and wonder what they did to deserve this horror.

I'm not saying your writing is insincere. It reads like life as you wish you could live it, but this is female passion. I spend most of my time with guys, and they hate these romantic, chocolate fantasies because they make them feel like objects. I think it's sort of like why we hate James Bond fantasies. From what you tell me about Josh, he'll be alarmed. He'll think you're in love with him, and he'll pull the plug not just to save himself but to save you from getting hurt. I can almost hear him thinking, the self-preservation current merging with his affection for you and his basic, decent desire to see you happy.

I wouldn't send him this. The parts of him I think you want to reach, the intelligence that loves a challenge, the aggression that loves a good fight, the libido that loves a good—you know—won't respond to this. I would go for that code you talk about, mysterious, so subtle that he wonders whether he's reading things into it even as he starts to heat up, so subtle that if someone else reads it, you can claim it's not about sex at all; it's really about your research. Do that, Leo. For God's sake, no roses or red satin. How about sending me a valentine? I accept roses, red satin scrunchies, and chocolate.

20:22, 12 FEBRUARY 1997
FROM: OWEN BAUER
TO: REBECCA FASS

I WANT TO STAY IN TOUCH, BECAUSE I REALIZE YOU MUST BE anxious. We are holding on here, and I have hopes we can overcome this. Work is going better than I deserve. We may have my top quark now, and we're scheduled for another accelerator run tomorrow. If we can confirm, we can publish, which would strengthen my chances for another three years here.

Trish is now with her mother under what sound like hideous circumstances. She's used up all her sick time and has had to apply for leave from work. I knew her mother before the disease, so I can feel how excruciating this must be for Trish. Her mother was clean and organized and efficient, gracious and generous, and her home was lovely. Now she's a monster, a hideous distortion of her former self. Her hair is a greasy mat unless Trish physically forces her to wash it, and she puts all her clothes on backwards. You'd think that just out of sheer odds she'd get some of them on right, but somehow, she doesn't, unless you dress her yourself. Technically she's still continent, but she defecates around the house and smears her feces out of spite. Trish told me that her mother sometimes tries to kick her or claw her with her nails. She thinks Trish is holding her prisoner, as the last nurse did.

I feel so sorry for Trish. Her mother will have to go into a nursing home, and the house will have to be sold, all these legal hassles, and meanwhile her sister is doing nothing herself but criticizing Trish's every move, saying she's mistreating the mother, trying to steal her money, etc. I talk to Trish for hours each day, trying to set things right again.

The biggest problem is insane, considering all the real ones we need to solve. Trish is overweight. She has been as long as I've known her, even though she eats well and is fairly active. Well, she does eat a lot of ice cream. Her whole family is overweight, so I think it's genetic. She's always been sensitive about it, and she's always had a near obsession that I'm not really attracted to her and someday I'll get involved with a woman who looks like a supermodel because that's what I really want. It's not true, but this isn't the kind of thought you can overcome with reason or reassurances. And now it's happened. It's such a shame. She's such an intelligent woman, I can't believe she thinks this way.

Living with her mother isn't helping, so for at least an hour each night I get, "What did it feel like to have your hands around a 24-inch waist and cute little breasts, huh, did it feel good?" If I tell her about you candidly, I feel as though I betray you. I say that you're not a supermodel, you're not conventionally beautiful, you're just a normal woman like her for whom I have feelings. She doesn't buy it, of course. She wants to know where the feelings came from. Do women really give us so little credit? Or is it maybe even worse for them to think the feelings come from respect for intelligence and a deep love of someone's way of being? I want to help Trish, but I don't know how.

Most of all, I'm concerned about how Jeannie feels with her. Under these circumstances, I think she'd be better off with me, but Trish is holding on to her with a ferocity that's disturbing. She wants to keep her away from me.

The images of you haunt me, and the memories of being with you are so strong, I wonder whether this obsession of hers could be right. It would be an awful thing to have to admit. No matter what happens, please know that I will never lose my admiration and respect and fondness for you. How are you? I wish I could hold you tonight.

20:27, 12 FEBRUARY 1997
TO: REBECCA FASS
FROM: LEE ANN DOWNING

HOW ABOUT THIS?

Une Flèche[1]

Les filles publiques, en écrivant, font du style et
de beaux sentiments; eh bien, les grandes dames,
qui font du style et de grands sentiments toute la
journée, écrivent comme les filles agissent. ... La
femme est un être inférieur, elle obéit trop à ses
organes.

—Honoré de Balzac, *Splendeurs*
et misères des courtisanes

C'est presque carnaval, et au carnaval, on parle une nouvelle
langue. Avec toi, j'ai découvert un nouvel espace, le cyberespace.
Je suis Alice au pays des merveilles; je t'ai suivi dans le trou. Voilà
deux niveaux de liberté: un nouvel espace; une nouvelle langue.

On dit que le cyberespace est une utopie. Je l'ai lu hier soir.
C'est drôle, cette idée. On dit que dans le cyberespace, on peut
satisfaire tous les désirs de la chair sans pécher. Mais c'est une
blague d'utopie; c'est une merde d'utopie. C'est une utopie où on
peut tout faire sauf toucher. Imaginer, mais pas avoir. Jouer. C'est
l'espace de Tantale, toujours la même histoire. On jou, mais y
a-t-il de la jouissance?

Voilà un nouveau poème scientifique. Prends. C'est le tiens,
c'est un cadeau.

Tantalus

Desire, the force that drives all,
Seeks its own end.

---

[1] See p. 271 for the English translation of this message.

Laura Otis

We live as a capacitor,
Two plates aglow with charge,
Forever split by that purposeful,
Maddening sliver of space.

No distance, no energy;
No wanting, no being.
And the flash-flow
For which nature screams
Is the death of the circuit.

Oh, for that end,
The leap of charges, the collapse of fields,
The touch that blasts potential
Into nothingness!

But being, we bear the charge of the world,
And as with the demigod
Straining toward the sweet fruit,
Our sin is wanting.

"Nous," j'ai dit. Mais je ne parle que pour moi. Alors, bien, je
voulais écrire de "la condition humaine." Mais je ne suppose rien.
Je ne peux parler que pour moi.

Mon rêve virtuel, il est simple. On danse, doucement. On
porte une robe de velours bleu, bleu comme minuit. On caresse
le velours bleu, partout, au-dessous enfin. Ce rêve est né il y a
quatre ans.

N'aies pas peur que je suis folle. Un rêve est un rêve, et la vérité
est la vérité. Le rêve: on danse, on touche. La vérité: on est pris,
on est content, on est loin; on était déjà pris, et content, et loin,
il y a quatre ans. Je suis professeur; je respecte la vérité. Ce soir je
déclare carnaval, mais je n'écrirai plus comme ça.

Entre le rêve et la vérité, le nouvel espace, la nouvelle langue. Il reste un espace où on danse, où on porte une robe de velours bleu. Il reste un espace où on dort, dans une paix absolue, entre des bras forts. De mes neurones, à mes lèvres—non, c'est un autre circuit, ça, un circuit parallèlle. De mes neurones, à mes doigts, à tes yeux. Je t'embrasse.

Joyeuse Saint Valentin.

7:57, 13 FEBRUARY 1997
FROM: REBECCA FASS
TO: LEE ANN DOWNING

No, Leo. You are not getting the concept. French is not a code; it's a mode. This is level 3 stuff. This you can only tell him when you're lying next to him. You send this over the net, you will alienate the man.

God, I wish somebody would send me stuff like this. Maybe I should send Owen a valentine. What do you think? I'm completely immersed in this grant proposal, and my neurons want to write something different.

10:13, 13 FEBRUARY 1997
FROM: JOSH GOLDEN
TO: LEE ANN DOWNING

Hey, what's goin on?

How's Sex and Death?

Was it somethin I said?

Like *Fatal Attraction*?

Don't be shy, Leo.

Now, there's a female who wants.

How about putting her in your book?

What do you think?

12:07, 13 FEBRUARY 1997
FROM: LEE ANN DOWNING
TO: MARCIA PINTO

OKAY, LET'S START WITH *FATAL ATTRACTION*. WHAT DID YOU think of *Fatal Attraction*?

21:47, 13 FEBRUARY 1997
FROM: MARCIA PINTO
TO: LEE ANN DOWNING

WOW. WHAT A WAY TO START. WELL, BASICALLY, THAT MOVIE made me so angry, I was ready to take up where Alex left off. It's just so RIGGED. It's set up so that the woman is 100% in the wrong, and any woman who's ever been upset about getting fucked and dumped becomes associated with this psychopath. In real life, the guy screws you until he's tired of it, then throws you away like a piece of garbage and gets a new one. But they have to find a way to justify this procedure and make themselves look good. So since they have all the money and the power, they make a propaganda film where it looks like the woman who wants more than a fuck must be a sadistic psycho.

They make him married. Poor guy, one little mistake, and look what happens. Even the women root for him. I mean, anyone can make a mistake. It's all the woman's fault. She knows he's married, and she wants him anyway. "You knew the rules," he says. Rules? What rules? Who made the rules? The rules say they tell you whatever it takes to stick themselves into you, and then they tell you whatever it takes to get you the fuck away from them. They tell you you're beautiful, you're intelligent, and your work is brilliant. Then when they've had enough, it's "I don't want to get involved here. I don't want to get your expectations up." Can't imagine what they could have done to raise your expectations— like coming inside of your body? When Alex says, "I'm not going to be IGNORED, Dan," I wanted to jump up and say "Yeah!" The script is brilliant at times even if the plot is warped.

In that scene where he fights her in the white kitchen, and it's sloppy and brutal and ugly, you can see the murderous hate in his face. He fucked her, and she won't go away, so now she's a threat to his life, and he wants her dead. I think every man has that in him, the desire to fuck a woman and kill her when he's done so she won't ever bother him again.

As you can probably tell, I just got dumped, and I think that's what he would like to do to me. We're sort of like garbage, the rotting remains of a meal they've finished eating that are starting to smell and creating a breeding place for infectious germs. I think he'd like to go at me with a can of Lysol. You know he won't even look at me? As if I were evil, as if he might catch the particles of evil I emit if he gets one in his eye.

So they make this movie where the woman they claim is a psychopath for being angry about getting dumped actually IS a psychopath, and everyone feels better all around. Wives even get into it, cheering for Dan Gallagher with his hands around her neck, screaming, "Kill the bitch!"

That's what I think of *Fatal Attraction*. Next question.

17:23, 14 FEBRUARY 1997
FROM: LEE ANN DOWNING
TO: REBECCA FASS

THIS IS YOUR CYBER VALENTINE. FEMALE SCIENTISTS ARE beautiful. Female scientists are gorgeous. Female scientists are sexy. Female scientists are wonderful. Female scientists look great in red satin.

By the way, I sent everything. I sent him both valentines. I didn't change a word. "Want to hear about Sex and Death?" I asked. "You got it." I keep thinking I could die tomorrow, and Josh would never see what I wrote for him. I could see him as I picked each word, so that if I threw them away, it would be like throwing him away. I want to make love to him with my words. It's the only way I can touch him, and I can't live anymore without touching him somehow.

22:07, 14 FEBRUARY 1997
FROM: REBECCA FASS
TO: OWEN BAUER

I DIDN'T KNOW A PERSON COULD BE THIS TIRED AND STILL LIVE. I should go home and sleep, but I'm too tired to get out of this chair. So how about a virtual valentine? I rub you all over with the warm, sweet-smelling foam of my clean good wishes. I miss you, Owen. Be with me tonight.

11:59, 17 FEBRUARY 1997
FROM: JOSH GOLDEN
TO: LEE ANN DOWNING
SUBJECT: UNE FLÈCHE

LEO, WHAT YOU'RE SENDING ME IS INAPPROPRIATE. I WORRY about you.

You don't have to play the capacitor. Flow is beautiful. Let your energy rip, but send it a different way. Desire DOES seek to extinguish itself—but you shouldn't.

I can't let you do this. Let's take a break, so you can shine your brilliance toward some guy who is reasonably nice, reasonably good-looking, reasonably intelligent, and reasonably available. Then you can make nice and talk to me about stuff your university wouldn't mind payin for.

You know I love ya, Leo, but this is gettin outa hand.

Do not write to me again until you have accomplished this mission.

17:40, 17 FEBRUARY 1997
FROM: LEE ANN DOWNING
TO: REBECCA FASS

WELL, HE'S DONE IT. HE'S PULLED THE PLUG ON ME, THE LOUSY, patriarchal son of a bitch. Maybe I shouldn't have sent the French and the chocolate. Guess I was still trying to experiment—like if you want to see if the space blob is alive, you poke it with a stick. Well it's alive, all right, and it just zapped me with a phaser on stun. If I write again, he might change the setting. His message came cloaked in for-your-own-good, but Marcia is right, boy, is Marcia right. He wants me to stifle myself with some Nice Guy and refrain from projecting my libidinal energy onto his computer screen. I feel sick. I feel as though I was floating in space and someone cut my lifeline, and I'm going to drift alone in the black until I die.

20:42, 17 FEBRUARY 1997
FROM: REBECCA FASS
TO: LEE ANN DOWNING

OH, LEO. I'M SO SORRY. I KNOW HOW YOU FEEL ABOUT HIM. WHY did you do it? I'm sure he's afraid. He sounds as though he has a pretty good life, and you could screw it up royally. You're funny sometimes. The stuff you write, it's like you're an exhibitionist, a flasher. You have to show yourself. Think about the perspective of the viewer. It's scary when people expose their private parts on your screen. It's more of a turn-on for the flasher than for the viewer. I would guess that he saw your emotion naked on his screen, undressed and uncoded, and he freaked out.

Probably he means well. Maybe he's even thinking of you and imagines you'll be happy if you find a guy who can spend time with you. This is probably what he was telling himself as he went at your lifeline with the garden shears.

There could be a lot of reasons why he cut you off. Maybe he has people out to get him at work, the way Owen does. He's got to make sure that if anyone checks his account, regardless of what he's receiving, the messages he sends are above reproach.

It could be something at home too. Maybe his wife suspects something. How good an actor is he? Can he walk around with his head in virtual reality where a black-haired, hundred-pound sprite is bouncing on top of him, and carry on a normal conversation? Maybe your valentines activated his VR implant.

Why did you send them, Leo? Why do you write to him? Excuse me for being the scientist, the Seeker of Truth, but WHY?

What are you getting out of this? The brutal, smelly, shaggy, snuffling truth seems to be that he doesn't want you to write to him.

I know you, Leo, and I know that right now you're composing the most scathing, vicious, outrageous, deadly reply of all time. Do NOT send it to him. DO NOT DO IT. Don't even think about it, Leo. Send it to me instead, and I'll tell you what I think of it. He'll go after you. I can see the guy has a strong preservation instinct, and guys like that will destroy you if you threaten them.

Besides, I don't think any one guy can cut a lifeline by himself. Life-support systems have backup batteries. Go on backup for a while and write to Marcia instead. Use her as a lifeline, and you can be hers. God knows, she needs one.

Tonight in the lab it was the saddest thing. Killington's lab is across the courtyard from ours, and his lights were on. Marcia kept watching. Sometimes you could see him flash past the window, a tall, fast-moving silhouette, and I know she was waiting to see if Bonnie would come. He doesn't want Marcia anymore, but she keeps looking, trying to absorb all those flickers. I wonder what puffs of ions make people want. If I knew, I'd look for a blocker and try to shut them down.

Nothing from Owen. I feel worried.

17:47, 18 FEBRUARY 1997
FROM: LEE ANN DOWNING
TO: REBECCA FASS

YOU'RE RIGHT ABOUT THE MESSAGE. I HAVE NOTHING TO LOSE anymore, so now I can say what I think.

I've been writing to him because that's how I live. When I'm typing my thoughts to him as fast as I can, I'm living, and after I hit Control-Z and see I've sent 116 lines, I feel the peace, comfort, and sense of purpose you get when you collapse back after making love. In the morning, everything passes in a rush and a blur as I race toward the moment I live for, the beep telling me I have new messages. Reading his thoughts on my screen, even if they're just funny seaweed thoughts washed up from the ocean of his consciousness, that's what I live for.

I love his mind. Once a year I go scuba diving in it for hours, and there's nothing in the universe more beautiful. I won't rest until I can get back in there. Whatever it takes, I'll plunge into him again and swim in that silent, mystic beauty. The surface is tricky, with whitecaps of self-deprecating humor and squalls of self-righteous anger, but underneath is wonder that welcomes you as it closes softly over your head.

His hands are fabulous, and his tongue is a marvel. He's so lingual! It's rare for a guy to be so into language. He is one of a kind, an ocean of verbal intelligence spiked with hormones. There isn't anyone else like Josh. Writing to someone else—writing for anyone else—wouldn't be the same. I've got to get him back somehow.

You know, you're in this as much as the rest of us, watching the window and trying to snatch at figures as they flicker by. Write to Owen, for God's sake! He's a flicker-snatcher too. Guys seem to like it, that figures flash by and then disappear, but Owen sounds different. He may have been further back in line when they were handing out the hormones. Josh talked his way into first place. I can see him now, sweet-talking God.

I don't know what wanting is. What I feel for Josh is more than wanting. He cuts me off to survive, but I can't survive if he cuts me off. I wonder what he wants. I wonder why he ever wanted to dive into me. I wonder if he dove in and didn't like it. Am I a polluted ocean?

I like your idea about Marcia. I'm going to write to her right now.

20:37, 18 FEBRUARY 1997
FROM: LEE ANN DOWNING
TO: JOSH GOLDEN
SUBJECT: LIFE IS WHAT KICKS BACK

DEAR JOSH,

I'd be delighted to honor your last request, except that you asked me some questions, and I presume that you wanted answers.

"How about *Fatal Attraction?*"

To watch *Fatal Attraction* is to watch rampant injustice while you are bound and gagged. The film vindicates every man who ever slept with a woman, wiped her out of his life, and heaved a sigh of relief. The woman who watches is bound and gagged because if she dares to voice the slightest murmur of sympathy for Alex, she's an advocate of selfishness, sadism, and child abuse. In a witch hunt, if you defend the witch, then you're a witch too.

He's married. She knows he's married. She dares to desire him anyway. She's in the wrong. Of course she's in the wrong— IN CONTEXT THE FILM SETS UP. The gag comes from the manipulation of the context: the whole damned thing is a synecdoche. One situation in which a woman is wrong represents a whole host of possible relationships.

Both men and women desire. Both men and women abandon people to whom they've made love, abruptly, maladroitly, driven by habit or fear. This film, in which the man has good reasons to shake off his lover, makes it seem as though every man who's ever wanted to leave a woman after one night is justified. He may be guilty of a misdemeanor, but the sympathy is all on his side.

Have you any idea what it feels like to watch this film as a woman? With whom can a woman identify? Not with the man, not by a long shot. I suppose some marketer thought we would identify with the maligned wife—but who can identify with a victim, a minor character who doesn't act but reacts, someone to whom things happen, an object? As an active subject, a woman can identify only with Alex, beautiful, mad Alex with her ringlets and her great big knife. These are our choices: an alien, a victim, or a psychopathic killer.

Alex doesn't play by the rules. The rules say that a man can sleep with a woman, then tell her to disappear, and remain in the right. If he could, he would throw her on the transporter, set the coordinates for deep space, and put it on scatter. Yes, women do it too. And women are wrong.

Hasn't this ever happened to you? Have you any idea what it feels like to have someone tell you you're beautiful, tell you you're wonderful, and touch you as you've never been touched before, come inside of you with his body and his mind so that he can explore every convolution, every hidden part of you? To *know*—they knew what they were doing when they assigned that verb all its territory. And then to have him disown you—no more talk, no more touching, no more knowing, to refuse even to look at you, to turn his eyes away as though you were something deadly, a virus that could land on his retina and be transported to his brain through his optic nerve.

Do you know you did this? Or was it a survival instinct so basic that you did it without being conscious of it? I can't tell you how many times this has happened to me. To meet, to touch, to come together, to learn about each other, then to split up because you decide you don't want to bond, that's one thing. But not even to want to get to know someone! Not even to care what she's like—just to penetrate her and then will her out of existence, to do whatever it takes not to see her or hear her anymore—that's murder. That's a death wish.

I know you're married. I'm not going to call you, I'm not going to go to your office, I'm not going to go to your house, I'm not going to trash your car, I'm not going to kidnap your kids, and I'm not going to boil your fucking rabbit. You know I don't even know your wife's name? You're so fucking paranoid, you won't tell me anything. It's humiliating, Josh, it's insulting!

Since *Fatal Attraction* we have all become Alex, every woman who ever wanted to maintain a connection that brought her to life. Alex makes it all right for you to cut me off.

I just want to write to you, Josh. I want to touch your mind. I can't touch you the way I want to, and I accept that; I have no choice. But I can reach you with my words, and you can still know me. Don't you want to know me anymore? Four years ago, I saw you, and you were making a whole bunch of people laugh. You sought me out and said, "Hi, I'm Josh, how ya doin?" You wanted to know me, and now you don't. It's not right; it just isn't right. The affinity is there, the desire is there, desire like a wind, like a flood, like Niagara Falls. We can still touch each other. It doesn't have to be all or nothing. Please, Josh. I beg you, please, don't do this.

Second question: "How are Sex and Death?"

Sex: came at 6:30 this morning, massively, explosively, with your name in my mouth and your image in my eyes and your ghost on top of me.

Death: died at noon yesterday when I saw your death wish on my screen.

19:23, 19 FEBRUARY 1997
FROM: LEE ANN DOWNING
TO: REBECCA FASS

THIS WOULD BE FUNNY IF IT WEREN'T SO FRIGHTENING. WE talked for an hour in Sex and Death about Madame de Merteuil's advice on letter writing: a letter is always for someone else, and you should see the words with that person's eyes even as they come together in your mind. You should write not what you feel but what you want to make him feel. A debate broke out, and two camps formed: the Feelies, who thought you should write to convey truth, and the Lawyers, who thought you should write to make people think and do things. I love teaching *Liaisons dangereuses*.

Another near riot broke out between people who thought Madame de Merteuil was a sociopath and people who thought that by manipulating everyone, she was doing the same thing Valmont and the men were doing. As a scientist, you'll be interested to know that there was no correlation between the Feelies/Lawyers and the Pro-Merteuil/Anti-Merteuil factions. I poked and prodded each faction in hope that deep truths would emerge, but in the end, it came down to taste, a personality test. People either wrote to purge (the Feelies), or they wrote to bring about an effect (the Lawyers), and we couldn't get beyond that.

I'm a Feelie. You—you hand out Lawyerly advice, but you're a closet Feelie. Owen has got to be a Feelie. Josh is a Lawyer. I don't think he's ever typed a word into his keyboard without considering how I'd react to it. Me, I just go at it, and his reactions happen. I don't make them happen.

Well, he's going to react now! He made the mistake of asking me about *Fatal Attraction*, and inspired by Marcia, I let him know. Oh, you have dynamite working in your lab! Just set the charges so that she blasts away obstacles to knowledge, because she could blow the place sky-high. I love Marcia. Hearing her voice, I'm starting to write my new book in my head. I'm going to call it *Boiling the Rabbit*.

So anyway, a funny-dangerous thing happened because I'm just learning to print emails. For a long time, I never even wanted to. It was sort of an honor system, creating the messages and then wiping the system clean, like those bright sidewalk paintings washed away after a few days. Well, I tried to print what I was sending to Josh, and it was about as personal and incriminating as you can get, and it wouldn't stop coming out of the printer! I sent it once, "print stream," but then the message sent itself again, and again, this big window flashing up on the screen telling me it was printing when I hadn't asked it to. Luckily it was late, and there was no one around, so I ran downstairs and turned off the printer and quit out.

I left campus and went to Starbucks, but then I started to have misgivings and went back to campus and turned the printer back on. The message came out again! It kept rolling out, laughing at me, my own vituperative, incriminating words, available for the whole department to see. I sent a few boring documents to clear out the system, like Roto-Rooter. Probably I activated some safety mechanism, saving the last job before you kill the power, but the system's safety could have been my ass. I am never printing email again.

Last night I had a strange nightmare. I was in the Louvre, and suddenly I discovered I didn't have my little black purse. I was trying to get back to the coat check place, but there were three of them, and I couldn't reach any of the three. I scrambled up a dirt embankment and jumped off what looked like a balcony into a sculpture hall below. As I jumped, the hall grew infinitely more remote, and I floated down eerily, breaking my fall with a bounce on each successive ledge. Finally I landed gracefully, as if I were holding a parasol. Then I remembered I'd forgotten to bring any luggage, and I was in Paris with no clothes, no money, no credit cards, not even a hairbrush. I woke up thinking over and over, "I'm not prepared, I'm not prepared, I'm not prepared." But I had read the 50 pages of *Liaisons* and 40 pages of *Bovary* and 20 pages of Nietzsche I was supposed to teach.

11:13, 20 FEBRUARY 1997
FROM: JOSH GOLDEN
TO: LEE ANN DOWNING

You need help, Leo. Please find a psychologist who can listen to you the way you need. Do not write to me again, I mean it.

17:17, 20 FEBRUARY 1997
FROM: LEE ANN DOWNING
TO: JOSH GOLDEN

You murdering son of a bitch, I hope someone DOES boil your goddamn fucking rabbit.

10:17, 21 FEBRUARY 1997
FROM: JOSH GOLDEN
TO: LEE ANN DOWNING

What you're doing is sexual harassment. If you write to me again, I will contact the head of computing at your university, tell him I am receiving harassing messages from you, and ask him to look at your account.

17:21, 21 FEBRUARY 1997
FROM: LEE ANN DOWNING
TO: REBECCA FASS

WELL, IT'S HAPPENED, JUST AS YOU PREDICTED. I LOST IT, REALLY lost it and screamed at him in cyberspace. I was telling him everything I felt, practically begging him not to turn me away, and he tells me to go see a shrink. I can't believe it. I can't believe it's the same guy who told me I was so wonderful and he'd always dreamed about running his hands up my skirt. Was he lying? About the first part, I mean. I feel completely, utterly humiliated. He's cutting me off like a gangrened foot, and I can't believe he ever liked me or respected me. I'm diseased, and he's severing the connection. That's it, no more to say. But I have so much more to say! He's threatening me now, and I'm as scared as I am furious. If I write again, I could lose my job. He's not kidding. That steel that frightened me when he pulled me against him ("C'meah") is defensive as well as aggressive, and if I advance one more step, he'll blow me away.

I am dealing with power, and I just hit the Maginot Line. He would endorse this metaphor: I'm the Nazis trying to march into his life, and he's going to blow me off the map. How did I become the Nazis? For the first time I understand how you feel. What did I do wrong? How did I become the aggressor, trying to invade and conquer and kill and destroy? Well, the Nazis won this one, and I'm going to march around the Maginot Line. If he sees me as an evil Nazi, at least I get to be smart.

19:07, 24 FEBRUARY 1997
FROM: REBECCA FASS
TO: OWEN BAUER

ARE YOU THERE? I KNOW I SHOULDN'T BE BREAKING RADIO silence at a time like this, but I wanted to make sure you're all right. How is everything?

19:15, 24 FEBRUARY 1997
FROM: REBECCA FASS
TO: LEE ANN DOWNING

LEO! I AM HEARING YOU, BUT I'M DESPERATE. THIS GRANT proposal has to be postmarked in four days. Just DON'T WRITE TO HIM. Hang on! Write to me, write to Marcia. We want to hear from you!

20:45, 25 FEBRUARY 1997
FROM: OWEN BAUER
TO: REBECCA FASS

I'M SORRY I'VE TAKEN SO LONG TO WRITE. THANKS FOR THE valentine! I was waiting for something to happen before I wrote you again but finally decided that was the wrong strategy. Things are happening all the time, just nothing big enough to qualify as something.

They've found a bed in a nursing home, and we're negotiating financially. To get her mother in at all, Trish had to understate her behavioral patterns. They like patients who lie there and gurgle, and one who's mobile, verbal, kicks, and smears shit is their worst nightmare. Money-wise, it looks as though Medicaid is the way to go. If you do that, the person or guardians can't have more than

$70,000 in assets. This is no problem for us, since we'll probably never see that much money in our lives, but Trish's mother has that much. Either way, the house has to be sold.

Trish's sister continues to criticize, accuse, and sabotage her at each step. She never wants to do anything herself, but she wants to be consulted about everything, and screwing up other people's attempts to solve problems gives her a feeling of power. She comes over when Trish is giving Jeannie her dinner and the mother has escaped and is making her way across the yard. Trish says it's Murphy's law: if she takes care of one, the other creates a crisis, and either way, the sister shows up just as the chaos hits its peak: the mother making her way down the icy driveway, clutching a pair of scissors and muttering about cutting them all up, or Jeannie crying because she's hungry and bored and Mommy is busy cleaning up the mess Grandma made. The sister sounds off about that day's chaos, watches while Trish cleans it up, and then leaves.

I never know what keeps Trish going, but she always does. She's a bulldozer rolling over rough terrain, leveling problems one by one—and now I'm one of them. I have complete confidence that she'll do it too: park the mother where she needs to be parked, soothe the sister, be kind to Jeannie, sort through the house, clean up the mess. She has never run out of gas.

I shouldn't tell you this, since I've vowed not to talk about our personal relationship, but Trish got me through hard times years ago when I was ready to give up on life altogether. I feel like I'm a problem now, one more bad thing happening to her that she has to solve. I even think she sees Jeannie that way sometimes, although no one could be a better mother. She just never seems to need or want any help. Now that I've screwed everything up, it's almost as though she expected it.

I can take the nightly phone calls because I know the hell she's living in. I know she's living mainly on ice cream, and I know that everything she's telling me, I deserve to hear. Do you look at my lingerie catalogues, she asked me last night, do you picture her in that stuff? (Actually, I hadn't thought of it, but now that she mentions it, it seems like a good idea.) Pretty soon we'll have to make a choice. The mother can either go into a home in New Jersey, or we can put her in one here in Chicago. With the sister, Trish loses either way: if Mom gets parked in New Jersey, she's abandoning her and dumping all the work on the sister; if Mom gets parked in Chicago, she's excluding the sister from the decisions and taking her mother away from her.

Dismantling the house is proving to be an adventure in archaeology. You're never conscious of the stuff you accumulate over a lifetime until suddenly, it has to go. It's a lot harder to get rid of it than to get it. Records! What are you supposed to do with records? Who wants them? Clothes you can generally give away, but what about stuff like dishes, beat-up furniture, curtains, garden tools? If only a house could decompose like a body when you die. Actually, I suppose it could, but no one would want to look at it.

I want to get Jeannie out of there. That grim, half-stripped house is no place for her. Trish knows I'm right, but she keeps finding excuses to keep her there. It's as if she thinks I'm infected and I'll contaminate my daughter with some disease.

I'm getting increasingly worried that Trish isn't planning to come back. If she doesn't, I don't know what I'll do. This is awful to say, but it's Jeannie I couldn't live without. Whatever it is that makes you want to get up in the morning, she's it for me, watching her grow and change. I can see I'll have to fight to get her back, and I'm doing everything I can to convince Trish I'm still a decent human being.

This is hard since, inspired by my wife, I picked up a lingerie catalogue last night and began imagining you in all sorts of things. Right now, a virtual you is sitting on my console wearing them, legs wide apart, and I can't tell you how aroused I am. I wonder if Trish could be right after all. She almost always is. I've always been attracted to her, and everything has gone great in that department. What happened in Germany came as a surprise, yet it seems as though something that powerful has to have been a long time in the making. You know what happens when I see you. If only I could have it all—be worthy of Trish and a great dad to Jeannie and still feel the foam of your clean good wishes. I miss all three of you.

In keeping with some other law, not Murphy's, my work is taking off. Work seems to be inversely proportional to life. We've got my top quark. "Got" is a funny word. It existed for about 10^{-19} seconds, but we've got the evidence—traces of the tiniest flicker that we're scrambling to inscribe so that we prove it existed.

Now that things are looking better, Rhonda is riding me. She calls me "lover boy." Where is she getting this? You know that physics is a macho science, and I can do the physics, but I'm no macho guy. So few women make it in this business, the ones who do are more macho than the men. Rhonda is bright, so they promoted her as fast as they could to prove they're not sexist. Now she's running the show, and they have it all, because with her, physics stays in the hands of machismo.

It's as if she can smell weakness. It reminds me of when I was a kid and the guys called me faggot and beat me up. Every time she says "lover boy," I hear "faggot." It's as if she knew. She picks on me because she senses I'm a fissure in the housing, a weak point through which something might leak. Today it was "How are those calculations, lover boy, you ready to publish yet?" Christ! How do you answer that?

Dave and the other guys think it's a riot. They think she may have a thing for me. I think she wants to get me the hell out of here and replace me with a more hermetic guy. Maybe she thinks she's motivating me, and these are her management techniques. I'm doing everything I can to keep her from finding out about my home situation, since this would reinforce her notion of me as a wimp and make her more sadistic. Well, I can't put it off any longer. Time to make the nightly phone call.

All my love,
Owen

20:30, 27 FEBRUARY 1997
FROM: REBECCA FASS
TO: OWEN BAUER

WHAT'S HAPPENING, LOVER BOY? GOD, THAT'S HORRIBLE. I CAN'T believe she calls you that.

Our chair sleeps with the grad students and leaves them depressed for life. Other than that, he treats me decently. I think his respect for our work may even have increased since he hooked up with my student Marcia. The imminent uncoupling had me more scared than it did her, but he seems to have retained his interest in the cat's occipital cortex after dumping the woman who inspired it. He's always asking questions at beer hour, how's it going, how are the cells, and he's really bright.

But nobody here sees me as a lover. Should I be grateful? You're just about the only one who ever has. I still haven't figured out how or why you do it, but I'm thankful.

Given that this may never happen to me again, the next thing I'm going to say may sound insane, but I think you should go to New Jersey. I think about Jeannie all the time. It must be so wonderful to have your own little girl. How horrible it must be for her out there, with a grandma who's crazy, a mother who's hurting, and an aunt determined to drive her mother nuts. I feel half-responsible for it—look what happens when I finally get somebody to see me as a lover. I should stick to the cats. And you—you must miss her like crazy. Why don't you just show up? It would be harder for Trish to say no to your face. I can see it all happening by default, and it's such a shame. Save your kid!

Me, I can keep going on the images you've given me and on any new virtual ones you can supply. I am so flattered! I still can't believe you see me that way. It makes me want to laugh. Oh—gotta go—Dawn has some new electron micrographs to show me.

21:45, 3 MARCH 1997
FROM: OWEN BAUER
TO: REBECCA FASS

I APPRECIATE THE PEP TALK, ESPECIALLY COMING FROM YOU. I'VE thought of flying out there, but Rhonda is after me like you wouldn't believe. She wants me to publish as fast as possible, but I don't think we're ready. I want to do some more experiments to confirm some things, but of course she's against it. There are rumors they've seen this top quark at the National Lab, and we might get scooped. So she's dealing with it by giving Dave all the accelerator time, so I can't do anything but write. She and Dave seem to get along pretty well. I can't imagine how, but I often see them talking together. She stops in several times a day to check my progress, dropping hints about fellowships and how you don't get them renewed without publications.

I wonder how she got this way. I wonder what her family is like. I wonder what she does when she goes home at night. Dave is sure she's into S&M and swears that what she really wants is

Laura Otis

for me to tie her up. Go for it, he says, then leave her there, bound and gagged, and we'll say she ran off to Brazil, and Murray can be chair. I'm starting to consider it.

As you can imagine, I'm barely writing anything. Even so, I can't go to New Jersey, because Dave is promising to give me any accelerator time he can spare. I could get access at any time, and I can't leave. Even if Dave weren't such a good guy, it would be the end of me if Rhonda knew I had run out before the article was done. Only a wimp would run out on his quark to save his family, and wimps don't get grants.

I have managed to sneak out to look at nursing homes nearby, which is my real hope. If Trish can bring her mother here once the house is sold, it will anchor us in Chicago. Trish will feel better if she's away from her sister, the emotional leech.

Have you ever been to one of these places? It's terrifying, the thought that we may end up there. They smell of steam and bland food and sometimes of urine. The "residents" (inmates, more like it) sit in wheelchairs with their mouths hanging open, and every now and then an alarm squeals when someone tries to stand up by himself.

Herself, I should say. At least 90% of them are women. What can I say, you're a superior model. You outlast us, although looking at these places, I see no advantage in it. The residents are all crazy in different ways. One bangs endlessly on the table, and another keeps calling for something, but nobody understands her because she only speaks Polish. Another is clutching an enormous blue rabbit. The nurses try hard to care for them, but they can't pacify each one every minute. Some of them call out every 15 seconds, "Is anybody there?" It makes me think about neurons firing— why every 15 seconds? I timed it, and it was perfectly regular. I wonder if it's a circuit that's normally deactivated.

If I were there, I'd be calling for you. I'm not supposed to be thinking these thoughts, but the harder I try to write the article, the more I miss Jeannie, and the more I want you. Those loops of longing may be the last active circuits when my brain dies someday. My body/mind has assigned those loops top priority: life support.

Good news! I just got off the phone with Trish, and she's coming out with Jeannie to talk face-to-face. Her mother is in a home on a trial basis, and the house looks good enough to be shown. She says she's sorry to have been holding out on me and wants to see how it feels to be together again. Two days! They're going to be here in two days! I feel as though I've been on death row and the governor just pardoned me! I can't tell you how this feels. She even put Jeannie on the phone, and she said, "Hi Daddy."

I don't know what to tell you except what you already know: I want you, and I love my family. You mustn't count on me. My joy and relief at this moment make me realize this. We're going to look at nursing homes here and try to spend some time together. I picture you out there in your lab, at your terminal, with your cats, and I wish I could hold you. But I should go: I'm going to write an article.

18:12, 4 MARCH 1997
FROM: LEE ANN DOWNING
TO: MARCIA PINTO

I FOUND YOUR COMMENTS ON *FATAL ATTRACTION* INSPIRATIONAL. Sorry to have been out of touch. I've been overwhelmed by work. I wish I could tap into every woman the way I've tapped into you. I get the feeling we could all be one big brain, but something keeps us from firing in sync, as Rebecca would say.

I can feel this book bubbling, thanks to the snakes and lizards you're throwing into the cauldron. It's supposed to be about female desire, but really, it's about female rage. I'm starting to think that female desire and female rage are inseparable. Rage is the sound of desire unfulfilled, and I'm beginning to hear it everywhere. So far, you've been an enormous help. Can you keep going? Have you read *The Crucible*? I need to know what you think about that. And there's more: real life, if you're willing. You said you had a lot to say. I'm holding out a mike to you: talk to me, Marcia, talk to me.

21:36, 4 MARCH 1997
FROM: MARCIA PINTO
TO: LEE ANN DOWNING

GOD, I WISH I COULD DO ENGLISH AND WRITE ABOUT FEMALE rage. Can you work on anything you want in English? We spend our days sticking electrodes in cells and trying to figure out which is the signal and which is the noise.

I don't know how much I can help with *The Crucible*. I read it in high school, but the real book has been erased by the movie I just saw. I know why you're asking me, because it's so much like *Fatal Attraction*. I can't tell whether the story was always that way or whether they played up the similarity because *Fatal Attraction* has remade the mold for every movie about adultery.

Same deal. It's even harder to identify with Abigail pointing fingers and calling everyone a witch than with Alex leading Dan's terrified kid through the amusement park. The married guy has fucked her and dumped her, and she goes berserk and destroys everything like a supernova. No, not like a supernova, more like a virus, because it's a progressive, self-propagating destruction.

The guy is so virtuous, so repentant, such a lover of truth. He's hiding one thing, one huge, ugly, festering thing, but you have to root for him anyway. The girl takes the rap and does all the lying for both of them. Same as with Alex: she's so hideous that you feel guilty for feeling sorry for her.

This one scene really got me, when they meet alone in the woods for a showdown. You see how happy she is, thinking he wants her again. He can't deny that he wants her, and her body beams triumph. She lets her pretty brown hair spill down over her shoulders. And then he grabs her, shakes her, curses her, calls her a whore, and throws her on the ground, so that her pretty brown hair is mashed into the cold, wet dirt. "We never touched," he says. These guys, they make their own truth, and they believe it.

That's all I have to say about *The Crucible*, but if you're serious about real life, I don't mind telling you. What do I have to lose? I can be an experimental animal, and we can win fame and glory, and you can write the greatest book ever about female rage. I suppose we could get sued, but I'll let you worry about that. It's like Abigail in the dirt: the guys make the laws; the guys make the truth. They screw you, and then they sue you.

The guy who screwed me is the chair of our department. Until a few weeks ago, I was living with him. Then I was living on Tony's couch, because my guy decided he would rather screw Bonnie, this new grad student in Gordon's lab. As of this week I've moved into a house with a bunch of people from genetics.

At the time I didn't see it as screwing. It lasted six months, and what kills me is that at the beginning, he was so nice to me. I don't know what English is like, but around here you never hear anything good about yourself. You're in competition with everyone, always being watched, and every day you have to show them what you're made of. You have to have a great mind, a great body, and big balls, and you keep having to prove it. You get tired.

Laura Otis

If someone tells you you're smart or you're beautiful or your work is good science, you just melt.

And if it's HIM! He's a well-known guy, and his work on serotonin receptors is amazing. He has about 20 guys in his group, really hot DNA guys. They make point mutations to figure out where the transmitter binds and how much of the protein they can knock out before it stops working. They should have the receptor sequenced before too long. To have a guy like that tell you that you do good science—shit, who wouldn't want to believe it?

I fell in love with his work before I fell in love with him, but he's an attractive guy, no fat anywhere, great posture, moves well, has eyes that see everything. I couldn't resist believing. A few people tried to warn me, but I thought they were jealous. I figured they hated him because he was so hot. I couldn't believe he could be interested in me. It was such a rush. He would step over to me at beer hour and ask me what I was working on. Sometimes he would smile, and I would smile back when I passed him in the hall, as if we were sharing a secret joke, but I didn't know what it was.

It happened so gradually, I didn't realize it was happening. I would hang out in his lab and talk with them about a new mutation in a region they thought might be a binding site, and then we would all go out for pizza. Except then it was just me and him, and we would go for Chinese food, or we would take it back to his place and watch a video.

It happened the night we got this scary video about twin brothers who are mad gynecologists designing weird, curled instruments for mutant women. I screamed and covered my eyes when they started to operate, and he laughed and put his arm around me so I could bury my face against his chest and hide my eyes. After that he kept his arm around me, and when the crash of static hit because the tape had run out, he was on top of me on the rug, and we laughed our heads off as he grabbed for the remote. He told me he felt so good with me, so natural, so relaxed.

After that I went to his place each night, and we would talk science. Sometimes on weekends we would go mountain biking. His lab accepted me, and even though I was a physiologist, they listened to my ideas about the receptor. They seemed to like being hooked up with a physiologist, someone who listened to real, live neurons each day.

It was weird for Becky, me sleeping with her boss, but it was also good publicity. I got Killington interested in synaptic connections, and he's a brilliant guy, so he started giving us ideas for experiments. While it lasted, it was paradise, nonstop science. I wish I could be like him. He thinks about science 24 hours a day, and his mind questions everything. I felt stupid in comparison, always believing, taking things for granted. He kept telling me how bright I was and how interesting my work was and how much I turned him on. He wasn't kidding. Our record was five times in a 24-hour period, a time being defined as an independently inspired bout, separated from the previous bout by at least an hour. You know I still feel the same way about him? Why doesn't he feel the same way about me?

The trouble started when I moved in. I had been living with him, pretty much, but when I moved the last of my stuff out of the house I shared with med students, something happened. He had to go to all sorts of university dinners and receptions, and there I was with him, this grad student. People talked about funding and mortgages and restaurants and kids, and I only knew how to talk about grad student stuff—like where to get the best burrito and which professor was the biggest asshole. Sometimes I'd have to switch modes in one day, listen to complaints about the asshole in the afternoon and have dinner with him that night. I felt afraid of forgetting who I was, like Mrs. Doubtfire switching between a woman and a man. I could tell he felt uncomfortable too, fearing security leaks and conflicts of interest.

As long as we talked science, we were on common ground, but sometimes I'd come up and they'd be talking science, and they would change the subject. I was a woman, a pleasure machine. I was one thing, and science was another. It did give me a sick thrill to see the fading, thickening wives of the ones who'd stayed married. I could feel the men looking at me and thinking, "God, how lucky Killington is, if only I had the nerve …"

He got rid of his wife, a controlling bitch. She has the kids up in Seattle, but they never see him. She kept telling the kids what an asshole he was until they became convinced. She never appreciated what he was doing in the lab. Now I wonder. What he's done with me makes me reconsider everything he's ever said about her. Maybe his definition of a controlling bitch is someone who gets pissed when you dump her.

Well, at any rate, I figured out he was annoyed by having my name paired with his. The whole department knew about us. It irked him, having to plan how to include me when people invited him to do something. I got the sense it embarrassed him to have me around, and we made an agreement to avoid intimate contact in public. The definition of intimate contact expanded until it included conversations.

We were leading a double life, avoiding each other on campus and then trying to switch modes and become lovers at home. We saw each other less and less. Becky had been concerned I wasn't working enough when I was spending evenings with him, and once the first rush was over, he felt wrong about not being in his lab too. Finally we hardly saw each other at all. We both came home in the middle of the night and crawled into bed.

One morning at breakfast he said, "Marcia, I'm sorry. This isn't working. I want to see other people, and I think you should too." I remember staring at the scrambled eggs and raisin toast I had made until everything dissolved into grayness. Did you know that you have to keep moving your eyes and changing the focus, or everything dissolves?

It was horrible. I cried so hard I practically howled, and he tried to comfort me. He said it destroyed things if you tried to hold on to them. The beauty of life was its wild, random motion, which let particles collide and separate and allowed transient regions of order. You couldn't force order. That did the system an injustice and showed limited understanding. You had to let the order organize itself so you could enjoy its fleeting beauty.

A new patch of order had emerged in the joyous nonlinear system of his life: Bonnie. I went out for margaritas with the female grad students, and they told me what nobody had been able to make me believe before. Since he left his wife six years ago, he's gone through at least one new grad student or lab tech each year. We laughed like crazy about it, and then we plotted the data on a napkin. We recorded the length of each relationship vs. time to see how he was doing. The trend was that they were getting shorter. Mine came in fourth. The mean length was eight months, with a standard deviation of plus or minus two weeks. Then we made bets on Bonnie. I have $10 down that she'll go four months. They tried to get me to talk about what he was like in bed, but I wouldn't. When I got home, I threw up.

I hope you'll put this in your book. He doesn't have a rabbit to kill, but he has a fish tank. I remember looking up at the striped fish gliding when I was upside down on his Persian rug. What if I put tetrodotoxin in his fish tank?

I can't believe this is happening. She wants to divorce me. That's what she came home to say. I can't believe it. I never knew she was this good an actress. At the airport she seemed genuinely happy to see me, and Jeannie was all over me like a puppy and wanted me to carry her around. Trish was laughing, and I was sure she was happy when she saw the house and told me I had given her living proof of the second law of thermodynamics. Order has always been her concept, not mine.

She managed to keep this up until Jeannie went to bed, and I was feeling relieved that everything was all right. We were on the couch talking after dinner when she turned to me, and the smile that had seemed real faded from her face. "I've had a lot of time to think about this," she said, "and I'm sure." My heart galloped toward the next sentence, eager for the reprieve I knew was coming. Then she told me, "I don't think we should be together. What happened isn't going to go away. I can't trust you anymore. I've thought about it, and I think I would be better off by myself than with you. I don't need you." She has always been direct.

I lost my breath, and I couldn't speak. When I finally did, it was about Jeannie. What about her? She was half Trish, half me. Didn't that give us a reason to stay together? Trish was quiet, nothing like that awful first time, but I could tell that her disgust ran deep. She asked me how this had failed to occur to me— twice—when I had climbed into bed with another woman.

What really got her was that it had happened twice. All that time I'd been in Germany, she had been home alone, pregnant, listening to me tell her on the phone how much I missed her. It was true, I did—but I'd also been touching someone else. Her clear, civil words were all the more terrible for the obscene details and sarcastic jabs I knew she was repressing. I had lived with her four years since that first time without revealing a word; only the second time had I felt a need to confess. It sounded like an immune response: had four years of hidden guilt-antibody production been necessary to make something happen with the second exposure to the foreign body? If it had happened twice, it could happen again.

I swore it would never happen again, I'm sorry to tell you, while inside, I wasn't sure it was true. I could feel her suppressing a bitter laugh. I've never been able to hide the truth. Someone once told me that everything I feel is written on my face and you can watch the thoughts pass by like clouds. Trish has always been my best reader, and she saw the truth.

I swore that for Jeannie I would give up anything, that I loved her more than anything else in the world. Here she lost control, but what came out was sorrow, not rage. "What about me?" she asked. "What would you give up for me? Does it really feel like such a sacrifice?" There she had me.

As she sat there, reading my face, she saw you drift before my eyes. I was seeing you the first time I put my arms around you, strands of your hair blowing loose in the moist German wind and your eyes sparkling in the night. There was no way I could hide it. From the moment Jeannie was born, I've loved her more than I've ever loved Trish. I've wanted you more than I've wanted Trish. If I didn't want her, or even if I were subject to lapses, why should she want me? What good was I as a husband?

There on the couch, I fought for my daughter and for my life. Had she ever needed me? I asked. Why had she wanted to marry me? Wasn't there anything left of what we'd built together? Trish told me straight out that she had never needed anybody. Her father had died when she was young, her mother had worked all the time, and from the time she was 10, she had taken care of the house and her crazy sister (her sister has always been crazy). She had always been fat, and guys had rarely paid any attention to her. She had liked me from the first because no guy had ever cared so much about her feelings, and she had never in her life seen anyone with such a beautiful face. Also, it seemed as though I needed someone to take care of me, and that was what she could give. That was her thing, taking care of people. Even the day we married, she had never been able to believe that such a beautiful guy would want to be with her.

And she'd been right. Once Jeannie was born four years ago, I had pretty much ceased to pay attention to her. I was almost always in the lab, even at night, and when I did come home, it was Jeannie I wanted to see. These past few weeks, she had seen it all. I was divided like a pie chart between physics, Jeannie, and you; she had thought it was just physics and Jeannie, but now it was even clearer why she had had no piece of the pie.

"Know what decided me?" she said, smiling bitterly. "It was this physicist joke that a high school friend of mine told me. I ran into her a week ago. She's married to a biochemist, and they joke about physicists a lot. This physicist comes home at three in the morning, really out of it, his clothes all messed up, lipstick on his shirt, and his wife demands to know where he's been. 'Well (hic), gee, honey,' he says, 'I was out with the guys, and I ran into this old girlfriend, and one thing led to another …' His wife looks at him, outraged, and screams, 'You're LYING! You were in the LAB!'"

Again she had me. I'm in the lab too much to keep a wife but not enough to keep a job. "Therapy?" I asked feebly. She shook her head. She told me there was nothing new for her to learn about me, and she could never respect me again. She was filing for divorce on the grounds of adultery. They would serve me with the papers soon—in the lab.

Jeannie needed both of us, she said, and although it turned her stomach to think of her with me, maybe meeting you, she wouldn't deny Jeannie the right to see her father. She was moving back to New Jersey, where she had lined up possible jobs and day care centers and where she could look after her mother and sister. Jeannie was coming with her; after that, custody was negotiable. I sat there in shock and let her dictate terms. Any argument I brought up to make her stay with me, she turned against me, even the argument that I loved her. "You know you don't mean that," she said with a smile. "Saying it won't make it happen."

So here I sit in my hole, in shock. She went around with her usual efficiency, packed their things, made arrangements for work and day care. Within three days it was done, and they were gone. I even helped. Jeannie doesn't know yet. She thinks they're just going back to Grandma's for a while.

PART II

SPRING

You must see that when you write to someone, it is for him and not for you: you should therefore try to tell him less what you think than what will please him more.

—Choderlos de Laclos, *Les Liaisons dangereuses*

8:43, 11 MARCH 1997
FROM: REBECCA FASS
TO: OWEN BAUER

ARE YOU ALL RIGHT? I'M SO SORRY. I DIDN'T EXPECT THIS ANY more than you did. I want to help any way I can. What can I do? I never imagined this could happen. Although I also want Jeannie to be happy, my main concern is for you. Are you eating? Are you getting up? Are you going to bed? I wish I could be with you, even though I know I'm the cause of the problem.

My parents divorced, so I know the pain splashes around everywhere, like a mild acid that only starts to burn minutes after it hits. I respect what Trish is doing about Jeannie, not wanting to cut her off from her tainted father in a burst of rage.

I was also spared the horror of a custody battle when I was a kid, but for different reasons. My father just didn't want to deal with the hassle. He was seeing this beautiful Chinese woman who was kind to him, and to me. She used to look at me as though she felt sorry for me. Probably he was telling her my mother was a monster and that's why he had left her. His girlfriend had such sad eyes. I remember once she gave me a red packet of good luck money for New Year's. He dumped her a few months later.

Once my mother got the court order, I hardly ever saw my father, just heard from her what a bum he was. Even though I was seven, I didn't believe it. How could a guy have that much money and let us be so poor, and how could a guy go out with that many women and just leave them? I thought there must be some good part of him that my mother had never turned on. You know, I still do? He's an old alcoholic now, too ugly and disgusting to attract any woman. I see him about once a year and don't tell my mother about it. I've never seen any sign of goodness in him, but

Laura Otis

I won't give up. Maybe he'll repent on his deathbed. My mother just hopes that he'll die before she does. She hates his guts.

So Trish is doing a wonderful thing, I don't know if you realize how wonderful. Divorcing you—well, that depends on your perspective. I wouldn't do it. I think I could forgive you just about anything.

I know I said I would do anything to be with you, but that's not quite true. I'm anchored to this lab—no, I'm the navigator, and I can't leave my console for a minute, or it will crash. In science there's no such thing as autopilot. From the kitties to my students' love lives, it's all on my shoulders. You are what gives me joy, and learning how the synapses form gives my life meaning. We all want both, but hardly anyone gets it all. Nothing and no one could make me give up this lab voluntarily. The National Institute of Health could divorce me, I guess. Then I don't know what I'd do.

This week I think you're going to find out how much physics means to you and whether it's enough. I hope it is. And Jeannie loves you, and she's still there. As a kid who went through a divorce, I'd advise you to keep in touch with her as much as you can and keep letting her know that just because you and her mom don't want each other, that doesn't mean you don't want her. Just live, work, write your paper word by word, and know that I am with you.

20:12, 11 MARCH 1997
FROM: LEE ANN DOWNING
TO: REBECCA FASS

WHAT'S HAPPENING WITH OWEN? MY VIRTUAL LOVE AFFAIR IS down, so maybe I can live yours, twice removed—virtual and vicarious. Is everything virtual vicarious?

I missed Josh so much yesterday that when I got out of class, I went to the library and found his latest book. We have most of his books, and I couldn't believe I had never thought of this before. This one was beat up and defiled by notes. On the title page, someone had written that the thesis was on pp. 68–69: "*Great Expectations* is a novel about misreading and about the failure of written language to convey the true nature of human relations."

I went for the acknowledgments, my heart beating wildly, knowing what I was going to find. His wife's name is Beth. His boys' names are David and Jeremy. *Misreading Dickens* was dedicated "to Beth, David, and Jeremy, whose love warms me in my Hard Times and teaches me how to imagine and to wonder."

Reading this dedication, I felt like a disease. My heart was pounding with the guilty excitement of the voyeur. I felt as though I were seeing something I wasn't supposed to see. It's crazy—I mean, this is a library, for Chrissake. Anyone who wants to can pick up his book and read that dedication, but I felt as if I were committing a violation, looking right through their bedroom window. I xeroxed as much as I could as fast as I could, cursing, dropping my quarters. This is what I'm going to do for now, read all his articles and his books. I can't be with him, and I can't talk to him, but I can still kayak through his mind. Know thine enemy! I want to glide around inside of him, and reading his books seems constructive. It doesn't hurt anyone, and I might even learn something.

I haven't started reading yet, but I peek at that dedication daily. Along with the guilty heat, I feel jealousy. Then I feel more guilt for feeling jealous. Josh was with me when he wrote this book two years ago. I know, because he talked about it. What would it take for me to get into that dedication? I bet I taught him a thing or two about how to imagine and to wonder. When he was thinking about writing and human relations, was he imagining

Laura Otis

human relations with me? I'm going to comb his books for any sign of myself. I'm going to read them like Freud, as if they were one big dream, one big portal to the nether regions of his mind. I'm going to study those regions, and then I'll pass through the portal and go there as soon as I learn how. I'm going to walk around the Maginot Line.

I wonder what it feels like to be Beth. I wonder how she warms him in his Hard Times and teaches him to imagine and to wonder. They've been married 12 years, and they had the kids right away. I wonder what she does. He's never talked to me about her, not a word. I don't wish that I were her. I like to sleep with him and turn him on and inspire him occasionally, but I wouldn't want to be a wife.

Do you ever think about what it's like to have kids? You swell up. You get fat. An alien is growing inside of you, and you can't stop it. You feel sick. You throw up. Your husband isn't attracted to you, and he sleeps with someone else. I know. I have been this someone else, and so have you. How could you love something that sucks your blood, grows at your expense, expands inside you until you're hideously distorted? I would hate the thing from the moment of conception.

Then come 50 hours of excruciating agony, blinding, soul-killing pain. Maybe they rip your belly open so that you're scarred for life.

Once it's born, things get worse, because you become its slave. All day long, all night long, it screams and shits, shits and screams. You can't rest, can't work, can't sleep, can't think. You cease to exist as a human being. You exist only to serve the monster and to respond to its screams. The mother-in-law moves in to bully you and tell you a hundred times a day that you're inadequate. Your house, your body, your life, your time, your money, none of them belong to you. You scheme; you grovel for scraps of time. You rage against the monster that's enslaved you, the one you created by mistake because you didn't know what it would be like. Everyone lied to you and told you that tending this thing would give your life meaning. You have to masquerade and pretend to love the screaming, shitting thing because you're evil if you don't. You live a lie. As far as I can tell, everyone lives the same lie, and everyone perpetuates it, in the interest of perpetuating the species. No one would ever have a kid if she knew what it was like and could do something to prevent it.

You hate the monster, and you hate your life, and you can't express your feelings to anyone. The beast grows, and as it grows, it gets smarter and senses that you hate it for killing your life. The thing opposes you from the start, and it hates you back, and it keeps getting smarter. Along with your husband, it plots to control you with guilt and eat up all your time. If you don't do what they want, you're selfish.

You can't work. You can't go to conferences. People ask you what you're working on, and you try not to cry. You don't get your students' papers back, and you miss your office hours, and they look at you with accusing, self-righteous disgust as you stammer excuses.

You can't exercise, and you get fat. You can't use your mind, and it gets fat too. You become mediocre in every possible way, half-dead. Life rushes by, keen and exciting, but you're trapped in the miserable phone booth of your existence, barely able to breathe, unable to communicate with the outside world because the phone is dead.

The monster keeps growing. It uses all its intelligence to torment you, because it senses how much you hate it. It watches you constantly, looking for weakness. It laughs and jeers at you when you make a mistake, continually challenges your intelligence and your judgment, tests you, experiments on you, tries to sabotage your work, accuses you, rages at you, curses you, mocks you, tortures you psychologically. It hits the neighbors' kids, and the neighbors call to tell you what an awful mother you are. The creature does badly in school, and the other mothers talk to you with pseudo-sympathetic, knowing smirks about their children's successes. Their eyes say, "See, I always knew, the truth will out: you're stupid, and you're a horrible person. You can hide it, but it comes out in the kids the way it comes out in the wash."

When the thing becomes a teenager, it takes drugs, has sex, drops out, and runs away. Everyone says it's your fault, because you're such a selfish person and such an awful mother. And then you're 50, you're fat, your body is ruined, you're exhausted, you're stupid, your mind is dead, you've written nothing, and everyone around you is telling you what a horrible human being you are. That's what it means to have kids.

That's what it was like in my house, and that's what it's like in every house, but people won't admit it. My father was out of it, writing books all the time. My mother, I came between her and her music, and there was nothing I could do to make up for it. I tried as hard as I could to do what she wanted, but what she wanted was for me not to be there. Once I got mad and poured a jar of honey on the piano keys. They had to take the whole instrument apart to clean it, but even then, it never sounded the same. That's what my kid would do to me, pour a jar of honey on my computer. Like Alex Forrest in the movie—they do that, and then they wonder why you don't love them. They want you to love them, and they throw acid on your car and pour honey on your computer. Maybe I've always been Alex, Alex facing the Maginot Line.

Well, from now on I'm going to be logical, rational, reasonable. I am going on a campaign. The goal: to be connected. To have him want me, and admit it. To have him think, as he's typing the dedication of his new cell book (*Middlemarch*, neurons), "To Leo, whose lascivious language has been there for me in my Hard Times and taught me how to imagine and to wonder." He can't write it, but I want him to feel it. I want to be joined to him, to be part of him, to live the delight of a connection no one sees. The strategy: to know him, to know what he wants, to fly through every dark tunnel of his honeycombed, wanting mind. What do you think?

22:07, 12 MARCH 1997
FROM: REBECCA FASS
TO: LEE ANN DOWNING

You frighten me, Leo, you and your guy, but I know the truth when I hear it. I don't think everyone sees life the way you do, but you write the truth as you see it. Just don't write it to him, at least not for a while. He would blow you away. Reading his books seems like a reasonable idea, as long as it doesn't take too much time away from your work.

Whatever you're saying to Marcia, she thinks you're the greatest thing ever. You sound ripe to write your rabbit book. I say go for it, start writing! Maybe it could cross over from academia and become a best seller. I would buy it. All the women in science would buy it.

Me, I feel like I just won the lottery because I got five numbers right and the woman who got all six numbers right has been hit by a truck. Trish is divorcing Owen! Can you believe it? Here I've been, this vulture circling their marriage, and I guess it's time to swoop down. I wonder if vultures feel any sense of satisfaction. I don't. I made their marriage die, and now this poor kid has no father. Trish will do fine. I like her more and more from his descriptions. Even knowing what he did with me, she's not fighting for total custody, so that her kid can have a father.

I wonder if it ever occurs to people that they could win the lottery. I mean, they make plans, but how do you live once you've won? I wonder if he would even want to live with me. I wonder if I want to live with him. He's a high-maintenance animal, not like one of my cats. I wonder if Jeannie will hate me.

Well, he's there, and I'm here, and for now neither of us is going anywhere. Marcia, Tony, and Dawn all have data coming in, and we need to do something with it. I'm so worried about Owen, though. What if he won't eat? What if he stops working? You and me, we never freak out, but he might. I have to keep him going somehow. He's so wonderful.

I feel ashamed for being glad that Trish is fat. Do you think Beth could be fat too? I think I could handle being married to Owen. Having a kid, I don't know. I'm in this lab 80 hours a week and can barely keep things going. I have no clue how other people do it, although they seem to be reproducing. I want a wife, that's what I need, someone to put dinner on the table each night and take care of the kids and tell me how wonderful I am.

9:15, 13 MARCH 1997
FROM: LEE ANN DOWNING
TO: REBECCA FASS

WOW, JACKPOT! THIS IS A NEW ONE! FORGET THE MACK TRUCKS and the vultures, it's not as much your fault as you think it is. Remember she's the one who's divorcing him because she WANTS to do it, and she sounds like she knows what she's doing. What did you, rape him at gunpoint or something? Artificially stimulate his brain? He knew the risk, and he took it.

Verbs always say it all. That's the great thing about making yourself write things down: I seduced him; she's divorcing him. Is this guy never a subject? Didn't he do something to you, and her too? Poor Owen. I have to admit, he's pretty alien to me, not my type at all, but for your sake I'll try to understand him.

Josh is my type—wit, chutzpah, aggression. I miss him so much. If he were a dog, there would be this big sign up: Beware of Dog. Josh bites. God, I miss him! He bites to defend his home and family against intruders, and that's me, Cathy in *Wuthering Heights*, beautiful Cathy in flight, half over the wall, almost out of there, when this great, big, snarling dog chomps his teeth on her delicate white ankle. I am a big-time intruder.

Me, I am always the subject. I always command the active verb. To tell you the truth, I'm not sorry about Owen's divorce. As far as I can see from my own family, there's nothing particularly good about having two parents. Jeannie will be fine.

18:57, 17 MARCH 1997
FROM: LEE ANN DOWNING
TO: REBECCA FASS

I MISS JOSH. I'VE GOT HIS WORDS ON PAPER NOW INSTEAD OF ON a screen: clear, forceful, direct, brilliant. He writes the way Fred Astaire dances. His writing flows naturally, logically, one idea leading effortlessly to the next, but you know it got that way only through years of the most strenuous thinking and slashing and despair. I have the secret delight of knowing that during all that grueling rehearsal, at least for his Dickens book, his mind was dancing with me. Now I scan his words hungrily for hints of unconscious activity.

I think I see signs of his urges when he talks about interpreting patterns of light and dark. He has a lot to say about pale skin and black hair, but the problem with reading code is that if you're cut off from the guy who created it, there's no way to know whether you're right. There's no external reference point. There's no feedback except from your own desires, and they're pushing you to read things into the text based on excitement generated by what you think you've found. I feel like the early 19th-century Europeans trying to read hieroglyphics, poor fools. I'm driven by a delusion of grandeur, thinking that I've permeated his consciousness and seeped into his work and that even in his books, I'm present as a force in his mind and in his words.

I sit here trying to write my rabbit book, my chin resting on my stuffed lion, Leonhardt. I stare out at the pink and purple streaks in the west behind the black capillaries of my oak tree. Instead I read Josh's words, still looking for myself. His words on the screen were better, brief and brutal, because they were glowing and alive, and I knew he wrote them for me. Now there won't be any more of them. I can't stand the pain.

I begin to understand these characters I've laughed at, the ones who killed themselves for love—Romeo and Werther and poor little Michael what's-his-name in "The Dead" who stood in the rain until he got pneumonia. What's the point? When I log on now, the silent, blinking paragraph sign mocks me, inviting me to ask for mail in the absence of new messages. Or worse, the beep comes, and the announcement "You have three new messages," and I grip the edge of my desk and try not to faint, and one is yours (no offense) and two are about changes in the dental plan. No matter how many times I tell myself, "Face it, it's over, he's not writing to you ever again," my heart speeds up when I hear that beep. I guess I haven't given up. I still think he's bluffing.

We've been done with *Liaisons* for weeks now. Valmont has died valiantly, and Merteuil's soul has become visible in her face. The students still insist these manipulators were different: he just wanted to have sex, but she wanted to destroy people. The students are so certain, they almost have me convinced, but there is something wrong with their idea. To write the rabbit book, I have to map the fault in the logic, but in the meantime, we've plunged into *The Red and the Black*, and I'm immersed in the mind of ambitious, angry, calculating, beautiful Julien Sorel. Julien has always turned me on. When he says, "I will have that woman," he inspires me.

I am going to have Josh. I am going to do it. I'm not going to do anything rash or stupid, but I have a plan. I am going to do a Valmont. I will have him, and it will be my greatest campaign and my greatest triumph. When I say "have," I mean it just the way Julien and Valmont mean it: to make love and then to part, but with the knowledge that I have made him want me and that I am forever inscribed in his consciousness.

I am going to turn myself into a cyber genie, a great, swirling, pink cloud of words. He's such a hungry reader, he'll devour anything and won't be able to resist or erect barriers against me. He can control what he lets out, but not what he lets in. After transforming myself into digitized energy, I'll swirl out from his screen into the living blackness of his eyes, and then, as digitized energy, I'll rocket down his optic nerve and explode into his brain in a cascade of sparks. Since I'm a smart bomb, I'll head straight for his pleasure center. Tell me what to do. I'm going to write my way into his consciousness. Meanwhile, I'll write my book to purge myself of thoughts that he won't want to hear but I might let out.

19:15, 18 MARCH 1997
FROM: REBECCA FASS
TO: LEE ANN DOWNING

YOU ARE DANGEROUS. I MEAN, THERE OUGHT TO BE A LAW. I'M actually starting to feel sorry for this guy. Just don't get yourself fired, that's all I can say. I'm not as sure as you are that he's bluffing. I would wait at least a while before sending something, and if you do (I still don't think you should), send something harmless, something the email police couldn't find fault with. Don't tell him what color panties you're wearing. I think you could seduce anyone, because you've already seduced me, the supposed Voice of Reason.

I can't resist your plan and want to play Mr. Spock (or Uhura? or Sulu?—the voices of science, communications, and navigation) and give you the coordinates. Once you get into his optic nerve, follow the flow of traffic to the lateral geniculate nucleus, but then you should split your signal. Part of you should head for the occipital cortex, where you can dance until you create a conga line of all his visual memories of you, but another part of your nerve-storm should go to the hypothalamus. Your target is the core, deep inside, the amygdala for emotion, the hypothalamus for bestial hunger, and maybe the rest of the limbic system for emotions and smells, intertwined. Be sure to hit the hippocampus for encoding new memories. The neocortex lies on top of all that like a big, wet sponge trying to muffle the wild party going on below, but if you get all those neurons fired up at the back and in the core, he won't be able to handle it.

What I can't predict is what he'll do when the sponge dries out and blows away. Have you thought about that? When this happens in the books you teach, don't people get killed? My idea of "having" is different from yours. I could deal with having

Owen, waking up in the morning and finding my nose wedged against his wonderful broad back.

20:22, 25 MARCH 1997
FROM: LEE ANN DOWNING
TO: JOSH GOLDEN
SUBJECT: THE LIFELINE

I HEAR IT EVERY MORNING AND LATE INTO THE NIGHT; THE chugging and scouring, the warning hoot to get ready. It hasn't changed in the 33 years I've lived here: the ugly, dependable, inevitable blue-and-yellow beast that carries us into the city. The view through the windows is scratched and dim, barely revealing the red brick and white houses that fly by. At night I see only lights and my face in the window, white, ghostly, with shadows under the eyes.

In the morning between 6:30 and 8:00, people hurry to the beast the way they hurry to the shaft in a Welsh mining town. The women wear high heels, and their great masses of curls are still wet; the men wear woolen coats and carry briefcases. Commuters clog the bagel shop and listen for the bright, demanding chord. They climb into the machine and vanish, only to be replaced by a second swarm.

Sometimes a foot of snow will stop the train, but nothing cuts this lifeline between people and their work. They tumble out at Jamaica, dirty, icy nexus, where they dash through trains to reach their platforms and curse the cold in fine clothes that don't keep it out. They try their best not to press against each other in trains that smell of burnt wiring and bitter heat. There are never enough places to sit. Fathers commute each morning and night for 40 years, and then their sons and daughters start, feeling important with their suits and their talk of the real world. Jamaica, Queens, is the real world, waiting for the clicking, humming electric creature that will carry you to your final destination once the scouring diesel has brought you this far.

The train that carries us to the world brings fear; it is too big, too strong to stop. It hurtles through stations, rushes past the flashing arms of crossing gates, and though it sometimes derails, it runs over everything. It flattened the pennies we used to leave on the shining silver rails. We knew it would roll over us if we let it, and our mothers told us never to play near the tracks. We did anyway, and we thrilled in the danger as we balanced on the rails and listened for the warning chord. We ran screaming when we heard the monster snorting and saw its yellow snout appear.

In high school I used to write poems. I haven't written any more until recently, when passion brought back my voice. I had a fan back then, my friend Jodie's sister Charlotte. Jodie organized parties for us, her life force asserting itself despite her paralyzed mother and Charlotte's shadowy pain in the house crammed with books, papers, mildew, and dust. We used to gather there, and we talked and danced. Sometimes I played their piano, and we sang. I loved Jodie for defying the misery around her.

Jodie loved Robbie, the anchor of our group. At 17, he had the kindness and wisdom of an older man. He and Jodie worked side by side, campaigning, laying out the yearbook, sometimes all night, but he never wanted her the way she wanted him. Jodie wasn't beautiful, not to look at, but her strength was beautiful, her will to live in the midst of madness.

When Robbie started seeing this Thai exchange student, Jodie almost lost it. I think he knew about her desire, and he tried to be as kind as he could without giving up his own. Once we were all on a field trip, at Jamaica waiting in the cold. Lovely May, that was her name, leaned out over the platform, looking out at the approaching train. Jodie stepped slowly forward behind her, thick arms tingling, itching to give one terrible push. She didn't, of course, but I felt the urge with her. It would have been so satisfying.

Both Jodie and Charlotte cut themselves, and straight white worms on their wrists marked the times they had tried to open themselves and let their lives flow out. We took turns stopping Jodie, who always warned us somehow, but Charlotte was harder, because she stayed alone in her room. At parties she would slip out of her space, and she would look for me. She wore a limp maroon bathrobe, and her brown hair hung half in a ponytail, half out. Her black eyes glowed with pleasure when she told me in her whispery voice how much she loved my poems. I told her thank you, and she asked me when I was going to write more.

In the end, no one could stop her. Charlotte went for a walk in the early morning and laid herself crosswise on the tracks, resting her head on a shining cold rail. The blue-and-yellow monster with its load of commuters ran over her as she wanted, and they never felt a thing. Someone called the police days later, when he found what was left of her. The train had separated her head from her body.

I wrote poems after that, but they had no force to them. Finally I stopped, and I began again only this year, when I found the words to say what Tantalus felt.

Even today, I awaken to the insistent chord of the approaching train. So many people pass along its lines, in and out, the respiration of a massive creature horribly alive. I hear the train in my office and in my bed at dawn, the demanding voice of life in motion, running over everything in its path.

Laura Otis

12:14, 31 MARCH 1997
FROM: MARCIA PINTO
TO: LEE ANN DOWNING

Hey, what's been going on? What's happening with your book? Serving as a data point is giving me so many ideas that now I need to transmit them spontaneously.

So, are you saying that men keep making movies about women who refuse to disconnect? There's something to that, the recurring story of the woman who won't go away. You've got something there. She won't go away, and if you ignore her and hope she'll leave, she gets madder, trashes your car, trashes your pets, trashes your marriage, shit, she trashes the whole town.

What I'm wondering is what the male equivalent would be. I mean, is there a female version of this story? I can't think of any story about a spurned male lover who won't leave. What you get are stories about psychopaths who hunt down the woman and try to kill her when *she* tries to leave him: *Sleeping with the Enemy*, the monstrous husband determined to regain control of his fleeing wife. The situation is close, but it's different. What do you think is the difference?

What about your life? Are you going to put your life in the book too? I am still eyeing the tetrodotoxin.

18:03, 31 MARCH 1997
FROM: REBECCA FASS
TO: LEE ANN DOWNING

What are you transmitting to your cyberlover? Be careful! I can picture him licking his chops—I know you love that—but don't let him sink his teeth into you. How about running it by me? I could use the entertainment, and I love reading your stuff. I wish someone would write to me the way you write to him.

I'm doing a lot these days. Know what's amazing? Marcia and Dawn have this project going that shows that if a kitty grows up in the dark, with his little eyes covered, the connections still form almost normally with the cells in the visual cortex, but if you block the activity of the retinal neurons, so that they can't fire at all, they never hook up with the cells they're supposed to talk to in the brain. The cortical cells must be relying on some sort of noise that happens whether the retinal cells are seeing anything or not. We've got to get this out, and soon, so I'm taking Marcia back from you for a while.

19:22, 4 APRIL 1997
FROM: LEE ANN DOWNING
TO: JOSH GOLDEN
SUBJECT: NOISES IN THE DARK

My friend Rebecca the neuroscientist says that retinal cells still form connections with neurons in the brain even if you're blindfolded and can't see anything. Apparently, they make noises even though they can't see, and as long as the noises are happening, they can still hook up with the cells they're supposed to find. It's only when you poison them so they can't talk at all that they can't form the connections.

Tomorrow is opening day for the Mets. The forsythia has turned the parkway into a chute through yellow canary feathers, and the trees are purplish at the tips. In the morning we shiver, but the force is inevitable: more light, more heat, the momentum of biological time.

What is it like to have children, Josh? My friend Rickie had a baby once.

Rickie's real name was Rachel Rubin; nobody knew why we called her Rickie, not even me, and I started it. She was my friend for as long as I could remember. At the bus stop, this idiot Bobby Deegan used to make fun of her. RU-ben, he would say to her, RU-ben, yawruh JEW. Rickie would look down, her face bright pink. I would go over and stand by her. I didn't titter like the other kids. I hated Bobby Deegan.

When I hear about the Mets, I always think of Rickie. Her father used to take us to Mets games, a whole group of girls, and beforehand he would take us to a Chinese restaurant in Queens so he could eat. He had a huge belly, and at home her mother starved him. With us he would eat great round heaps of glistening meat with strange vegetables and let it settle under a sweet blanket of ice cream. We would have to promise not to tell. I loved going with him, and sometimes the Mets would win.

Once Rickie got her license, it was just us two, careening down Grand Central Parkway, jumping from station to station in search of the song "Fame." They played it so often, you could catch a new piece of it as soon as one rendition ended, and we followed a never-ending splice of inspiring tune. I can't remember whether the Mets won that day. Instead I remember climbing on the seats to reach down to a player so he could give us his autograph. The seats were wet, and this lady yelled at me for leaving black, watery blobs where she was going to sit.

That night we went to Rickie's sister's house, and we ate at a diner that had dishes of red Jell-O revolving in a refrigerator next to six-inch strawberry cheesecake. Rickie's sister had been to college, and she was married and talked about the importance of marrying a Jew. We listened to the Kinks, and she complained about the way people had printed up her résumé.

Next day she took us to a party at a mansion surrounded by an endless green lawn. Rickie felt anxious. There was this guy, and she was wondering if she was going to see him.

I was always so fascinated by Rickie. She was huge on top, every man's dream, thick, wavy black hair, big brown eyes. Me, I was this little scrap, and she was an entire meal. She beat everyone in gym at the flexed arm hang, this fitness test where you had to curl your fingers and cling to a bar like a drowning animal. All her weight was in her upper body, and Rickie hung on longer than anyone. She was good at that, just hanging on.

Rickie's mother had always been crazy. The whole temple knew it. She would envision these huge projects that would make the world feel the spirit of Judaism, and she would call the rabbi in the middle of the night to tell him. Once when I was at her house, I heard a terrible fight between her and Rickie's sister. The whole thing was insane: the sister claimed she had washed her hands, and the mother swore she hadn't. "That soap is as dry as a bone!" she screamed. Then came the sudden, sharp sound of slaps, followed by more screams. "You LIED to me!" shrieked the mother. The sister screamed back that she hated her. Rickie got very quiet and wouldn't say a word. I remember how upset she got once when she saw a mother slapping her little girl in a supermarket. Rickie was so quiet, she hardly ever spoke, but I remember her saying how terrible it was to hit a child.

When her mother called the party's host, no one knew where Rickie was. Whoever answered looked around, didn't see her, and said, "Rickie can't come to the phone right now." Her mother lost it, because she was sure Rickie was off having sex with this guy. Everyone knew about it, I learned afterward, her mother, her sister, everyone but me. He lived there in that house with the endless green lawn. You see, he wasn't Jewish.

When Rickie spoke to her mother, I saw the joy drain from her face. We had been so happy listening to the music, wandering from group to group. On the way home, we left the radio on one station, and we hardly said a word. I went in with Rickie, thinking her mother would go easier on her with a friend around; instead, she attacked us both. "Young people today ah SHITHEADS!" she screamed. "Yawr all SHITHEADS!" She yelled about the perils of "intuhdating." Intuhdating led to petting, and petting led to the worst evil of all, intuhmarriage. I wasn't used to this; my parents never raised their voices, only stroked me with a brush dipped in acidic guilt. My throat grew hard and tight, and my head filled, ready to explode. I was shaking. "You—you don't look good," her mother said finally. "Don't make huh cry!" Rickie burst out. I couldn't help it. I cried. I always cry when people scream at me. I was even vile enough to stroke Rickie with guilt afterward, telling her that no one had ever spoken to me like that in my life. I'm sure she thought it was all her fault, and I let her think it.

I didn't see Rickie much after that. I went away to college, and she studied at a school nearby. Then when I had graduated and come back from six weeks in France, she came to see me. "She's about nine months pregnant," my mother said. It was Rickie, all right, still beautiful, still with her shy giggle, enormous and ready to burst. She didn't know who the father was. "Oh, I'm wild now," she said, and she threw back her head and laughed crazily. She had stopped getting her period, she told me, but she had thought that she was just, you know, not getting her period. Then her mother told her, "You look like you're about five months pregnant," and she was, and it was too late. She was going to give the baby up for adoption. Her mother had arranged for it to go to a Jewish family, and she was urging the hospital to record the birth as the removal of a growth, so that it wouldn't go on record and prevent Rickie from marrying a nice man someday.

I was busy, getting ready to start grad school, and I missed her delivery a week later. She showed me a picture of a red little thing with black hair plastered down on its sticky head. "It was a boy," she said, "the most beautifulest baby boy you ever saw." I showed her my pictures of France, and she asked me quietly if she could see the picture of the synagogue one more time. That was the last time I saw her, and I've always wondered what became of Rickie and her most beautifulest baby boy.

The light is golden now, my favorite part of the day. Are you out there, Josh? What's it like to be a Jew? I have tried so hard to understand. When I was growing up, all my friends belonged except for me. The mothers screamed at their sons if they asked me out, and no matter how much time I spent with everyone, there was always that difference. I loved them so much, and I think they even loved me a little, but somehow, I was an intruder. Twenty years and I'm still at it, still reaching out, still daring. Same yellow canary plumes on the parkway, same Mets, same Passover, same spring, and same me, still out of place.

So many guys have told me I'm incapable of love. I can't imagine what it's like to create new life, or to live with someone for a lifetime. But I do know how it feels to be connected and to know that I've made the right connection. That connection can be many things; it can create wonders, and it need not hurt. Please let me transmit, please let this connection live.

The light is dimmer, pinkish now, and the images are so strong I don't trust myself to write. "Jewish women light Shabbat candles, 18 minutes before sunset, 7:14 in New York City," say tiny letters at the bottom of my *New York Times*. I imagine candles glowing on your dining room table. I imagine you smiling, laughing in the fading light. The same light is withdrawing from this café window, and these limp red silk flowers form a feeble reflection of your candle's glow.

Laura Otis

Live well, Josh. You always live well, and I will live, as I always have, in my own way.

18:32, 7 APRIL 1997
FROM: LEE ANN DOWNING
TO: MARCIA PINTO

I'M SORRY TO HAVE STOPPED THE QUESTIONS, ESPECIALLY AFTER you told me your story. You have been an inspiration, and I have been thinking about this book somewhere in the back of my mind.

You're asking what's the difference between *Fatal Attraction*, Alex leading the terrified kid onto the roller coaster, and *Sleeping with the Enemy*, the control freak husband feeding his wife's blind, old mother her dinner. You've hit on the main problem: how to be fair to the guys.

Even though I may call my book *Boiling the Rabbit*, I don't want it to be a man-bashing book. I want people to be able to learn from it. I want to people to think. It's so stupid to write off half of humanity, over three billion people. With your help, I want to show everyone what stories we're writing and what these stories are doing to us. When I can answer your question, I'll be able to write a book: a theoretical chapter, a chapter on *Liaisons dangereuses*, a chapter on *The Crucible*, a chapter on *Fatal Attraction*. In my business we always know what chapters we're going to write before we know what we're going to say. That's where you come in—helping me figure out what to say. Is this parasitism?

The difference between *Fatal Attraction* and *Sleeping with the Enemy* seems to lie in the titles. We've got to be fair: there are movies about both male and female psychos stalking people with whom they think they're in love. The male ones tend to be husbands and boyfriends who are trying to retrieve a woman who's escaped. I can't think of any movie about a man who goes crazy and harasses a married woman to death because after one night of passion, he has fallen madly in love with her but she's dumped him. They don't do this; at least, we don't watch them do it on film. In the movies they have more pride: they take what they can get, and then they move on to a new one.

Suppose you switched the titles. "Sleeping with the Enemy" would work fine for *Fatal Attraction*: Dan and Alex are enemies almost from the start, as though they're competing for something only one of them can have. But "Fatal Attraction" doesn't work for *Sleeping with the Enemy*, because that movie's not about attraction. It's about an unusual situation, a poor, sweet woman trying to escape slavery imposed by a psychopath who never seems normal. *Fatal Attraction* was designed to be the story of Any Guy, who feels an attraction Any Guy can feel and who makes the "fatal" mistake of indulging his lust with someone who, for a while, seems normal. I have to keep thinking about this.

My book has been deferred lately because I've been thinking about a friend of mine and her guy, who is worrisome because he doesn't fit these patterns. He's married, and my friend was with him once four years ago and once three months ago. He told his wife, the fool, and she left him and took their little girl with her. What's worst is that at the same time, he may be losing his job. My concern is not for him but for my friend, who is susceptible to guilt. He's not like the guys I'm used to (or you, I bet). He seems to need companionship and support to stay alive, and my good-hearted friend may spend her time providing it instead of doing the work she needs to do to survive. Is this fatal attraction? Seems more like female attraction. She keeps saying how wonderful he is, and I try not to laugh loud enough for her to hear. What would you tell her?

And my own life? My own life is in everything I teach and everything I write, like a perfume that permeates everything that's yours but only other people can smell. Probably you've smelled it. Yeah, there's a guy. Yeah, he's married. Aren't they all? Two kids, boys, computer wizards like him. I see him once a year at conferences. Yeah, we've done it. I'm afraid to activate the cascade of praises that rushes through my mind when I think of him, but, oh, boy, here I go: he's brilliant; he's hilarious; he's written 5 books and 50 articles; he's such a good writer it scares you; he works the words like a Language God; and he knows your thoughts before you know them yourself. For a while we wrote, and it was like a Vulcan mind meld, but I wrote too much, or maybe he doesn't like my mind, and now he thinks I'm Alex Forrest. You get the picture. How does tetrodotoxin work?

19:30, 10 APRIL 1997
FROM: REBECCA FASS
TO: LEE ANN DOWNING

A GOOD DAY TODAY. AT GROUP MEETING WE DECIDED THAT Marcia and Dawn have enough data to write, and that guy Jacobsen called from Marin's lab. He really is coming to do a postdoc here starting in August, and he's flying out in three weeks to check out our setup.

I'm struggling to keep my mind on the lab while I grapple with my concern for Owen. I've held back from writing, thinking he'll find his way better without me, but the picture of him alone in Chicago remains fixed in my head. Anything else I envision pops up on a corner of the screen, like on those TVs where you can check out one channel while watching another. I am tuned in, permanently, to the Owen channel, with little cat neurons reaching out to each other down in the corner.

How is the Josh situation? You're not doing anything crazy, are you? How is your book going? Whatever you feel for this guy, can you channel it into your book?

18:12, 11 APRIL 1997
FROM: LEE ANN DOWNING
TO: REBECCA FASS

CHANNELING, THAT'S NOT THE WORD: WRITING WHEN YOU FEEL this way is more like telling your mind it must be a dam holding back a million billion tons of water. The dam has one pinprick in it, and through this you're supposed to let the water emerge in a perfect, needle-fine, linear spurt. It's easier not to let anything through at all.

The hardest thing is avoiding clichés, which gets harder the more water you hold back. Remember that guy Dieter in college who we called the cliché police? He'd listen carefully to everything you said and snap, "That's a cliché!" when he detected one. After a while you couldn't talk at all. What made me maddest is that he never expressed himself in any way that was mildly interesting. At some point, I incorporated Dieter into my head, and whenever I write, he pops up and crows triumphantly, "That's a cliché!" It's like he thinks he should get a prize whenever he finds one. The words that get through the Great Dieter Dam run pure enough, but they lack the force of that million billion tons. If I'm going to write a decent book, that's the force I need to summon.

All I do is write. Every thought that comes through is directed to Josh, in a message I write in my head. I write notes for the rabbit book, notes for teaching other people's books. I write email; I write in my diary. My sensations become messages as soon as they register; my memories become messages anytime they bubble up, and all day and all night I splice together memories and sensations

Laura Otis

into a designer virus I hope will set off uncontrolled production of memories and sensations when it infects his mind. Just imagine if Alex Forrest worked in biotechnology!

But what I'd love best would be if I could transmit to him directly from a chip in my mind, like Molly in *Neuromancer*. Remember that science fiction class we took? That's how we got to know each other, isn't it? I thought you were so cool when you related ideas in that book to the way the brain works. Could I send Josh data directly from my brain, have him jack into me and live in me, seeing everything I see and feeling everything I feel? Without having to be a Great Dieter Dam, could he turn it all into writing? I wonder if he could take it. He'd probably recoil like Spock from the Horta who was in agony. It hurts to hold back a million billion tons of pain.

20:09, 14 APRIL 1997
FROM: LEE ANN DOWNING
TO: JOSH GOLDEN
SUBJECT: LOSERS

RHONDA USED TO SAY SHE DIDN'T WANT TO BE LIKE HER PARENTS; her parents were losers. Her mother taught sociology, and her father taught computer science. Neither one of them got tenure, and they ended up teaching courses here and there at community colleges. Her mother finally left academia altogether and went into personnel work.

Rhonda's father was a superannuated hippie with bushy hair and a beard. He and her brother, a math genius, used to love playing Dungeons and Dragons. They would invite all the guys over who were good at math and physics, and they would create monstrous characters. That's what her father loved, filling his house with scheming 16-year-olds. I used to go because my boyfriend went, but I never joined in their collective fantasies. It was a weird place, stacks of papers growing like crops, barely any furniture, just a huge scrap-metal statue of a dinosaur and a refrigerator with nothing but beer.

One night when her father had had a lot to drink, he sidled up to me, and I felt his moist, beery breath on my neck and his bulk pressing me from behind. He said, "Hey, darling, wouldn't you like to come upstairs with me and warm my bed for a little while?" He stroked his hand over my forearm like a crab crawling up a Rodin nymph. I was 15. I think I smiled when I said no; I should have punched him in his algorithmic balls.

From then on, I liked Rhonda better. Nobody could stand Rhonda. When she was 10, she told us she was going to Caltech, and she was going to major in physics. She had to beat everyone at everything. The guys hated her because she could do math and physics better than they could; the girls hated her because she despised them.

As she got older, she got more and more gorgeous. Her body seemed to be made of bronze. She went running and did aerobics five days a week, and she had the kind of body guys dream of: big on top, no hips to speak of, and legs that never end. Somehow, she found clothes for nothing that made her look more mature.

Rhonda took all AP courses, got an 800 on her math SAT, 700 on her verbal, but she explained that she had never felt any affinity for "soft" fields that didn't require real intelligence. As a writer I was beneath contempt for her, like the guys dumb enough to let their hormones rule and put moves on her. She would tell about those episodes in detail and laugh her head off.

Toward the end of senior year, Rhonda got this crazy idea to sing in the high school talent show. She got up on stage in a merry widow and looked so good, it was almost frightening. She was a great singer, but as far as we were concerned, it was payback time. "Boooooo!" we howled, hundreds and hundreds of us. Math nerds and cheerleaders combined their voices to scream her off the stage. Rhonda just put the mike up to her mouth and swiveled her hips and sang louder. She was singing "The Time Warp," and she looked better than anyone in *Rocky Horror*.

When Rhonda was 17, she got into Caltech, early decision. She bragged about how she would be warm when we were freezing our butts off in the Northeast. New York was for losers. Her whole life was an attempt to prove she wasn't a loser: her science, her body, and someday her marriage and kids would all furnish evidence for that proof.

Rhonda liked men, just hated most of them the way she hated most women. I always wondered if she could love a guy. Maybe at Caltech, but it would have to be a guy who looked gorgeous, had established himself in his field, did hard science, was hard to get, was hard all over, and wanted to live with a one-woman war on softness. I heard she was with one of her professors until he dumped her. She wouldn't talk about it; that at least had changed.

Lots of things remind me of Rhonda. She's a voice I never exorcised from my head: disgusted, mocking laughter at anything imperfect. She's like that killer robot on *Star Trek* that got its instructions crossed when aliens reprogrammed it. It had been sent to search for new biological life-forms; the aliens wanted it to sterilize soil samples and seek out errors in computer programs, and it ended up seeking out new biological life-forms and sterilizing any that were imperfect. In the end, Kirk talked it into self-destruction when it was forced to admit it had made an error. I always felt sorry for the thing, the changeling, Kirk called it. I was rooting for it for a while, just as I was rooting for Rhonda while I booed her. The robot just wanted to wipe out all the losers. Sometimes I feel like that probe, floating out there alone, half-smashed by asteroids, with aliens fingering my circuits.

Are you out there, Josh? I miss you. I am harmless. I wouldn't ever hurt you or anyone else.

12:37, 18 APRIL 1997
FROM: OWEN BAUER
TO: REBECCA FASS

I KEEP THINKING OF YOU, AND I SENSE YOU THINKING OF ME EVEN though we've been quiet. It helps me to know you're out there in your lab, with your cats and those beautiful hands fingering the keys. It's just been hard to find the will to write.

You know me too well. Physics is not enough, never has been, never will be. Whatever force it is that makes me love chasing quarks isn't enough to get me up in the morning. I have gotten up this past week and shown up when I'm supposed to, and I've written things that sound like an article.

I told Dave right away. I had to, and he's been sympathetic. He thinks Trish will come back, and he's reading over what I write each day—writing it himself would be more like it. We're trying to hide the divorce from Rhonda. Whereas a lot of bosses might like it (no wife and no kid means more energy for physics), we both have this gut instinct that she'll hold it against me, the final piece of evidence that I'm a sinking ship.

You know me well enough to guess how I feel. Work for me means existing, surviving. The meaning and purpose you speak of, like the joy, for the past four years have come from my daughter, and before that from Trish and her faith in me. She's lost that faith now, for good reason, and I'm left wondering why anyone should have faith in me again. I'm afraid to ask myself why you do. I want to be as good to all of you as I can— you, Trish, Jeannie—Rhonda!—all my women, after the terrible mistakes I've made. One thing you can be sure of is that you know everything just as it is. For some time now, I've been incapable of hiding anything from anyone. It's just a question of time before Rhonda finds out. In answer to your questions, I do eat, go to bed, get up. I just never know what I've eaten five minutes later, and in the night, instead of sleeping, I think alternately of you and Trish.

There are a lot of other things to think about. Trish made good money, more than I did, and I'm going to have to move out of this place. I can't pay for it myself. Hopefully this article will mean my fellowship will be renewed, but there's no guarantee; it will depend on what Rhonda writes about me. If the renewal doesn't come through, I'm unemployed, and I'll have to figure out what other kinds of jobs I can do. I suppose I could be someone's technician, or I could do something with computers, or I could try teaching physics somewhere. I think I would like that. I do like what I'm doing now, or pretending to do—oh, no, she's coming, gotta

7:48, 21 APRIL 1997
FROM: REBECCA FASS
TO: LEE ANN DOWNING

HOW ARE YOU? OWEN IS HANGING IN THERE, JUST BARELY. His boss, Rhonda, seems to want him out of there and may be divorcing him from his job on top of everything else. This woman intrigues me. She really seems to hate him, for reasons I can't fathom. How could anyone hate Owen? It would be like hating ice cream, or hating the earth.

18:06, 21 APRIL 1997
FROM: LEE ANN DOWNING
TO: REBECCA FASS

Her name is RHONDA? Listen, this may sound crazy, but I think I may know this woman. I know a Rhonda who went into physics, and how many of them can there be? If it's her, he doesn't have a prayer. Not to be rude or anything, but I can see how someone could hate Owen—all love, no control. I have a feeling I shouldn't look at this one too hard. But seriously, ask him what Rhonda's last name is—or no, ask him what she looks like.

21:45, 21 APRIL 1997
FROM: REBECCA FASS
TO: OWEN BAUER

The force of your honesty and your human feeling would inspire faith in anyone, and from me you can be sure not only of trust but of undying admiration and respect. I'm trying to think, and I can't imagine anything you could do that would turn me against you. I trust you because of what you are, not what you do, and that isn't going to change. If you think you're capable of nothing good, I can assure you that what you've done for me alone ensures you've accomplished something beautiful in this world. You've given me a few hours of happiness so intense that no matter what happens now, I'll fight to keep living in the hope that I'll know such moments again. Hardly anyone has ever seen me as a woman, and sometimes I wonder, but you've made me appreciate what I am, and I hope I can do the same for you. You've made me love being alive.

Well, I'm glad to hear that you're eating. But what I really want to ask you about is Rhonda. I'm intrigued by this woman.

Maybe I can help you deal with her—the gender frontier, that's my territory. What's her last name? Where's she from? What does she look like?

00:27, 24 APRIL 1997
FROM: OWEN BAUER
TO: REBECCA FASS

WRITING IS THE LAST THING I SHOULD BE DOING NOW, BUT I can't help it. I just got done talking to Rhonda. Well, "talking to Rhonda" isn't the right words for it—being threatened and bullied, then vomiting everything out all over the place, that would be more like it. It's actually getting to be funny, and it would be if it were happening to someone else. What kind of job should a person have who, when cornered, can think of nothing to say but the truth? Not physics, that's for sure. In physics you have to tell the truth when you do it but lie in order to be able to.

Rhonda isn't usually around this late at night, so she took me by surprise. Just as I was starting to write to you, she burst in and demanded to see what I had written in the past week. I said Dave had it, which is true, and she asked me, "Who's writing this article, lover boy, you or him?" I suspect she knows he's covering for me, and she's been looking for hard evidence. Technically there's nothing wrong with him helping me, but collaborations bug her, especially any she hasn't set up herself. Possibly she smells a conspiracy.

Tonight "lover boy" hit me like a wet towel in the face, and something happened, I don't know what. Suddenly I stopped caring. I wasn't afraid of her anymore. "Don't call me that," I said, and I saw her slow, spreading smile as she prepared for the combat she's been wanting so long. I shouldn't be so sensitive, she said. Take it easy; it was a joke. What really concerned her, and what had led her to use it, was my inability to find a balance between my personal life and my work. I asked her how well she was doing in that respect. It was fun. It was as if I were listening to someone else talk to her. I have no idea how I was coming up with these things. I didn't care.

As I watched her conceal her rage (I'd landed one that time), I thought of what Dave had said about how she was really attracted to me and wanted me to overpower her. It was inconceivable. She barely seems like a human being, let alone a woman I'd want to make love to. But I guess what Dave meant has nothing to do with love. "Look," she said, "you know the truth. You're not cutting it here. This is big time, not some nine-to-five job to support your family. You put anything before this, you don't belong here. There are a hundred guys out there willing to give twice what you give. You've got the brains, but your passion is going somewhere else." I asked her what she thought passion was and where hers was going. She never hesitated. "Passion is wanting something bad enough to give everything," she said. "And I want this group to do good physics. I give everything, and you give everything, aw yawr outa heah." Her New York accent gets stronger when she's trying to intimidate you.

I stood up. I had been sitting in my chair looking up at her, feeling like Don Giovanni talking with the statue. She is statuesque, maybe 5'10" and built, but as you know, I'm a lot taller. My height didn't faze her. She just mocked me with her eyes. "How did you get this kind of power?" I asked. "You know nothing about motivating people. We DO good physics here, but it's in spite of you, not because of you." Her voice was level, disgusted, as she told me my attitude was completely unprofessional.

Her eyes kept going to the picture of Jeannie, all blond curls and happy smile, over my desk. Finally I answered her accusing stare. "The fact that you have not succeeded in combining good physics with a family life," I told her, "doesn't mean it can't be done." She smiled at me, a chilling, mocking smile, as she retorted that she wished I could think as clearly when doing my job as when defending my lack of commitment to it. Her personal life was not relevant here.

That's when it happened. I wanted to hit her on her square, bronze jaw, but instead the truth bailed out of its own accord. I was crashing and burning, and the truth bailed out. I told her she didn't need to worry about my family taking time away from physics anymore, because I no longer had a family. Trish had left and taken Jeannie with her. This fazed her. I saw the impulses run across her face (she does have a striking face, in her own way), and the mocking smile disappeared. For a nanosecond, she considered that maybe I would have more time for physics, then rejected the thought, realizing that the misery involved would rob me of what little worth I had. There was also scorn. Whatever she may think of families and traditional gender roles, she was disgusted I hadn't been man enough to keep my wife. And she also felt sorry for me, even as she hated me for being a loser. I could see compassion, treading water in contempt and drowning. Sympathy is too dangerous for her. Sympathy keeps you from destroying losers, who pop up everywhere and undermine your ability to achieve. People like me are an infectious disease to her.

"I'm sorry," she said. "I didn't know." I just looked at her. "You write a good article," she said, "FAST, and show me what you've got, and I'll take it into consideration in the rankings. Just put this behind you and write." I told her I WAS writing a good article. "Right," she said, "you do that." And she was gone.

The shock hit me only afterward. I think she respects me more for standing up to her and less for having lost my family, so I've come out even. This probably means I'll be out of a job by the end of the year. But who cares? I've always felt like an impostor here.

Oh, about Rhonda. I don't think her background matters, but if you're interested, her name is Rhonda Tiedemann, and she's from somewhere near New York where they say things like "Yawr outa heah." Looks? Somehow the concept doesn't apply to her: tall, athletic, good figure, I guess, not a pretty face, but dresses well. Not someone I'd ever consider to be in my mating pool. Please write me something from the world where there are sane people, and thanks for your kind words about me.

8:30, 25 APRIL 1997
FROM: REBECCA FASS
TO: LEE ANN DOWNING

THIS RHONDA IS SCARY. HER LAST NAME IS TIEDEMANN, AND HE says that she's tall and well put together, sort of like the bionic woman. Is she the one? I wonder how she got this way. She hates him, and I can't understand how anyone could.

12:01, 25 APRIL 1997
FROM: LEE ANN DOWNING
TO: REBECCA FASS

SHIT! THAT'S HER! I HAVE TO TEACH IN FOUR MINUTES, AND I'VE got a stack of papers coming in. He's going to have to get out, because with her in charge, he has no hope.

19:06, 28 APRIL 1997
FROM: LEE ANN DOWNING
TO: MARCIA PINTO

How goes it in the lab? The book on female rage keeps growing in my head, and each new example leads me in new directions. As soon as this semester ends, I'll be free to write, and I can't wait. I envision days at my desk, watching the oak tree and listening to the ice cream truck's melody, writing about myths of women on the rampage.

To be ready, I need to ask you one more question: What makes you maddest? What do you think makes a woman angriest? In this book, you get to be Freud, the "approximately normal person." If you did put tetrodotoxin in the fish tank, what would put you over the edge? What is this stuff anyway?

20:20, 28 APRIL 1997
FROM: MARCIA PINTO
TO: LEE ANN DOWNING

It's great to hear from you! We've been working nonstop, trying to write up this new finding on how darkness affects synapse formation before Becky heads for Germany next month. She's going to be there for about two months, studying this new technique they have for intracellular recording.

Oh, before I forget, tetrodotoxin is a sodium channel blocker. If you put it anywhere near a neuron, no sodium ions can cross the membrane, and the neuron can't form an action potential. This is real good if it's your lab and you want to study other ionic currents, and real bad if it's your neuron. It would fry his fish. I may still do it. He just needs to do one more thing to put me over the edge.

Let's see, what would do it? Maybe if he walked by me one more time as if I weren't there. What gets me is when they think you don't feel. Guys have this amazing ability to shut down feelings when they think the feelings aren't good for them: getting angry won't do me any good, so I won't get angry; wanting this woman isn't good for me, so I won't want this woman anymore. And then he just doesn't. They decide what they're going to feel, and then they feel it. And they presume you can do the same thing. They tell you to feel only the emotions that suit their convenience.

But that still isn't it. It's something about the wanting—yeah—it's when they think you don't want. It's when they deny your desire—not deny WHAT you desire, but deny THAT you desire. It's when they see the connection between you and them as an arrow going one way, from them to you, so that when their desire stops, the connection ends. They can't seem to believe that we want them as much as they want us, or that we can't stop wanting them on demand. When he walks by, greets the people next to me, and looks right through me, I start to wonder whether I exist. Wanting someone, wanting anything, having feelings, feelings that you generate yourself, that's existing, and when they deny your desire, they deny your existence. I don't want to think about this anymore. Better go back to the synapses. Ask me more questions, though, this is fun.

18:08, 29 APRIL 1997
FROM: LEE ANN DOWNING
TO: MARCIA PINTO

I FIND THIS FASCINATING. I THINK YOU'VE GOT IT. HOW ARE YOU supposed to act when people refuse to accept that you have desires? How can you prove you have feelings without smashing something? But I'm still concerned about being fair to the guys, much as I want to go on the rampage.

Imagine some dork adores you and lusts after you, and you tell him you're not interested. Aren't you denying his desire? Aren't you denying his existence? What would you say is the difference? How do you treat guys when you want to get rid of them? Also, if a guy doesn't want you anymore, there's nothing you can really do about it, is there? I mean, you can't make a guy want you. If a guy is trying to get rid of you and you hold on with a death grip, I can imagine him asking, "What do you want from me?" How would you answer that question?

20:06, 29 APRIL 1997
FROM: MARCIA PINTO
TO: LEE ANN DOWNING

GLAD I CHECKED MY EMAIL. THIS IS A GREAT BREAK FROM choosing which scan to use as a figure. Okay, so Case One: Desired by a Dork. Well, I wouldn't encourage him in the first place. I wouldn't have sex with him just because he wants to, that's for sure. And when I told him I wouldn't go out with him, I'd say I was sorry. It's all in the way you look at someone. I would look at the dork as if he were really there. A guy I did like and had been with for a while, I would tell him the truth, but I'd still talk to him and look at him unless he treated me badly. I wouldn't treat him as if he weren't there, even if I wished he weren't.

Case Two: I Desire Him, He Dumps Me. Sounds familiar. What do I want? To feel significant. To have him smile at me when he sees me and tell me with his eyes that he remembers. I would feel significant if I could believe that he would always remember, but evidence shows he's trying to erase the memory. Killington hasn't smiled at me since he told me to get lost. Maybe he thinks I would come panting after him if he smiled. But that would mean he believes I have desires. How can a guy be afraid of something and not believe in it at the same time? But I think that's what they do.

19:33, 30 APRIL 1997
FROM: LEE ANN DOWNING
TO: REBECCA FASS

HE STILL WON'T ANSWER. WE'RE DOING THE LEBANESE THING now, me shooting at him, him not letting himself shoot back, yet somehow he has all the power. I'm the outlaw; spring is torture this year. I want him so badly I could scream, and I wake up at 3:30 each morning and writhe and sweat for hours in bed. Then I get up and teach Thomas Mann, always Mann for the end of the semester.

My neuroendocrine system is on a hair trigger. I see frizzy brown hair and a blue cotton shirt and start as though I've been hit, like those baby birds that will follow a stick with a red dot on it because they think it's their mother. Funny how in our eagerness to see what we want to see and be near people with whom we've bonded, our sensory systems let the most minimal cues suffice. We see people when they're barely there, or when they're not there at all. I'm always thinking I see Josh when he's not there and telling myself afterward, "It could be him." If he wanted to, he could drive here in an hour and a half. I miss his voice, low, light, mocking, lots of "uh," never any *r*'s.

I'll send you everything I've sent him so far so that you can tell me what you think. Does that mean we're experimenting on the guys again? I don't know what to do next. I wonder if he even reads the stuff. He may be blocking my messages, so that my passion is flowing into the black hole of cyberspace, deep space with the transporter on scatter. If I knew that were happening, I wonder if I would stop writing. Everything I live now is writing, and everything I write is for him, beamed directly to him. Is this an existence? Do I exist if he reads it? Do I exist if he doesn't read it? How can I make him want me again? What should I write?

18:14, 1 MAY 1997
FROM: OWEN BAUER
TO: REBECCA FASS

I couldn't write anything today. I was thinking too much. Writing and thinking shouldn't be mutually exclusive, but they are. Scientific writing is all formulas, which you string together according to what particle you're looking for and who you're competing with. Today the formulas seemed as inadequate as I am, just sitting there, not good for anything.

We spend our lives trying to show that these particles that exist in theory also exist in fact. The government gives us huge sums of money to create elaborate setups through which minute deviations in the tiniest fraction of a second provide evidence that these particles existed in a flicker. What does it mean to exist? I can't escape the thought that our "proof" of this top quark's existence is something we generate ourselves. We create the existence as an idea, and then, with millions of dollars, overgrown equipment, and hundreds of people's lives, we make that existence happen. My equipment isn't made for listening, like yours, to something already happening. My equipment creates and destroys by smashing things into each other.

Becky. If only I could touch you. Would my top quark exist at all if Wendell hadn't theorized it should, and I hadn't been down here in the dark for three years shooting particles into each other? But that isn't the worst. Even if this top quark does exist, even if we've visualized something that exists rather than fabricated proof of our fantasies, what does it matter? When the sun goes out and we're all dead, if we don't destroy ourselves first with the knowledge about particles we've gained so far, what difference will it make whether we know about everything that exists or not? Supposedly science slowly uncovers what exists, but it's tempting to say that what exists is what is known. I made a top quark exist, and now I get to write about it, my top quark. (As far as Rhonda is concerned, it's "our" top quark.) Who cares? Why is this news? What has changed? I feel as if the universe is laughing at me.

And I—do I exist? My parents made me exist, but they're gone now. As I lay in the dark, alone in our apartment last night, I asked myself what I was, and whether I was. No one would invest the energy or time to visualize me. In my business, to exist is to leave traces: bubbles, debris, knocking something off course. What traces have I left, or will I leave? I made a child, a beautiful child, and her mother has taken her away from me. In 10 years, what will she think of me? Memories are traces, but it won't take long until we're all forgotten. The biological traces, those seem to be the strongest, passing on our DNA, but that's not the reason I love Jeannie. She's always looked more like Trish than like me. I love her just because she's there. I think that may be what existence means: being loved because you're there. I love my top quark because it's there. I wish the same were true for me.

Because of my actions, there's no longer anyone who feels that way about me, and I'm responsible. I undermined my existence myself. When I'm not in the lab and I work at home or take Metra to the city, I go through whole days without talking to anyone. You're my last link, although I've tried not to say so, because it would put unfair pressure on you. I walk through the streets, and no one sees me. I eat, and I wonder why I'm worthy of being fed. All of us, all human beings, are we really so wonderful that our existence should continue? Think of everything we've destroyed. I go on because the will to live defies any rational analysis.

What should I do? I'm going to be kicked out of here sooner rather than later. Suddenly, without a wife or child, I realize I could go anywhere, do anything—write software, teach 14-year-olds, write poetry, serve soup. What does it matter? In 20 or 30 years, when my heart gives out (nobody in my family has made it past 60), what difference will it make? I can't see myself writing or teaching or creating anything good enough to be remembered, except my daughter. I'm sorry to be sending these particles of depression slamming into you. Something tells me you get a lot of them. Well, I'll grit my teeth and try to write some more sentences. Dave should be here in a few minutes to help me.

8:42, 2 MAY 1997
FROM: REBECCA FASS
TO: OWEN BAUER

YOU'RE SCARING ME. I WANT YOU TO KNOW THAT I'M HERE AND listening and rooting for you as hard as I can. I know who you are, and I know how beautiful you are, and I know you can do anything. Your work is real, and your work matters, but more important, you are real, and you matter.

You are wrong about Jeannie. She will always love and respect you, no matter what her mother says. I know because even now, after 30 years of hearing that my father was shit in human form, I still want to see him. And if he were YOU! My father IS pretty close to shit in human form, and if someone can love him, how could she not love you, who are ambrosia poured into the same mold (after they washed the shit out of it). Even if you had done nothing else productive in your life, the time you've spent with me has given me such joy that you would have earned your right to exist just with that. And you've done so much!

Science—tonight isn't the time to ask me to defend science, with everything here all messed up. Both of our best oscilloscopes are down, and the new postdoc from Marin's lab arrives tomorrow. Tony is on the phone now, begging companies to get someone the hell down here to fix the scopes. This double whammy would hurt at the best of times, but it's especially hard when I'm rushing to get work done before I leave for Germany. I'll be over there in June and July, back in our old place listening to German cells. With the mountain of work standing between me and Cologne, I won't be able to write, eat, or sleep much before I go.

But I've never questioned whether neurobiology is worth doing. It's a kind of arrogance, maybe. I think it's our brain, and we have a right to know how it works. I don't see why we can't say the same thing for the universe. Okay, so maybe it's not our universe, but we're here, aren't we? As long as we're here, we might as well figure out what it's made of. You have a right to do that.

What you're saying about the quark is interesting, whether it's really there or whether you make it happen. It seems like 99% of what we think is here in life, we make happen ourselves. Why should science be any different? The cells I listen to fire on their own. In the lab I make them fire by controlling what my kitties see. As far as you know, the top quark is out there, right? I only see a problem if the theoreticians say it doesn't exist and you try to make it exist anyway. But wait—didn't Columbus do something like that? Maybe there isn't anything you can do wrong in science.

What I'm trying to say is, just write the article. String the formulas together even if you don't believe in them right now. Do it on autopilot. Some of my best articles have been written on autopilot. If you don't, somebody else is going to step in and take credit for your project and make your quark his quark, and I guarantee you, the truth will not be served. Science will continue to scream for the existence of this particle, and your résumé will be shorter, that's all.

No matter what happens, it's worth being alive. There is nothing that could happen to me that would make me want to die, and I wish I could mind-meld with you to make you feel the same way. Live for Jeannie, for me, if nothing else, but most of all, live for yourself. I wish you could see how meaningful, how beautiful your life is. I wish I could show you. If I were with you, I would show you right now.

19:15, 2 MAY 1997
FROM: REBECCA FASS
TO: LEE ANN DOWNING

I'M SCARED ABOUT OWEN. THINGS HAVE CAUGHT UP WITH HIM, and he's more depressed than I've ever heard him. He doesn't sound like he's going to kill himself, just slowly wind down into nothing. He doesn't seem to want anything anymore. I feel as if I've wounded him, and now he's got gangrene. No—I amputated something, and he's developed blood poisoning. I'm going to send you the stuff he's been sending me, so you can see how his mind works and maybe give me some advice. Should I ask him to come out here? I'm not sure this is what he needs, or what I want. To be taken in right away by another woman might be more demoralizing for him than rebuilding his life by himself.

Your guy—I've read your stuff, and I don't get the logic. You're trying to seduce him with decapitation, bigotry, gender confusion, sadness, and failure? He's from Long Island, so you show him Long Island—at its worst? I think you're onto something. Memory is the ultimate aphrodisiac, but you've got to send him something more upbeat. What about beaches, ice cream, that way of talking you have out there, that outrageous sense of humor? That's the main thing I remember about Long Island from the time I visited you: driving, the songs we sang on the radio, crowded beaches that smelled of french fries, Italian food, and the mall.

What is he into besides Dickens? I mean, do this scientifically. I still get the feeling you're writing what you want to let out of you rather than what he wants to hear. I am against this whole project, but if you're going to do it, do it right. It's an interesting experiment, to see if you can seduce a guy in cyberspace. I want to know what happens.

Food. Is he into food? How about a *Tom Jones* type of deal, images of you eating, your luscious lips and tongue sucking on a chicken leg? God, I can't believe I'm saying this. I must be in some sort of evil mood today. Figure out a way to involve your body. My guess is, he's into you. Your hair, maybe. You've got such great hair. Or that teeny-tiny waist of yours. God, you've got such a great body. Why don't you use it? What are his favorite parts?

Is this the logic? "You come from here. You ARE here. I come from here. I love it here. I AM here. Therefore, you are me; you love me." I think it could work. You just don't have it right yet. Lace it with your body, and let me know what he does.

If he hasn't freaked yet, I think you're right; he isn't going to. There's something I like about Josh, such a diversion from Owen. I mean, I don't want to switch guys or anything, but this is comic relief, the difference between wooing Hamlet and Falstaff.

My cells are getting restless tonight.

19:02, 3 MAY 1997
FROM: LEE ANN DOWNING
TO: REBECCA FASS

I always knew you had it in you. Wooing Falstaff, that's a good one. Josh isn't Falstaff, though. He seems like it until you get to know him, and then you realize you're wooing Richard III.

21:33, 3 MAY 1997
FROM: LEE ANN DOWNING
TO: JOSH GOLDEN
SUBJECT: SAILING TO BYZANTIUM

You always know what season it is depending on how cold you feel at Jamaica. Today I'm just a little cold because of the wind that blows my hair up into my mouth and eyes. I crack through the tunnels and clatter up the steps in my black high-heeled boots. My blue silk shirt flutters in the foul wind from the subways. On a rooftop on 81st Street, a Japanese cherry is blooming, pink blossoms against blue sky. Yes, spring has come even to New York.

I've come to see the Byzantium exhibit, and instantly I'm engulfed in a swarm. I hear the hushed, caressing tones of French, the ringing vowels of German. I am so restless that I can't look at the treasures the way I'm supposed to. I dart along, stopping only when the glittering gold icons draw me like a magpie.

What arrests me today is the writhing torsos of the Rodin sculptures. Rodin is a genius, intrigued by transformations, bodies wanting, twisting, suffering. He stops movement, but he shows it happening; he stops time, yet he reveals its flow. One of his women looks just like me, tiny, twisting, hair spilling all over, flat on her back yet with every part of her going a different way.

After Byzantium, I eat an orange whose peel falls away almost as I touch it, with a hollow into which I eagerly plunge my thumb. I write for an hour, the light fleeing and returning as thick gray clouds drift between the skylight and the sun.

Then an angry African man who is bussing trays tells me that I have to go. "You can't take THIS"—he gestures toward the single chair, the round table, and the tray littered with orange peel—"for THAT"—he waves disgustedly at the sheet of loose-leaf paper covered with writing. I think he is a pathetic bully, taking his anger out on the smallest woman he can find. It's hard to find a place to write. Writing is not worth a table, a chair, or a tray.

For the past weeks, images and memories have awakened me at four each morning, and I am too restless to study anything closely. I walk rapidly through the pleasure dome and visit my favorite places: the 18th-century French rooms, with their gold and pastels; the Islamic room with its blue-and-white ceramics and gurgling fountain; the hazy blue Monet haystacks that look like muffins; the medieval Madonnas with their long braids; the gray light that floods the Temple of Dendur; and my favorite, the Indian wing, to visit Ganesha, Mover of Obstacles. I love the roundness of Indian art, the breasts like globes, the reaching arms, the gods that smile and dance. Ganesha has the head and trunk of an elephant and the round body of a man who indulges himself. He wields strength and power combined with pleasure and humor. In one hand he holds a battle-ax, and in another, a sticky sweet. To Ganesha I make my supplications, like today when I want an obstacle removed. I gaze on his mighty trunk and his bulging belly and feel a quiver of energy between my thighs.

After I walk through the Egyptian wing, I can't concentrate at all. I clatter down Madison Avenue in the uncertain sunlight and warm, irritating wind. I stare at the glittering jewelry in the windows and pick strands of hair from my mouth.

I go to see *Anna Karenina*, unmoving except for the resounding music and the actress's jewellike face. One woman comes in late and can't find her husband. "Antonio! Antonio!" she calls, while the audience titters. Then she and Antonio find a solution. He whistles like a bird in the dark, and she answers as his mate. He whistles again, and she answers until they home in on each other. I have the strangest urge to sabotage the process with an extraneous whistle, but I'm not sure I can. They seem to know each other's calls.

A wave of Tchaikovsky washes us out onto the street, and I crack down Fifth Avenue, past Atlas, past the cathedral, past the shining jewels and creamy lipsticks of Lord & Taylor. By 35th Street, I find that in my mind, Tchaikovsky has been replaced by a song from the radio, bouncy, insistent, and bold. The chords, on a synthesizer, seem like a cliché: minor one, held for a heartbeat, then minor four, the systole of the phrase. Then comes a surprise, a fall into major, the four of the four. I wonder why, but before I can think, the minor one returns to start a fresh cycle. The words make even less sense, phrases that work individually but won't mix when combined: "Another night, another dream, but always you ... I feel joy, I feel pain, 'cause it's still the same. When the night is gone, I'll be alone." In the final, descending phrase, the words fall deliciously off the beat.

My black heels crack, and as I twist past tourists and shoppers, the words slide into the spaces in between my steps. I feel light, flexible. I weigh nothing. I am pure dance. My silk shirt is a blue flash in the darkness; my black boot kicks up over my head. I turn onto 34th Street, *Crack! Crack! Crack!* Another night, another dream, but always you. Spanish, plastic shoes, the smell of burnt sugar. I slip down the gullet of Penn Station. This is no country for old men.

19:42, 5 MAY 1997
FROM: LEE ANN DOWNING
TO: REBECCA FASS

THE SEMESTER IS CAREENING TOWARD ITS END, AND TO THE LEFT of me lies a stack of 50 papers I'm supposed to read. To the right of me sits Josh's mirror book, which won him that prestigious prize. Now that I don't have him on my screen, I'm stalking him in the stacks. I still have these odd feelings of guilt and fear. I blush when I see his name in print. I know his books and articles are public, but I read them privately, as though they were written for me. His mirror book has appeared since he pushed his way inside me, since he came with my hair tumbling in his face, since he told me I was the most gorgeous, crazy vixen he had ever seen and he wanted to fuck me from here to kingdom come. That was four years ago when he was writing *The Victorian Mirror*. The book came out a year later.

If that encounter existed, if it continues to exist, it does so only as a memory. I've relived that memory so many times, reinforcing it as it wears, that I no longer trust my own records. I don't know what's original and what's a patch. I can know the truth, if there is a truth, only by comparing it to his memory. But he's not talking, and God only knows how he's patched up his own version.

My memory of my time with him is like my father's *New York Times* shirts. My mother used to say it's time to replace a shirt when you can read the *New York Times* through it, and I tested my father's shirts and undershirts all the time. I can read right through this memory now, and there's no template of truth to which I can compare it if I want to restore it.

The only reality is that ecstatic stab of level 3, and that's inaccessible now. I may never know that again. The motions are dissolving before the words. I can't remember now, last fall, if he asked me who won the Mets game before or after he pulled me down on top of him. I just remember the sound of his voice, no *r*'s, ironic, full of fun: "So, Leo, you heah who won the game tuhday?" and I threw back my head and laughed until he flipped me expertly so that he was on top of me. Yes, that's it, you remember the words, and then the actions follow.

So I'm looking for the memory in his book. I fear that if we cease to remember it, it will cease to exist, and I'm staking everything on my certainty he wrote it into his work. One day, he was sitting there writing about Victorians looking in the mirror, and he looked into his screen and saw me under him on the edge of a scream, pushing back so that I strained every muscle. As his fingers reached for the word, his virtual ones dug my upper back, and inwardly he screamed with me and typed me into his book. It has to have happened, and I have to find it. I read like Freud, looking for desire in each word.

Josh has a thing about mirrors. His book centers on George Eliot's pier glass metaphor in *Middlemarch*. Have you ever read it? She describes a metal surface, shiny enough to use as a mirror but covered with thousands of tiny random scratches. If you hold a candle up to it, the scratches seem to fall into a pattern radiating outward from the light; the randomness becomes centered and ordered. But that's an illusion, since a new radial pattern emerges each time you move the candle. The beauty of this parable is that you're never quite sure what it's about. The standard reading is that the false circular pattern is an individual's perception of her community, viewing all connections and meaning as radiating outward from herself, when in reality she's a point in the network no more significant than any other.

But the parable also refers to the novel. The coolest thing you can do in literary criticism nowadays is prove that a novel is really about language. But the critics are creating a pier glass illusion themselves, reading Eliot's scratchings in the light of their fascination with words. I'm no worse than they are, peering at Josh's words and watching them fall into concentric circles around the illuminating truth that he wants to fuck my brains out. Desire in language, what can I say? I bet I'm closer to the truth than many other readers are. Writing, driven by desire, fills the space where there's an absence. You write about something because it isn't there. The most basic, implacable desire of anyone who ever picked up a pen is to be wanted.

Josh is fascinated by our comical, bumbling attempts to use language to turn chaos into order. In this book, he argues that Victorian fiction is a mirror that tries to reflect chaos back as order but ends up incorporating the chaos it's trying to airbrush out. As data, he uses the astonishing number of instances in which Victorian heroines look at themselves in mirrors. The scenes, in which chaos lies just on the other side of the glass, become the ironic context for the reflected images.

As far as I can see, all his books are the same book. They're about misreadings and the motives for misreadings, and they're about illusions of order and control. And they're all dedicated to Beth and the boys, in one way or another. I wonder if she reads his books. I take a secret delight in knowing that she—that no one—can read them as I do, with the same candle lighting up his scratches.

Josh picked mirrors for a reason. He loves mirrors. Back when he was writing that book, that first time we were together, he wanted me so badly, he grabbed me the instant he kicked the door shut, and he lifted me up and said, "God, Leo, you weigh nothing." There was a full-length mirror in the room, and he undressed me in front of it, watching me watching him, watching him watching me, devouring every part of me with his eyes as it appeared in the image before us. Then he took me standing up. He was strong enough to do that, with my back smashed up against the silver coolness and him staring into his reflected eyes as he enjoyed me. He never closes his eyes when he does it.

But oh—horrible thought! What if he's done the same thing with his wife? What if he's done it in the mirror with 20 other women? Would they all read *The Victorian Mirror* the way I do? If that were true, I would feel as if I didn't exist. Beth and the boys. I wonder if he made those boys looking in a mirror. I keep searching through his book, searching and searching. The mirror is "alluring," he says, a "seductive" device, "one that promises pleasure and truth at once."

I go with Nietzsche on this one: truth is the abyss. Truth is what you see when you ram Leo up against the mirror and push and push and push until it shatters.

20:12, 6 MAY 1997
FROM: REBECCA FASS
TO: LEE ANN DOWNING

I UNDERSTAND NOW. FOR THE FIRST TIME, I UNDERSTAND. I always wondered what drew you to this guy who has one hell of a mean streak and doesn't seem to want you. Sounds like at least part of him does. I would wager you're right, and it's you he's got up against the mirror when he's writing for Beth and the boys.

Significance? Mirror encounters mean whatever you want them to mean. I've long since learned that when a guy wants to have sex with you, it means that he wants to have sex with you. It doesn't mean he thinks you're brilliant; it doesn't mean he thinks your work is fascinating; it doesn't mean he likes you as a human being; and it doesn't mean you are a good and worthwhile person, although he may tell you this, or you may think you hear it. If a guy wants to have sex with you, it means he wants to have sex with you, period, and any other significance that sex has is the significance you give it.

But you know this. Why am I telling you this? I should be passing this wisdom on to Marcia. Or should I? I've never experienced the kind of sex you're talking about. (By the way, do you think you should be writing this stuff over email?) It sounds wild, violent. One reason is pure logistics. You don't do it standing up with a five-foot-nine, 140-pound woman. Gee, now I'm talking about it over email. The best I've ever had was with Owen, and (don't laugh) it had a religious quality to it: beauty, tranquility, goodness, peace. My guess is you bring out parts of Josh he would rather not think about. I can understand how you could do this to someone. Josh sounds like pure aggression, maybe a little sadistic too. He hasn't ever hurt you, has he?

The central, illuminating truth that gives the scratches a pattern and a meaning—you called it right, Leo, he wants to fuck you. Is that a truth? I wonder. In my business (actually in yours too, right?) we try to separate the signals from the noise. Theoretically, the signal is the meaning, minus the noise—no, relative to the noise. The kind of wanting you're describing strikes me as noise. The problem with associating meaning with this firing pattern is that he's probably wanted to fuck a thousand other women just the same way. It's biology.

Of course, who's to say what's the noise and what's the signal, and listen to me dissing biological drives in favor of beauty, harmony, tranquility, and the form of the good. Probably this is the mask biology wears for me when I'm with Owen. For you guys, it wears a different face. I'm sure Josh tells himself it means nothing. I can hear him now. They always say this when we catch them: "It didn't mean anything." He's right that there's no meaning beyond the event, no meaning apart from the experience. But the experience IS the meaning, so powerful for you, and even to me now, reflected in that mirror. In all our minds, it will live on and on. He'll never forget it.

What does it take to make meaning anyway? Meaning seems more like something that's agreed on than something that exists. Go get him, Leo, if that's what you want. I like that picture of you together, shattering the mirror of meaning.

22:06, 10 MAY 1997
FROM: LEE ANN DOWNING
TO: JOSH GOLDEN
SUBJECT: THE MALL

THE MALL IS ABOUT WANTING, WOMAN-WANTING. I LOVE THE sound of the word as we say it: *mawl*, lips drawn out, cheeks drawn in. I'm going to the *mawl*. *Cawl* me. The mall is a temple to desire, and this Sunday I have come to worship, as have all these others: Black teenagers, enormous in their bulky pants and jackets; Orthodox Jewish men and their sons in yarmulkes; a dazzled Central American woman and her daughter eating ice cream and staring; a tiny, old Asian woman rocking slowly to her own rhythm; a smiling Latina with dark red lipstick, soft, thick hair, and an attentive boyfriend. Above all I see girls, fat ones, thin ones, hunting, searching. Their lips are outlined with dark pencil and colored with lipstick a shade lighter, creating an eerie, puffy effect that some magazine must be praising this week. Here we all are, and we are all wanting.

You have to understand the mall. You come to desire, because you desire to be desired. If you buy, you buy to be desired, and you covet not with your own eyes but with the eyes of another. I look, I touch. We hop like magpies around bins of sparkling earrings.

You never know when the first desire will strike. It comes as a stab and a gift: a shimmering blue-green top that ripples like a veil with the slightest motion. "He would want me if he could see me in that," I think. He could see the shape of my breasts, just barely see them moving. I try on the top, and in the mirror, I see him seeing me, wishing he could slide his hands under that shimmering green veil. Maybe. Maybe I'll buy it. The desire peaks and then quickly dissolves the instant the lust generator is mine.

What is the object of this desire? Not the rippling green; that's the cue, the means to the end. The object is me, I hope; I'm the object of his desire, but I'm also the subject, the one desiring. I want him, but he's desiring too; I want him to want me, and I lose my way among the arrows. I think the object may be desire itself, desire that looks back at me from the silver blankness of the mirror.

I love wanting. I move in a slow dance; I finger what gleams, and I notice weary men watching as I fondle a camisole. They want me, wanting it, wanting him, wanting me. They imagine me imagining myself in it, and I am pleased by their entry into the vortex of my desires.

The lingerie store, that's the climax, the place where the mall admits what it is. With the rose scent of free lotion on my hands and the voice of a guitar in my ears, I rub the silks between my fingers and imagine their feel against my breasts. I see myself before a mirror, leaning back against him, his hands around my waist, softly, slowly creeping upward, under that silk. How would it feel to live this image? I come to the mall to dress myself for this image, to make myself ready, to rehearse it. That's the reason I buy, to prepare myself for this image.

A weary man in a chair gives me a sharp, quick look. He sees my mental picture, but there's only one man for whose desire I buy, one man I want in my image. Red, I decide, bright, shimmering, trembling red silk, with my black hair brushing softly against it. I want to be a glowing red jewel for him in the darkness.

The image dissolves as I wander on, the slow march, the din of a thousand voices. Sunlight spills through the candy-store skylights, and the puffy clouds of reality show themselves between the glass panels.

Sometimes a word alone can make you want, a word like *Rampage*. I rush straight into the Rampage store. "Watch out, Pip," says Joe, "she's on the RAM-PAGE." I picture Mrs. Joe with her apron full of pins, roaring and brandishing a wooden spoon. I could buy a dress just for that word, for the vision of me on the RAM-PAGE. In a flouncy skirt, I would run and scream and smash. Who knew that a woman would buy a dress for the image of herself on the rampage?

I am hungry, but I will not eat. To remain desirable, you can't satisfy your desires. I want to be wanted more than I want. In the candy store, people buzz around the bins like bugs, and I imagine the joy of thrusting my hand into chocolate pebbles as deep as it will go, grabbing as many as I can seize, cramming my mouth with as many as it will hold. Then I think of my hips, barely there, and his eager hands all over them. I think of my hips, globbery and gooshy, and him turning away in disgust. I force my eyes away from the candy store. My hunger presses my temples like a vise, but my image pushes back, enduring, reviving me with a throb whenever I pass a mirror.

I could be beautiful, the mirrors say, if only I could sleep. If only I could lose those dark tracks under my eyes, worn by the lust that summons me each morning before dawn, twisting and writhing inside me.

I don't buy anything, but today I have lived. I have wanted. I am dazed by the colors and sparkles and clamor—more than I can see, more than I can hear, but never more than I can want. Wanting is infinite. My desire has no end. As I grind circles into my mattress at four in the morning, I am insatiable. I am wanting itself. I have come here to cast myself into a wave, to be smashed onto the shore of 10,000 people's longings. They clutch at their bulging plastic bags, and they poke with plastic forks at their Chinese food. They want with me as I write my way through this dying Sunday afternoon.

12:36, 12 MAY 1997
FROM: OWEN BAUER
TO: REBECCA FASS

THANKS FOR BEING OUT THERE. I AM READING AND FEELING YOU, and I appreciate each word, even though I can't respond right away. Words come hard now. Writing the article is making it all seem like formulas. The craziest thing—Trish called last night, and we had a normal conversation, our own version of the rhetoric of particle physics, I guess. We talked for an hour, same in-jokes, same problems, complained about the same people as if nothing had happened. It's as if we forgot. Trish even had me laughing, telling me stuff Jeannie had said. And then we hung up, and they were there, and I was here alone in this half-empty apartment. I have no idea what brought us together or what split us up. It's as if we crashed into each other, we produced another particle, and then we got hit by something else and went flying in different directions. I don't know what's happening anymore, but thanks for being out there.

Laura Otis

20:47, 13 MAY 1997
FROM: LEE ANN DOWNING
TO: JOSH GOLDEN
SUBJECT: JONES BEACH

Why do people go to the edges of things?

I pick my way through the tunnel, cool and dark on any day, with evil-looking puddles along the sides. Always there's a child who squeals to hear the echo, like me when I was four, testing the power of my voice while the adults covered their ears against the shriek. The smell of french fries hits me when I turn the corner and find myself facing the nautical flagpole whose trim lines slice the sky. That's the smell of Jones Beach as long as I've known it: fried potatoes, coconut sunscreen, salt, wind, and greasy humanity clinging to the edge of New York.

Today the wind roars relentlessly, whipping up every loose wisp of hair. Cheerfulness reigns on the boardwalk, even on this weekday morning. My feet patter against bleached wooden diagonals where women walk in twos and threes. Smokestack trash cans curl their heads toward me. At the edge of the boardwalk, a skinny cat slinks along a patch of grass. He has a scrap of plastic in his mouth. Strange—is he making a nest?

I walk down to the water, and the wind roars in my ears, plasters my purple jacket against my skin, blows my purse out behind me. I am alone, since no one else is crazy enough to wander out here today. I walk west. To my left, the waves churn and foam, the water almost turquoise, with a greenish-brown aftertaste of New York. A great big seagull has found a horseshoe crab and is tearing it with his beak. The desperate crab is still alive, and its remaining legs wiggle in the air. Sandpipers race where the sun sparkles in the inch of water left by each wave. The wind whips up the greenish foam, which flies up the beach like wisps of dirty cotton candy. To my right, there is a continuous hiss of blowing sand. The wind has carved a million furrows, white along the ridges, red brown in the depths, so that the beach is tiger-striped and I am clambering over its hide.

I have seen this beach so crowded that the sand is one great radio broadcast and the coconut air slides into my lungs. On those days, I can see the waves only when a hundred heads bob in unison. Today I am alone.

I feel each muscle in my legs and hips, tight and hard as I fight wind and sand. I close my eyes and see only orange. With my eyes closed, I walk as fast as I can, knowing I will collide with nothing. I walk in the roaring orange nothingness until my ears ache from the blast of air. A dead horseshoe crab lies at my feet, its spine pointing at nothing.

Josh, why do people go to the edges of things? Is it that we want to fall off? This Atlantic foaming at the edge of my state also licks yours. It touches both of us. If I were afloat in it, bobbing in the waves, would I be touching you?

Once I came here late with my friend Rebecca when most other people had gone. A garbage truck, speeding along, slammed to a halt just inches from a sleeping man's head. I remember his girlfriend running up screaming, her hands against her face. I was sure the tires had crushed his head, but Rebecca said no. She spoke so calmly, her voice like a gray lake. When someone's in danger, her feelings vanish. If she needs to, she just acts. Rebecca is like that, but I think she respects life more than I do. She's a neuroscientist.

What does it feel like to die? I remember this Ray Bradbury story, three guys flying through space in different directions after their ship exploded. They could still talk to each other, but they knew that each of them would die alone once life support failed, sometime after they lost radio contact. That's how I feel, staggering over striped sand with the wind in my face, or careening alone through space toward nothing.

You are my target, my ground zero. I've been directed toward you, and I look forward to that impact, to slam into you and feel you grind me to pieces like the sea, in me and everywhere around me. It's wanting that drives us to the edges, and I want to fall off into your powerful arms, those arms I know are reaching even now.

17:39, 15 MAY 1997
FROM: OWEN BAUER
TO: REBECCA FASS

IT'S SO GOOD TO KNOW YOU'RE OUT THERE LISTENING. I WAS thinking earlier today, sitting here at my desk, if a thought falls in the forest and no one hears it, does it make a sound? For years now I've come home and told my thoughts to Trish, and she has told me hers. Now I have thoughts, they pass, new ones take their place, and they vanish like a dream, experienced only by me. Falling like injured birds, they don't go anywhere, and I wonder whether they exist at all. Why think if no one hears your thoughts? DO you think if no one hears your thoughts? I lack your sense of the inherent value of things. I need a reference point, and I've detached myself from mine. I feel like a moon without a planet. What good am I?

I sit here and think that the azaleas outside are brilliant in the sun, and I'm glad Mobutu will be leaving Zaire, but there is no one to tell this to. It makes me feel disconnected, as though I no longer count. You have been wonderful, but the screen has never quite done it for me. I need a face with eyes that see me and a mouth that speaks to me. You have such a lovely mouth. But these thoughts are not conducive to article writing.

Hey, good news! I (we, I should say) almost have a first draft ready to show Rhonda. That should make her less ferocious for a day or two. Trish reports that Jeannie can say her letters up to *M* and may get into a good nursery school.

All my love,
Owen

4:19, 16 MAY 1997
FROM: JOSH GOLDEN
TO: LEE ANN DOWNING
SUBJECT: FEARLESS LEO

Leo.

Oh, your name rolls trippingly on the tongue.

Can't bust you, babe.

You are the craziest, looniest, wackiest, sexiest, most fearless cyberbabe ever to fly into the net.

What do you want from me, Leo? Why are you sending me this stuff?

You want me turned on, I'm turned on.

Can't act on it, and am pacing like a leopard in a cage.

Jones Beach, wow. Summer I used to live at Jones Beach, was one of those hundred heads bobbing on the waves.

I have fallen into end-of-semester madness, wild to get to the cell book when I take the gang back to Israel this summer.

But now at 4:00 a.m., after/during an all-nighter of grading, I am crazy enough to write to you.

You tell me, babe. What's on your mind? What will satisfy those feline appetites of yours?

I know these little women: they tear to pieces what they love.

Fearless Leo, didn't your mother tell you not to talk to fuckin murderers?

9:26, 16 MAY 1997
FROM: LEE ANN DOWNING
TO: REBECCA FASS

TRIUMPH! MY QUARRY BROKE RADIO SILENCE! I GOT HIM HUNGRY and half-conscious at 4:00 a.m., still functional enough to hit me with a guilt trip. He has been listening all this time.

I owe it all to you, my cyberlover's return. I sent him his past and my body, virtually, and it has proved to be a potent aphrodisiac.

Actually, I think cyberspace is the aphrodisiac. I sit down and start tapping, and I'm turned on. I type out things I would never say in a million years. Inside I'm smiling, one great, mad smile, pure exhilaration, and my hands dance over the keys the way my mother's did over the piano. I think this is the rush that computer geeks feel, the superman rush. You step into the virtual reality phone booth, you whip off your Clark Kent suit, and voilà, super-geek. You leave your body, your past, your failures, and you drape yourself in a new super-identity, the cape of cyberspace.

But it's more than that. You can say anything about yourself, and people will believe you. How could they know? You type out your own mixture of life as it is and life as it should be, and nobody knows the difference. That's the rush: absolute freedom, absolute power. I knew he was hearing me all this time. I knew it.

Well, what do I do now? He's just hit the ball to me, and I have to hit back. What do I want to do?

18:47, 16 MAY 1997
FROM: REBECCA FASS
TO: LEE ANN DOWNING

YOU'RE ASKING ME? SOUNDS TO ME LIKE YOU WANT THE MIRROR back, although God knows why. I'm having a hard time thinking about the Mirror Prince right now because I'm leaving for Germany in two weeks and have to make sure everyone has something useful to do and everything is set up for the two months I'm gone. I'm also negotiating hard with that soon-to-be postdoc from Marin's lab. I want him to do anatomy here and bring in some of their staining techniques, but he wants to get away from anatomy, and they don't want him to take anything with him. It's a little like an engineer going from Ford to GM, and GM asking him to bring the plans for the Taurus with him. But that's the way it works. You try to gain as much as you can with each new person you bring in, and lose as little as possible with each person who leaves you.

I think that's also the story with Owen and this Rhonda woman. She wants him out, and she wants him divested of that top quark before he goes. I'm afraid she's going to do it too. He's in bad shape—sort of like you say, writing me things you shouldn't say to anybody, although not the kind of things you have in mind.

I've never known anyone who needs people the way he does. It's something beautiful about him. Me, I go home, open a can of soup, turn on NPR, look at the mail, and plan what I'm going to do tomorrow. You too, right? Different food, different station, but same concept. Sometimes I don't go home at all. But he needs to go home and tell somebody what he did today and what he wants to do this summer. "Isn't that what a computer is for?" I feel like asking him, but I'm not that mean. He's never had the same relationship with a computer that you have. Sounds like you make love to the thing.

I'm afraid to tell you what you want. It's been fun but scary, making this thing happen from afar. What am I, the woman with the remote? I tell you what to say, you say it, he does it, and maybe no more Beth and the boys? But okay, yeah, Josh isn't Owen. You want what you've always wanted, Leo, for him to want you so bad that his whole universe is one big mirror reflecting his desire back in his face.

21:56, 16 MAY 1997
FROM: LEE ANN DOWNING
TO: JOSH GOLDEN
SUBJECT: FELIX LEO

OOOO, YOU MAKE ME A HAPPY CAT. YOU KNOW WHAT I LIKE: I'M a hungry lion; I love a good mouthful of meat. I want the mirror back, want the mirror-back, want that mirror at my back, pleasure and truth at once. Come on, Josh. Tell me about your book.

11:20, 19 MAY 1997
FROM: JOSH GOLDEN
TO: LEE ANN DOWNING
SUBJECT: FELIS LEO

OKAY, YOU DEVOURING FELINE, YOU GOT IT.

Still in your mirror stage, huh? Welcome to subjectivity, the fall into language.

Swoon, and I'll catch you—right after I subvert your identity with my reflected images.

The cell book: actually, I'm calling it the web book. It's about representations of nervous systems, communication networks, and communication between people in Victorian literature: *Middlemarch* above all, but also *Dracula* and *Tess of the d'Urbervilles*. I'm totally into it. They're obsessed with communication, but their plots are built around miscommunication. Seems almost like you can't tell a story without miscommunication, like you can't get anything going in a circuit without resistance. Could it be a variation of the second law?

Hey, I wanted to ask you, this friend Rebecca, think I could write to her and ask her some stuff about neurons? It would really help.

And you, you queen of the beasts, you been pokin around in my mirror book or somethin?

In between stalkin me in the stacks and proddin my libido and my long-term memory, you been writin anything of your own?

18:43, 19 MAY 1997
FROM: LEE ANN DOWNING
TO: REBECCA FASS

THIS IS A NEW ONE. WANT TO MEET THE MIRROR PRINCE? HE wants to write to you. I mentioned you to him, talking about your work, and now he wants to write to you directly for his new book on nervous systems and communication nets. It could be interesting, not to say amusing. He has no idea you get daily briefings on his academic writings and sexual urges, which as far as I'm concerned are one and the same. He's hotter now than he ever has been. He gets really theoretical, really into word games, when he wants it bad. I think something could happen. I wonder if he'll play word games with you too?

19:15, 19 MAY 1997
FROM: REBECCA FASS
TO: LEE ANN DOWNING

THE MIRROR PRINCE WANTS TO MEET ME, IN CYBERSPACE? GEE, what'll I wear? Don't you know I'm one of the stepsisters and my feet will bust the glass slipper? Sounds dangerous. I mean, a Mirror Prince—what if he shatters, should I pay no attention to the frog behind the glass? If I break him, do I get seven years of bad luck? Do you?

Of course I want to meet him. I'm already recording from him extracellularly, so I might as well do it intracellularly. That's what I'll be doing in Germany, learning this new technique they have of intracellular recording, in exchange for collaboration on another project where they need a specialist in development. So Josh could help to get me into shape.

Gosh, I'm flattered. Me, a neurobiology consultant. But if he's a player like you say he is, why doesn't he go for Gerry Edelman, a theorist of consciousness? You can trust me not to let on that I know of Josh's penchant for reflections, and for you. There's nothing like science to teach you not to talk. I'll just think of this as one more experiment.

I'm going nuts getting ready to go to Germany, and I'm afraid I can't deal with one more thing before I go. Tell him to write to me once I get there. I'll give him my address there once they give me an account.

13:32, 20 MAY 1997
FROM: OWEN BAUER
TO: REBECCA FASS

SOMETHING WEIRD IS HAPPENING. I SAW DAVE TALKING TO Rhonda yesterday, and when they saw me, they started and got real quiet. Dave has been great about the article, reworking everything I give him, and he's going to get back to me tomorrow about the first draft. He says the piece is in decent shape, and we should be able to show it to Rhonda in a few days. So I may retain a shred of dignity.

The question is what to do next. Rhonda wouldn't recommend me for a job shoveling shit, let alone a postdoc at another facility. I know a guy at the National Lab, so I'll try giving him a call.

Right now, I don't feel like doing anything. The spring is so beautiful, I just want to live. It seems insane to spend a sunny day in a dark tunnel. I would go to the zoo, my favorite place, but the kids remind me so much of Jeannie, I don't think I could stand it.

I wonder what's happening with Dave and Rhonda. Probably she's pumping him for updates on my mental status, using a combination of threats and bribes to make him talk. He never will—not that there's anything good or bad to report, just nothingness. I feel no ambition, no desire, no pain, as long as I don't go anywhere or do anything.

22:42, 27 MAY 1997
FROM: REBECCA FASS
TO: OWEN BAUER

THIS WILL BE THE LAST MESSAGE I CAN SEND YOU BEFORE I LEAVE for Germany. I'm not going until the day after tomorrow, but I'll be working nonstop between now and then, planning all of

Tony's and Marcia's and Dawn's experiments for the next two months, making sure everything is ordered and signed, all while communicating with the Germans and asking them to set things up. They say they can get me a computer account, but they can't give me the address until I'm there. Hopefully I'll be able to access this account from there. I hate the idea of a blackout, but I see no alternative. Please feel free to call me in an emergency. But what am I saying—in transit I won't have a phone either. It hurts to think that I'll be out of touch. Until the account is set up, you can call me in the lab at 011 49 221 506 9021. The time difference is seven hours from where you are, nine from here.

Any word from Dave or Rhonda on the article? I don't like the sound of his new bond with Rhonda. Can you ask him what's going on?

This next thing I don't know how to say, but here goes: Life may suck now, but life can get better. I know who you are, and I know your life has value and that you have the power to make it good again. I know how much you're worth because of how you've made me feel. 99% of life is filling out forms justifying your use of money, cats, and graduate students. That's what life is: we consume, and we have to justify it. But 1% is hearing a cell react to light in ways you never expected, and feeling your hands slide over my back in the shower. It's worth the whole 99% to live that 1% of joy and wonder. You, Owen Bauer, have to keep on living because you give people their 1%. I don't know what's going to happen here, but one of the main things that make me want to keep living is the desire to see you again. I bet you've made many people feel that way and will make many more people feel that way in the future, as long as you keep getting out of bed each morning. Hang in there and take care of yourself for me and for your other fans.

18:52, 29 MAY 1997
FROM: OWEN BAUER
TO: REBECCA FASS

I GUESS YOU'RE GONE. I CALLED YOUR HOUSE TODAY AND THEN your lab, but at home there was only the machine, and in the lab, they told me you had already left. I don't know where you are, Becky. I called because things have gotten so bad, worse than I ever imagined they could be, and I needed your voice in my ear. Letters on the screen are nice, coming from you, but on days like today they don't cut it.

I called my friend at the National Lab this morning, and although he was sympathetic, he told me it's hopeless. The Department of Energy is cutting their funding, and the National Science Foundation is struggling. His department is cutting its staff, and things don't look good for a postdoc or even a technician's job there or anywhere. He told me a lot of guys are going into industry, using their math and computer skills. Industry—what is that? Until now it's just been a word.

I hung up the phone, and I was sitting at my desk, looking at the picture of Jeannie, when a guy in a suit came in and asked me if I was Owen Bauer. When I said yes, he handed me an envelope and asked me to sign for it. Until the last second, I thought he was a representative of some company, trying to sell us some equipment. I mean, no one ever comes in here in a suit. Then I opened the envelope. It said that Owen Bauer was being sued for divorce on the grounds of adultery. I'm not doing it justice. The official language was terrifying, words like a branding iron searing into me. Adultery. When did I commit adultery? Twice I let myself get close to a wonderful woman, kind, intelligent, wise, and beautiful, in her own way. This is a crime? All the hatred in this world, all the shooting, the maiming, the hurting, the killing, and it's a crime to love someone? There is something terribly wrong with this idea.

For a long time, I couldn't move, just sat there staring at the paper. They might as well have hung a scarlet A around my neck, because after that, one by one, 50 people came in to ask me about the guy in the suit. Everyone saw him, because a guy in a suit around here is like an elephant. You can't miss him. I told them the truth. It was interesting to watch their different reactions—squirming, twitching, sympathy, mostly false. It was the first real science I've done in ages, hitting them with the beam of truth that my wife was divorcing me and seeing what particles they gave off.

At some point I called Trish. She was home, and she was not in a generous mood. "You're surprised?" she asked. I didn't know what to say. I didn't know why I was calling her or what I wanted to hear. "What do you want from me, sympathy?" she demanded. "I've known you for years. When in hell are you going to learn that what you get in life is the result of your actions? This is not something bad that's happening to you! This is the RESULT of what you DID!" I stammered that I didn't want a divorce, that I wanted to be with her and Jeannie, and she told me, "Well, you should have thought of that when you were taking that bitch's clothes off!" She slammed the phone in my ear.

Something bad must have happened with her mother. I've rarely heard her like this. I hate the thought that Jeannie has to be around her when she's acting this way. What if she snaps at Jeannie? She could do a lot of damage. I sat there for a long time, just staring at her picture.

Then I tried to call you. Your voice on the phone sounds different from your voice in real life—none of those tendrils that reach out and tickle me. It was more comforting to hear the young woman's voice telling me that Dr. Fass had left for Germany. It gave me more reassurance that you exist.

I can't take any more tonight. It's 7:00 p.m., but I'm going to bed. Where are you? Overhead? Changing planes in New York? Or will you fly over the North Pole? Are you landing in Germany? Oh, I wish I could be with you again.

20:48, 29 MAY 1997
FROM: LEE ANN DOWNING
TO: JOSH GOLDEN
SUBJECT: REFLECTIONS

So, you want to fuck up my identity, using the surface that reflects pleasure and truth at once? Every book you write is a mirror-book, cyberlover. Your language is one big reflection, you know of what. You keep cranking 'em out, but the pleasure and truth are always the same.

Who has fallen into language? Language uses us to make more of itself. My book is growing as female desire uses me to propagate itself. I'll be writing it soon now, very soon.

Why don't you inject me with something?

00:27, 30 MAY 1997
FROM: JOSH GOLDEN
TO: LEE ANN DOWNING
SUBJECT: REFLECTIONS, PROJECTIONS,
INJECTIONS

Language, Leo, language …

Trouble with mirrors, babe: they only show you yourself. If my books are mirrors, who do you think you see in 'em? You want to believe you've been on my mind, you'll find the answer you're lookin for in my mirror-books. This ain't a controlled experiment.

You'd do better to ask me what's on my mind at 4:00 a.m., when the verboten is de-repressed, and I inject, interject, project, subject, object. I could inject, inject, fill you up with antidote to your female desire.

But then how would you write your book?

How about it, Leo? Can I talk to Rebecca the neuroscientist? Leaving for Israel in a week, like to open the hailing frequency before I go.

22:57, 30 MAY 1997
FROM: OWEN BAUER
TO: REBECCA FASS

I don't know why I'm writing to you when you're not there. If I had any sense, I'd wait for your new address, but I can't. Maybe it's a scientific impulse, the need to record. Maybe it's a reflex, a habit I can't break.

I still felt exhausted when I got up at nine. I was thinking about what you said, about how things have to get better, and I forced myself to take a shower and eat something and go to the lab.

As soon as I got in, Rhonda stuck her head in and said could I please come down to her office, she'd like to talk to me. She also made a snide remark about people schlepping in at 11—this to me, who has spent 60 hours a week here for the past three years. But I couldn't think of a reply. It was Kasparov and Deep Blue—no more fighting spirit left. I walked down to her office like a bad kid going to the principal.

Rhonda didn't waste any time. She told me she was sorry about my personal problems, but that they had been taking me away from my work for some time, and she could not recommend the renewal of my fellowship. I had spent three months trying to write an article that should have taken three weeks. I needed to be out by August, and she suggested that I start looking for a new position now.

I asked her what she thought of the article, and something happened to her face. She armed herself, as she had in our last encounter, but this time I had no power for the shields. "Dave showed it to me," she said, "and he explained what's been happening." I asked her what she meant. "It's his work, Owen," she said. No more lover boy, but her new tone was eerier. "He wrote it, and you know it, and I know it. As far as I can see, he's done most of the research as well. The work was done on his accelerator time. He's been doing your project and his for a while now. He's not going to carry your weight anymore. As of now, it's his baby. He's going to be first author."

I was stupefied. I had expected to be terminated, but not this. I told her this was not going to happen, that Dave would never agree to it, and she laughed. "Are you kidding?" she asked. "Man, are you out of it. He came to ME. He told me what was happening, and he asked for the top quark project, and I gave it to him. Why should I leave it in the hands of some walking personal crisis who drags his ass in here at 11 in the morning?"

I wanted to hit her, but the shock of what was happening knocked the wind out of me. She could have been lying. Isn't this what they do in brainwashing, tell you you're shit and your friends have all gone over to their side? But deep down, I knew she was right. I am a foreign body here, and I'm being eliminated, as I always had to be, for the good of the organism. Dave, my God. I've talked to him about everything, gone running with him a hundred times. People are like this, I guess. They see you going down, and they take what they can get. I wonder if he fucked her. I wonder if he was already planning to take my project the day he told me to tie her up.

I should be fighting for my project and my life. I don't feel like it, though. The slow-motion crash is so fascinating to watch, so unreal, I want to sit back and let it unfold. I never was a good physicist. I've never been much good at anything. Women. I love women. I love kids. But I've been a lousy husband and father. Rhonda, Dave, Trish, Jeannie—they'll find someone else, and their lives will work better without me. I've even been bad for you, despite what you say: you're a good person, and it must make you feel guilty, what's happened between us. I should have kept my distance after I told you how wonderful you are.

Where are you today? I can't stand this silence much longer. I'm sorry to write you this kind of stuff, but maybe you won't see it. I could call you and ask you to delete it. Maybe I'll do that.

17:32, 31 MAY 1997
FROM: OWEN BAUER
TO: REBECCA FASS

YOU WON'T SEE THIS UNTIL YOU COME BACK, AND MAYBE IT'S FOR the best. I tried to call your lab in Germany today, but I couldn't communicate. I'm not even sure I had the right place, because no one there could speak English. Despite my German roots, my four years of high school German, and my three months there with you, I couldn't say or understand a word. You know me and languages. You always did all the talking, didn't you? I really am useless. Well, I know what I have to do, what's going to be best for everyone. I am writing to say goodbye and tell you how wonderful it's been to be close to you. You're a beautiful person. I don't ever want to let you down or hurt you the way I've hurt my wife. I don't know how I'll do it yet, but I think I'll do it tomorrow. Everyone's life will be better when I'm gone.

All my love,
Owen

PART III

SUMMER

On errands of life, these letters speed to death.

—Herman Melville, "Bartleby, the Scrivener"

9:15, 2 JUNE 1997
FROM: REBECCA FASS
TO: OWEN BAUER

WHAT'S HAPPENING? I HOPE YOU GET THIS. I JUST GOT HERE THIS morning, and there was a note from the cleaning lady saying that you called over the weekend. She couldn't understand anything except my name, but she left a message on my desk that an American man had called, and I knew it could only be one person. What's going on? I checked in with Marcia, and she said you had called the lab too. So I called your apartment and your lab, but you're not there. Has something happened? Where are you? At the lab they said they hadn't seen you today and didn't know when you'd be back. Please send me a message when you get in. Now you have my address. Please let me know if you're okay!

9:25, 2 JUNE 1997
FROM: REBECCA FASS
TO: LEE ANN DOWNING

MADE IT! IT FEELS WONDERFUL TO BE IN GERMANY AGAIN, BUT I'm worried sick about Owen. He was trying to reach me, and then he disappeared. We've made the quantum leap to phone contact, but now we can't find each other on any level. So far, I haven't been able to get into my UC account from here. I'm thinking of asking Marcia to open up my email, giving her the password to see if he left me any messages while I was in transit. What do you think?

Laura Otis

18:50, 2 JUNE 1997
FROM: LEE ANN DOWNING
TO: JOSH GOLDEN
SUBJECT: THE F-WORD

WANT ME TO WATCH MY LANGUAGE? BUT DARLING, I'M AN academic; that's what I do all day: watch language, Laclos's, my students', yours. I watch language the way Audubon watches birds, seeking patterns in the flitting. Must I also watch my own language? When do I get to be wild?

The f-word, now there's a tough bird, too wild to enter a classroom or twitch in the net of cyberspace. First, it's a verb that means to create and destroy, a verb in which Eros and Thanatos meet: to fuck, to fuck up, to fuck over. To fuck something, as subject, is to penetrate and maybe wreck it, to handle it, use it, trash it, leave it battered and permanently altered. To get fucked, as an object, is to be entered, altered, or maybe betrayed. Fucked up, as an adjective: scrambled, ruined, drunk, drugged, twisted, complicated, disordered through mishandling. Only as a noun is the word more restricted to its literal meaning, a good fuck, a bad fuck, but even then, it can mean an idiot, you dumb fuck. This forbidden word can mean almost anything—anything that's bad. The only thing I see excluded from its territory is goodness. Now why should that be, when there's nothing better than a good fuck—depending on who with, of course. Is it that we commit all this destruction and then take our guilt out on the word? Is language our guilt hangover for the mad, drunken fucking of our lives?

Rebecca: you want her, you got her. She's just sent me her address in Germany: rebecca.fass@mpin-köln.mpg.de. Have fun.

11:47, 3 JUNE 1997
FROM: JOSH GOLDEN
TO: REBECCA FASS

Hɪ, I'ᴍ Jᴏꜱʜ.

Lee Ann gave me your address because I'm working on a book about how people thought about their contacts with others in the 19th century. I want to know how their ideas about relationships reflected their ideas about the development and growth of the nervous system. I'm mainly working with George Eliot, but on the scientific end I need to talk to someone who knows what a neuron is.

What is a neuron?

11:58, 3 JUNE 1997
FROM: JOSH GOLDEN
TO: LEE ANN DOWNING
SUBJECT: MOUTH

Yᴏᴜ ɢᴏᴛ ᴀ ᴅɪʀᴛʏ ᴍᴏᴜᴛʜ ᴏɴ ʏᴏᴜ, ʙᴀʙᴇ.

Should drive up there and wash it out with soap, except you'd bite my fingers off, wouldn't you, if I stuck 'em in there.

Mouth full of meat, now there's a thought, like to fill you up till your roars settle to a purr.

Trouble is, you talk too much, darlin. Why this compulsion to speak the verboten? The f-word, a speech act. To say it is to do it: speech acts.

Trick is to do it and not say it, but you are a performance artist in cyberspace.

You got it down, Leo, with you, best in the universe, but got to perform it in private, just reflections for company.

Leaving for Israel in three days, here all is chaos. Will be accessing my email from there, same account.

Write me a chapter of female desire, darlin, make your book your performance, roar for everyone, not just for me, and I'll read your pages and reflect.

Hey, thanks for Rebecca!

17:16, 3 JUNE 1997
FROM: LEE ANN DOWNING
TO: REBECCA FASS

GREETINGS IN DEUTSCHLAND. SORRY THE PRINCE OF PARTICLES is losing it. I wouldn't let Marcia into your account, though. Do you delete your messages? I mean, she's great, but she would see everything—not just the stuff we've been writing about her, but everything that comes in for the next month. Besides, didn't he know you were in transit? Why would he be sending messages into oblivion when he knows there's nobody there?

Josh is pissing me off again. He gives new meaning to the term doublethink. He's given up trying to foist me onto another guy, but he's telling me simultaneously that he wants to fuck my brains out and that it's too dangerous to talk about it. He says I should write all my lust into a mirror-book, into which he'll gaze to his heart's content. I wish I were strong and smart enough to wrestle him and win, pin him to the mat and push my face into his Beethoven hair.

19:16, 4 JUNE 1997
FROM: REBECCA FASS
TO: JOSH GOLDEN

A NEURON IS A BABY'S HAND REACHING OUT.

A neuron is life talking to itself.

A neuron is noise.

A neuron is a tree with more branches than you can imagine.

A neuron is infinity.

A neuron is trying to imagine something with more branches than you can imagine.

A neuron is a voice.

A neuron is almost touching, but not quite.

7:58, 5 JUNE 1997
FROM: REBECCA FASS
TO: LEE ANN DOWNING

JOSH DID WRITE TO ME, AND I DON'T KNOW WHAT CAME OVER me. He introduced himself and asked about neurons, and somehow I went crazy. Was I always crazy, was it the buildup, or does Josh just do this to people? Can someone have a magnetic personality in cyberspace?

10:07, 5 JUNE 1997
FROM: JOSH GOLDEN
TO: REBECCA FASS

I can see I came to the right person.
Tell me, darlin, what do you look like?

14:17, 6 JUNE 1997
FROM: OWEN BAUER
TO: REBECCA FASS

Becky! Yes, I'm still here. Someday I'll tell you what happened, but right now I'm too embarrassed. Can I ask you to promise me something? I sent three messages to your San Diego account after you were already gone. Please could you delete them without reading them?

When I called, I was really out of it, and I must have forgotten the time difference. Something did happen, as you can tell: Trish has filed for divorce, and Dave has fucked me over. He's trying to take credit for the whole top quark project, and as far as Rhonda is concerned, it's his. I'm going to fight, but it will be hard to find allies. No one wants to go up against Rhonda, and no one wants to be affiliated with a guy who's so clearly going down. I'm still deciding what to do, but now that the worst that can happen has happened, I'm starting to feel better. I'm sorry to have made you worry like this. Just please delete those messages. I hope to see you again soon.

17:43, 6 JUNE 1997
FROM: LEE ANN DOWNING
TO: JOSH GOLDEN
SUBJECT: WASHING MY MOUTH, WATCHING MY MOUTH

YOU WASH MY MOUTH, CYBERLOVER, THAT'S A GOOD ONE, AFTER all the, um, language you put in there. Shall I remind you of your own vocabulary? Watching my mouth, that's more like it. You always did love to watch my mouth, always loved everything it could do. You told me that: my talk on Hardy, first time you saw me, you kept staring at my lips, big and luscious on my little face, wondering what they felt like, until you had to find out.

What did Alec d'Urberville see in Tess's mouth, what turned him on? Now you know. You can wash out my mouth, but you can't wash away the feel. Only one thing has ever made my neurons fire that way, only one thing ever lit up the board like that. Neurons don't forget. You can't do a Lady Macbeth on my mouth.

11:15, 9 JUNE 1997
FROM: JOSH GOLDEN
TO: LEE ANN DOWNING
SUBJECT: WATCHING YOUR LANGUAGE

DAMN LEO, 110 DEGREES HERE, AND NOW YOU TURN UP THE heat?

This ain't your universe, darlin, one touch of those wicked, succulent lips of yours and we blow up on contact, matter and antimatter.

Hebrew word for language is lips.

Am accessing my email from here. Board is lit up.

Turn down the heat, will ya? Have to write, have to live, have my kids to think about.

20:02, 9 JUNE 1997
FROM: REBECCA FASS
TO: JOSH GOLDEN

DON'T CALL ME DARLIN. IF YOU COULD SEE ME, I CAN GUARANTEE you wouldn't. I'm no hundred-pound sprite like Lee Ann. Let's see: five foot nine, long legs, big feet, hair blond when I was a kid, now mostly brown, theoretically in a ponytail but really all over the place depending on how late in the day it is. Eyes blue-green-brown, somewhere in there. I always wear a T-shirt and jeans and sneakers, and usually the T-shirt says something. Today it has a cat on it.

I work with kitties—I guess Lee Ann told you. I love kitty cats. I have animal rights people after me all the time because of the kitties. "You Nazi bitch," the latest caller told me, "you cut open another cat's brain, and I'll strap YOU to a table and stick needles in YOU." I've learned to deal with it. I'm German—Rebecca Fass, meaning "tap," as in, "on tap," and this has been fuel for the more militant activists. But then, Alan Berg gets the same calls about his monkeys, and he's Jewish. Probably it's the same guy.

So this is who you're talking to: a 35-year-old assistant professor and Nazi bitch, in size nine Nikes, trying to get a blob of tuna fish off her keyboard. I'm not your darlin. What is this anyway? What do you look like?

11:14, 10 JUNE 1997
FROM: JOSH GOLDEN
TO: REBECCA FASS

SORRY, REBECCA ON TAP, DIDN'T MEAN TO RUB YOUR FUR THE wrong way.

Let's get back to neurons. When they reach out, how close do they come? How do they know where to go? How do they know when to stop? Wouldn't it be more efficient for them to be in physical contact? Why almost touch but not quite? Tell me, I want to know.

You're no Nazi bitch. People say these things because it makes them feel powerful to hurt someone. I know what a Nazi is: it's the guys who pushed my grandparents into the ovens. You weren't there. You keep on listenin to those neurons, and screen your calls.

Can't help you with the tuna fish. My specialty is poppy seeds, which are slowly filling in the cracks between my keys.

18:52, 10 JUNE 1997
FROM: REBECCA FASS
TO: JOSH GOLDEN

YOU ARE A NICE GUY, AND I'M SO, SO SORRY THAT THEY—THAT we—pushed in your grandparents. I wish I could undo it somehow. I've spent a lot of time in Germany, and it has always frightened me how well I fit in. I feel almost as if I did it personally. All those people. That pile of glasses. They stole everyone's glasses, and then they took a picture of it. I cry whenever I see that heap of dusty glass and twisted frames. Maybe we can talk about this sometime.

Anyway, neurons, from everything I've seen, have evolved to maximize the possibility of making connections. It's a neat idea, a special cell that does everything other cells do but is designed to influence and be influenced as much as possible. There's that word that always gets us in trouble, so un-Darwinian, "design." Do you believe in God?

If there were a real neural net and the cells were physically connected, you would gain speed but lose control. The real beauty of almost touching but not quite (and this is what I work on—I would only work on the most beautiful thing, of course) is that the connections can change. There are cells, like the pyramidal cells in the cortex, that have their bodies in the brain and reach all the way down the spinal cord, almost a direct line between the mind and the muscles. But these are the exception. Most pathways are interrupted at many points and include several cerebral equivalents of Grand Central Station. Because most neurons never quite touch, they can change what they approach or listen harder to one input than another, depending on what's happening. They can change not just what they're listening to but how carefully they're listening.

One guy here, Alan Berg, works with monkeys, and he finds that if you teach a monkey to do tasks requiring him to use certain parts of his hands, the area representing those parts in the cortex increases in size. Almost touching but not quite is the basis of the whole nervous system, and maybe of life. A direct pipeline would be death. It would convey information fast, but survival depends on every center responding to everything that's happening everywhere. If you just send a signal from A to B, you're not saying enough to keep the monkey alive.

Telling you how neurons work reminds me how beautiful this system is. Writing grant proposals, ordering supplies, reading articles with a pounding heart to see how far Marin's group has gotten, that's not beautiful. Hey, you never told me what you looked like.

18:58, 10 JUNE 1997
FROM: LEE ANN DOWNING
TO: MARCIA PINTO

How is life in the lab? Sorry I've been off-line for a while, but a stack of 50 papers fell on me that I had to grade, and then came finals. Now my book is coming out of me in a veritable explosion, and I wanted to keep talking to you as a reality check.

My thesis is that female rage and female desire are inseparable, because female rage arises when a woman is told that she can't desire. I'm starting with *The Bacchae*, where Dionysus makes the women run amok and Agave tears her son to pieces with her bare hands. I'm pretty sure that's what my mother wanted to do to me. Then I'll write about *Liaisons dangereuses*, witches, and finally *Fatal Attraction*.

And I've just had an inspiration! The mouth! The mouth is the most dangerous part of a woman, because that alluring slit expresses desire. I've got to get mouths all over this book. The mouth hungers, eats, speaks, screams, lies, takes in, bites off. Just look how we outline it in red, to suck them in. Then we devour them. They would kill to get inside of us, but they're also scared to death of it.

Do you have any thoughts on mouths? I hope you're being good while the boss is away.

12:02, 11 JUNE 1997
FROM: JOSH GOLDEN
TO: REBECCA FASS

I love what you're telling me. I just need to know whether they knew it in 1870, but I can find out.

George Eliot is always talking about webs, and she's always telling the same story. Some arrogant, clueless young person thinks he's an independent agent and can act on his own, unhindered by petty social squabbles. 800 pages later he learns that everyone's in a web and everyone's connected to everyone else. The smallest action by the smallest person creates a wave that washes away the arrogant, clueless young person with his plans for direct action. You can still act, but you have to keep in mind that everyone will be responding and influencing your capacity to act. Eliot knew a lot about science. Do you think she could have figured the nervous system out on her own?

Okay, all right, how I look: depends on who you ask. My female relatives are under the impression I'm so skinny that I should be taken to a hospital and fed kreplach soup intravenously. I've always devoured everything in sight, but I stay skinny. Too intense, I guess. If there were a famine, I'd be the first to go. I was born with Beethoven hair, and I gave my kids Beethoven hair, and while everyone around me is going bald and having an existential crisis, I still have Beethoven hair. Brown. When the three of us sit at the computer, it looks like it's being attacked by tribbles. I am not gorgeous, dar—oops, sorry. When I float on my back, they yell, "Shark, shark!" Didn't Lee Ann tell you? She should know.

By the way, long as you're in Deutschland, maybe you can answer another question I've had all my life. What's the story with that place? I've never gone there, and I'm never going there. I guess you understand why. Just the language would stick in my throat.

Someone asked me once what it's like to be a Jew, and I couldn't answer. There's no reference point, because I've never not been one, and I don't know what it's like not to be one. To me it means feeling you're the same as everyone else, and then learning that people want to kill you.

Here in Israel I'm a normal guy, but in Germany I don't believe they've gotten over wanting to exterminate us. It's like a gene, maybe not expressed right now, maybe skipping a couple generations, but at any moment it will be turned on again. If I were there, I can't predict what I would do. Here I am jokin to you about my shark-fin nose and Beethoven hair, but if a German ever said anything about them, I can't answer for what I'd do. I'd smash his Aryan face in, and then they'd throw me in jail and I couldn't write any more books.

So tell me what the story is with that place. Be a good little—oops, sorry, babe—sensory neuron and transmit me the picture.

21:21, 11 JUNE 1997
FROM: MARCIA PINTO
TO: LEE ANN DOWNING

DEFINE GOOD. OKAY, YEAH, I'M BEING GOOD. I'M DRAWING A blank on mouths, though. All I can see are hundreds of little kitties, as Becky calls them, with mouths full of sharp white teeth.

Oh—that song! You know that song on the radio, "Mouth"? "When I kiss your mouth, I want to taste it, and turn you upside down, don't want to waste it." Try scanning the teenybopper stations, the ones that play bouncy, girly music. I bet you could use it for your book.

We're actually getting a lot done here. The results are amazing but consistent. Even if you block the eyes at the critical time, you still get synapses forming. Not all the ones you should get, but some. It's incredible—sort of a cerebral insurance policy.

I like your mouth idea. Seriously, try to find that song.

21:58, 11 JUNE 1997
FROM: REBECCA FASS
TO: JOSH GOLDEN

YOU GOT ME AT THE RIGHT MOMENT, BECAUSE I'VE BEEN LOOKING for an excuse to think about something other than science and my own *Liebeskummer* (problems in love—do you speak this language?), and Germany has been on my mind.

Germans, let's see. From the moment you get off the train/ plane/whatever, you notice how big everything is: the people, the clothes, the food. At first you think maybe you've shrunk, but actually the world has grown. In San Diego, with all the Latino and Asian people, I feel like a giant. I tower over lots of grown men, but in Germany I blend in so well that no one gives me a second glance. The goal here is to be healthy, not skinny, although there are fewer fat people than at home. The Germans are just big—big bones, heavy muscles, strong arms, big feet. They look like me.

This profound sense of belonging causes guilt for just the reasons you say. You know when you walk along, how you tune in to one conversation after another, like scanning radio stations when you're on the road? Well, here I understand every scrap. I know the language—not just that, though—I feel the thoughts behind the words. My family left here over a hundred years ago, but I belong here, and it frightens me.

I love this place. It's hard to fathom that people with a genius for making life enjoyable could have committed such outrages against life. If you could see the passion for music here, the love of art, the mouth-watering lineup of fruity, creamy cakes in the cafés, the loaves of dense brown bread covered with seeds, the glinting towers of chocolate and marzipan in the candy stores, the menageries of soft stuffed animals crying out to be loved, the noisy, self-righteous pleas for "environmental friendliness," the lust for travel, the insistence on walking and bicycling in all weather—I don't know how to finish this sentence—if you could see it—would you change your mind? I doubt it. But you did ask.

I love living here, and I've always worried that this makes me a Nazi. People here like me instinctively, as though they recognize me as a member of their club, and it worries me because I know what this club has done. I feel guilty when I see how they treat nonmembers. They're tough people until they know you—won't form lines, tell you off the minute you do something wrong. Above all, they love to point out the mistakes you've made. As far as I can tell, it's culturally acceptable to go around telling people what's wrong with them. And they're formal—I'm Frau Professorin here, no more "Hey, Becky, wassup?" In this land where the sun rarely shines, the women run around all year with scarves around their necks, popping herb bonbons to keep from getting colds. They worship the thought of California and think that I'm insane to have come here.

But I love this place. I love the old ladies enjoying their daily slice of cake with whipped cream at 4:00 p.m., and I love the young people bicycling in the red lane just for bikes, dinging furiously if I stray into it. I love the way people wear green, and I love the sounds of their voices. I love the way everyone has big feet here and I'm the most normal person in the world. Hey, what can I say, we bigfoots don't tip over easily, superior design—oops, sorry, bad word. A more sturdy, less sexy model, that's me, proud bigfoot to the end. Well, enough of this, I should get back to my electrodes and see if Brigitte, Thomas, and I can get a cell. Hope this has been enlightening in a way that's not sick.

Laura Otis

00:23, 13 JUNE 1997
FROM: JOSH GOLDEN
TO: REBECCA FASS
SUBJECT: NOT SATISFIED

I'M NOT SATISFIED.

I have two boys, know the value of good candy and bears, but that doesn't make up for systematically murdering six million Jews. Yeah, I know, the gypsies. Didn't like them either—what did they, do a few mil of them too? After a long day's work roasting my family, they went home and listened to Mozart and had coffee and cake and played with their bears?

You can't imagine. Suppose somebody wanted to kill all the Germans, kill YOU, systematically, making lists, hunting you down, just because you're you, or maybe because you do things better than they do. Can you imagine how that would feel? And they still want to kill us, only now they know they can't get away with it—probably. Even here in Israel people want to blow us up. Imagine if people all over the world wanted to kill you, not because of anything you'd ever done, but because of what you are—live with that. Makes you want to have more kids, write more books, live harder, live better, screw 'em all.

Shouldn't be writing you this stuff, sorry. Barely ate anything today, then drank too much tonight. Life has been driving me nuts. Can't sleep. Bomb went off downtown today, right near where my kids were this morning. You seem sane, needed the relief. My wife's been freaking out.

00:30, 13 JUNE 1997
FROM: JOSH GOLDEN
TO: LEE ANN DOWNING

CAN'T TAKE IT ANYMORE, LEO, GOTTA HAVE IT TONIGHT.
   Talk dirty to me, darlin, want to live dangerously.
   Talk to me about Tess's mouth, tell me about communication.

17:36, 12 JUNE 1997
FROM: LEE ANN DOWNING
TO: JOSH GOLDEN
SUBJECT: TESS'S MOUTH

HOW NICE THAT YOU WANT TO HEAR ABOUT MY BOOK. IT'S
coming out like a geyser. I read film theory six or eight hours a
day, but sometimes I write what I think without waiting to read
other people's theories, pure insanity in academia. I work 14 hours
a day. The mouth, the nexus of female desire. The mouth is what
takes in. Is that what you want?

00:39, 13 JUNE 1997
FROM: JOSH GOLDEN
TO: LEE ANN DOWNING
SUBJECT: TAKEN IN

GOD, LEO, YOU ONLINE? WHAT A RUSH, REAL TIME! DO IT TO ME
in real time, Leo, you know what I want, taken in, taken on, lips,
tongue, langue, lick me with your language, Leo, take me in.

17:49, 12 JUNE 1997
FROM: LEE ANN DOWNING
TO: JOSH GOLDEN
SUBJECT: IN

IF THIS IS REAL TIME, WHAT TIME IS UNREAL? WHAT ALEC SAW: soft, ripe, wet vulnerability, the too-rich earth begging to be tilled. I always had a thing for Alec d'Urberville, forcing that sweet, warm, red berry into her mouth, not like that prick Angel Clare who fucked her with his Calvinism. Tess is excess, superfluous being, soft, full, yielding, surrounding. I am just as ripe on the way in, but I tighten, I clench, I push back. I take in, my wet, excessive lips, and then I wrestle, hard and tight, I muffle your scream in a shower of hair. Scream for me, Josh, in cyberspace.

00:51, 13 JUNE 1997
FROM: JOSH GOLDEN
TO: LEE ANN DOWNING

AAAAAAAAAAAAAAAAAAAAAAAAAAAAAAAAAAAAAAAAAAAAAAA!!!

17:53, 12 JUNE 1997
FROM: LEE ANN DOWNING
TO: JOSH GOLDEN
SUBJECT: COMMUNICATIONS

NOW WHAT DID THAT MEAN? AGONY, ECSTASY, CATHARSIS, frustration, too much, not enough, was it good for you?

00:54, 13 JUNE 1997
FROM: JOSH GOLDEN
TO: LEE ANN DOWNING

OH NO, GOTTA GO LEO ECSTA

19:50, 13 JUNE 1997
FROM: REBECCA FASS
TO: OWEN BAUER

I'M SO GLAD YOU'RE OKAY! YOU'RE RIGHT, I WAS REALLY WORRIED. I'm going to have to find better ways to stay in touch. You must have been expecting the divorce, I guess, but this thing with Dave is outrageous! Isn't there anybody above Rhonda you could go to? I know they don't like it when you do that, but this seems like an extreme case.

Being here is bringing back so many memories. My time here with you is real and alive again. Do you remember the zoo? That's how it all started, isn't it? We were at this party, and some guy said that the zoo here is great, and I said I'd been dying to go, and the others shook their heads, animals trapped in cages, screaming kids, and then you said you would go with me, you loved zoos, and I looked up and saw you for the first time.

I noticed how big you were, how broad in the shoulders, and how your eyes shone with sympathy, reaching out. We had been here two months, and neither of us had gone anywhere. I worked nonstop, and you didn't like to go out alone, because you didn't speak the language.

One day, some holiday we'd never heard of, we went to the zoo. I love to watch living things. The animals are marvelous: a big black dog barking nonstop at a donkey, outraged that such a creature could exist; a leopard asleep in the sun, ignoring the cries of the children trying to wake him; a red parrot hanging upside down, plucking leaves outside his cage; a mother orangutan with the breasts of a woman, gazing at you intelligently.

A giraffe glided around in circles while a crowd of children gazed up at it in awe. Looking down at the kids, who came up to my hips, I felt exactly like the giraffe. I loved the lions, tigers, panthers, anything that's a cat, but they just lay there, a disappointment. You liked the bears best, and we watched them for half an hour, with their rolling walk and fuzzy, round faces.

I remember how we talked. If you were trying to woo me, it has to have been the weirdest wooing of all time (maybe that's why it worked). You were telling me how you met Trish and how you were expecting a baby and were sure it would be a girl. You seemed lonely, and I never dreamed—not at first. Some guys complain about their wives, the old my-wife-doesn't-understand-me shtick, but you had only praises. In grad school you'd been down, so depressed you didn't want to live, and then you met her, and everything fell into place. She was a dynamo, all action, kept you going—you just felt bad about being in the lab all the time. She had even insisted on your coming here, when she was home pregnant, because it was such a great opportunity. You called her every night—that night was the first one you missed.

I remember how much I loved talking to you, how every thought I had came naturally to my lips, and you seemed to read them before I spoke them. You finished my sentences for me, and I could sniff out yours.

We both loved kids, and at the zoo it's more fun to watch the kids than to watch the animals. There was an American girl with a ponytail who kept calling to the owl and finally got it to answer, and there was a boy with a green backpack who roared at the lion, trying to make it wake up. Kids were swarming, squealing everywhere, louder than the flamingos, who were making an unholy racket. We watched the kids and laughed, and you told me you were made to be a father. You were looking forward to that baby so much.

I got a kick out of teaching you German, and you thought it was great how a polar bear was an ice-bear and a raccoon was a wash-bear, because it washes its food. I could see how brilliant you were from the way you questioned everything, questions I had never thought to ask. How odd it was that the German rolled off your brain as though it were made of Teflon. We were both German, but I took to the language, and you rejected it— different neuronal connections, I guess.

We spent that whole day at the zoo, walking around, talking about particle physics and neuronal development and animal behavior and babies, always the same circle: animals, neurons, synapses, intelligence, babies, round and round. At some point we stopped and had a beer, and you thought that was funny, beer at the zoo.

Afterward I led you into the city, and we wandered through the *Altstadt*, the narrow streets along the river. You marveled at the fairy-tale houses and the cobblestone streets you'd never known were there. We ate at a touristy restaurant with white plastic tables and chairs, and we talked until our pathetic past love lives entered the circuit, somewhere between animal behavior and neurons. We talked about what attracted us: honesty, you said, kindness; I said intelligence and empathy, a rare combination. It got dark, and the white ships on the river twinkled with lights.

Finally we got up, but we didn't want the day to end, and we kept circling the pedestrian zone. We were looking at a huge window full of stuffed animals, a mountain, an ark full of animals: bears, hedgehogs, pigs, frogs, raccoons, camels, owls, cats, parrots, mice, fuzzy and plushy with glinting brown eyes. I felt as if the rays of those eyes gave me a gentle push, the way the photoelectric effect makes metal leaves spin. I fell back against you, and you wrapped your arms around me, big bear arms, and asked me not to leave you that night. Slowly, slowly, I turned around …

I haven't been the same person since that moment, now over four years ago. We formed a *Beziehung* as they say in German, a connection that can't be broken. No matter where you are, what you do, I'll always feel connected to you.

Did you know they laughed at us? They called me Dial-a-Deutsch because you called the lab all the time asking how to say things in German. When I got here yesterday, two people remembered us and asked me how you were. As I walk through the *Altstadt*, past the black, lacy towers of the cathedral, the streets seem to be full of ghosts. I see us everywhere, listen to us talking, watch you slide your arm around my waist. You know, that same window full of animals is still there, looking out. Should I buy you a soft brown bear? I wish I could give it to you personally and place it in your loving, reaching arms.

I want whatever is best for you: Trish and Jeannie, freedom, or more days at the zoo with me. I have to get to work now, but take care. I know that I'll see you again soon.

Alles Liebe,
Deine Rebecca

20:10, 15 JUNE 1997
FROM: REBECCA FASS
TO: JOSH GOLDEN

SORRY TO BE PRAISING GERMANS TO YOU NOW THAT I UNDERSTAND your life better, but you did ask for my honest impression. I believe there are more good people here than Nazis. I mean, somebody's got to be painting all the graffiti that says "Nazis raus." But then again, I'm always Anne Frank, swearing that people are good inside even as the Nazis are tramping up the stairs.

That's scary, the near miss with your kids. I love kids. Tell me about your family. Is your wife a professor too? How old are your children, and what are they like?

What more can I tell you about neurons?

11:20, 16 JUNE 1997
FROM: JOSH GOLDEN
TO: REBECCA FASS
SUBJECT: KIDS

How does one neuron recognize another? That's the main thing I want to know. How do they all find the guys they're supposed to be connected to?

What I'm looking at in these novels is how people signal each other, how the signaling works on a social level, and what they think about how they're connected.

Speaking of biology, kids: David is 10, Jeremy is 8. Wife is Beth, wonderful gal, been together about 15 years. No professor, she: runs a cosmetics business, makes all of you more beautiful. We're a good match, same background, complementary neuroses, understand each other perfectly. Couldn't live with someone who doesn't know the kosher from the tref.

Kids are #1 with me, can't explain having kids to someone who has none, like trying to explain sight to the blind. It's just a whole nother realm, a whole nother way of navigating.

David is into sports and bad at all of 'em—gotta love him for his persistence, though. Someday he'll find one he can do and win a gold medal. Jeremy is a computer freak. I ask him stuff all the time, same as I'm asking you now.

Kids: you do less, you do more, and if you survive, you have a better sense of humor.

Now tell me about those neurons, ba— Hey, what do I call you? I need an epithet to help my phrases slide through cyberspace, a little butter on the cyberbread. You ain't no darlin, and I bet you ain't no babe. What are ya?

17:12, 16 JUNE 1997
FROM: OWEN BAUER
TO: REBECCA FASS

I THINK ABOUT YOU IN GERMANY ALL THE TIME, WHAT YOU'RE doing, what you're saying, what you're thinking. I wish so much that I could be there with you again. I know I can never get that back because of the way time works—not linear, progressive, but flitting, buzzing, settling, zooming like a fly. You can't recapture moments, not because they're behind you but because you can't predict what time will do next. Right now, I'm reliving my first days with Trish, which were ecstatic—watching *Tender Mercies* and eating frozen pizza under a blanket on a night when it was 10 below.

I faced the inevitable today: I met with a lawyer, and I talked to Dave. It's so hard fighting when you don't want to fight. I wanted a female lawyer and probably should have gone for a legal version of Rhonda, but in the end, I used the yellow pages. I said I wanted nothing but the right to see Jeannie, and she nodded and took notes with a client-is-always-right, disapproving air. They like a battle, I guess, and I must have struck her as too wimpy. I have no idea how I'm going to pay for this.

She told me that if it comes to a custody fight, I'm at a serious disadvantage, because I've admitted the adultery charge. She even suggested I deny it, in the absence of proof. But that seems so stupid when it's so clearly true, and I don't want you dragged into this. She also advised me to stay away from you—no visits, no phone calls until this is over. She doesn't recommend email either, although to use it as evidence, Trish would have to get a court order, plus permission from both facilities to open the accounts. Who thinks that something like this can happen when you reach out and put your arms around someone? Life is so insane.

After meeting with the lawyer, I felt ready for anything, so I went to confront Dave. That was more insane, if you can imagine it. He told me not only that he'd written the article, but that he'd done most of the work, and it was only right that he be first author. I always lose arguments because I stop and ask myself whether what the other guy is saying could be true. Dave did put a lot of work into the article, but he always started with text I wrote. But what is writing? I didn't create that text out of nothing any more than he did, just strung together a new combination of the formulas we use to communicate in this business. Doing the work, that's further from reality, although he did let me use his accelerator time, and we worked together some nights. I always had the impression he was doing it for fun. Was he setting me up from the beginning, or did he see an opportunity and create a version of events that would work to his advantage? We all tend to do that, rewrite history to our advantage.

To settle his conscience, he has so thoroughly convinced himself he's right that he blew up at me for confronting him. How dare I accuse him? I hadn't been doing my job, and he'd been doing it for me, and now I was trying to take credit for his work. He sounded so certain that I began to doubt the truth myself. I told him he was wrong, that he was taking credit for my work and he knew it, and this was unworthy of him. I knew he was a better person than this. I was trying to reach the guy I had

Laura Otis

known, who I hoped was still cowering inside Mr. Hyde, but to no avail. If Dr. Jekyll was still alive, he was bound and gagged.

I gave up. I may try going over Rhonda's head, as you advised. I'll ask around about who's best to talk to. A week or two ago I would have asked Dave. How terrible people are to each other. Looking back at my own actions, I wonder whether I've been as ruthless as the people around me. In my own way I have. The will to love can be as devastating as the will to power, two tornadoes with different causes and the same results.

I'd better sign off now before I depress you too much. I keep trying to call Trish and Jeannie, but Trish won't return my calls. She screens them with a machine that says, "We'd be glad to get back to you."

00:27, 17 JUNE 1997
FROM: JOSH GOLDEN
TO: LEE ANN DOWNING
SUBJECT: LICKED

PLEASE, LEO, MORE, PLEEZ, PLEEZ, PLEEEEEEEZ, MORE!

18:52, 17 JUNE 1997
FROM: LEE ANN DOWNING
TO: JOSH GOLDEN
SUBJECT: A LICKING

FULL MOON HERE, COULD PEEL OFF ALL MY CLOTHES AND HOWL. But then I'd get cold, and you know what I'm like when I'm cold, hard as gumdrops you have to lick and suck until they dissolve. When they do, I do, one great writhing moan clinging to you with a salamander grip.

But you, you don't frighten, you love a challenge: something grabs you, you wrestle it, you flip it, you pin it, you spread it out, and you nuzzle it and taste it and push it and poke it to see what will happen. Then you ram right into it, and oh, lots of things happen, lots and lots of things, it contracts, it undulates, it clings tighter, and you grab it harder and push harder until it screams, and then it lies quiet and whimpering in your grip.

So you lick it all over to comfort it, long, wet, masterful licks, over the belly, then back up to the gumdrops that need dissolving again. It licks back, tamed, down and down and down, until it's you who's helpless and gasping and begging, too big to dissolve, too hard to dissolve, only way out is to explode.

In the end it's a draw, one round to you, one to the monster, and exhausted, we sleep, confused and tangled, too tired to know what it means.

19:12, 18 JUNE 1997
FROM: REBECCA FASS
TO: LEE ANN DOWNING

HOW IS YOUR SUMMER DEVELOPING? I AM IN CELLS ALL THE TIME here, barely ever leave the lab. They tell me it's raining a lot. The technique they have is so fantastic—electrodes that slide right in, so you can stay inside for a long time and get a sense of what's happening.

I've been writing to Josh, and I'm beginning to see what you see in him—a forceful personality, but a lot of kindness too. His aggression seems mainly defensive, if that makes any sense.

My own guy is doing a little better. The Germans are on break, and I don't have much time for email tonight. Gotta write to the guys now. Writing to the guys—sometimes it feels like slopping the pigs. God, am I bad. I throw 'em out some mental scraps, and I can just hear 'em slurping it down, grunting with pleasure, their little tails wriggling with excitement. I've been working too hard again. Just don't slaughter 'em, Leo. I love fattening 'em up, and I want them to live long, happy, porcine lives, rolling in the mud and the clover.

19:29, 18 JUNE 1997
FROM: REBECCA FASS
TO: JOSH GOLDEN
SUBJECT: CALL ME BIGFOOT

GEE, YOUR COLLECTION OF EPITHETS SEEMS LIMITED. WHAT DO you call the guys you write to—do they get cyberbutter too? You do write to guys, right? Just think of me as one of them.

You have asked THE question, the one we all want to answer and the one I'll probably spend most of my life trying to solve: How do neurons know what to connect to? Nobody knows. There's nerve growth factor, which can make the little guys grow in a particular direction. Then there's Gerry Edelman's "neural Darwinism" idea about neurons competing to form connections. He thinks it's not completely planned. A whole bunch try to hook up with a particular cell, and in the end only some can. He says the molecule on the surface that gets recognized is a ganglioside, this big, hairy brush of sugar. This molecule binds to itself, on the surface of other neurons—no opposites attracting in synapse formation. Well, time to go stick another cell. Think about it—a great big, hairy brush of sugar, like cotton candy.

10:52, 19 JUNE 1997
FROM: JOSH GOLDEN
TO: REBECCA FASS
SUBJECT: GENDER IN CYBERSPACE

LOVE THE BRUSH. BUT WHAT'S THIS I'M HEARIN, YOU THINK you're a guy?

You don't write like a guy, bigfoot, you got that twinkle in your touch. You are a female somethin, don' know what.

Now, what's all this about *Liebeskummer*, your guy let you down? We do that. You go find a better one, one you can stroke till he purrs with your big ol' sugar brush.

I'd volunteer, but I'm taken, boy, am I taken. Just don't stick 'im, bigfoot, no intracellular recording.

Now, tell me all 'bout it—need an alternate epithet—what do you suggest?

By the way, how would you describe the human neural communications network? Give me your top 10 words for it— science-speak would be best.

20:32, 19 JUNE 1997
FROM: REBECCA FASS
TO: JOSH GOLDEN
SUBJECT: WORDS

THE HUMAN NEURAL COMMUNICATIONS NETWORK: ONLY A humanities type could come up with that.

> Okay:
> Reaching
> Changing
> Dynamic

Sensitive
Tangled
Delicate
Intricate
Active
Electric
Beautiful

Not too scientific, but that's the best I can do tonight. The best word is German, I'm afraid, *Beziehung*, which means connection and relationship at once.

You really want to hear about this? I should not be telling you. My guy is the greatest in the universe, perfect for me, kind, loving, caring, brilliant, gorgeous. Met him four years ago when we were spending a semester in Germany. Instant affinity. Big-time bonding. Just one problem. Yeah, you got it, the usual: his wife and daughter wouldn't approve. So I've sort of been in limbo, wanting the synapse but with no right to it. It would hurt if I didn't work 80 hours a week. That's the whole story: potential difference, opposite charges, with some intervening space. I can't believe you've got me talking about this. What's your story anyway? How have you stayed happy for this long?

11:11, 20 JUNE 1997
FROM: JOSH GOLDEN
TO: REBECCA FASS
SUBJECT: STAYING HAPPY

THIS SOUNDS BAD, BEAUTIFUL. (LIKE YOUR NEW CYBERBUTTER?)
Get yourself another guy. Don't waste energy pining for one who's taken. Save your brush for an unconnected cell.

No perfect guy or gal for anyone, just a number of workable possibilities if you're willing to do the work. Kids, companionship, teamwork, that's what it's about, giving up what you think you want, getting a surprise that's better than what you thought you wanted.

Keep your wanting dynamic, that's how to stay happy. Never want too much, and always be ready to receive.

Bend your knees when you catch, and don't look too hard at what you've caught.

Like my paternal advice? Why do I hear you laughing in cyberspace?

11:31, 20 JUNE 1997
FROM: JOSH GOLDEN
TO: LEE ANN DOWNING
SUBJECT: BASTA

GUMDROPS? DON'T THINK I'VE EVER SEEN ONE. SOUNDS LIKE something out of *Little House on the Prairie.*

Jujyfruits I like, gummy bears, but you don't suck 'em. You chew 'em, scrunge 'em around in your mouth, then spend the rest of the day pullin 'em outa your teeth.

Flawed metaphor.

We gotta stop this, Leo. It's gettin outa hand. Almost got caught a couple of nights ago, cyber interruptus.

Yeah, I know, I asked for it, an' now I'm askin you to cool it.

It's all clichés anyway. Last message was a jumble of recycled erotic bubbles. You can do better.

Funny, clichés do the job anyway, pleasure center is not discriminating, no taste. Almost exploded at the terminal.

Can't take it anymore. Let's take a break.

Be home on August 7, then we can talk. Be good.

Laura Otis

16:56, 23 JUNE 1997
FROM: LEE ANN DOWNING
TO: REBECCA FASS

HEY, WHAT ARE THE NEURONS SAYING? IS JOSH STILL WRITING to you? I'm mad because he's just cut me off again. I'm like his own private cable channel that he can turn on and off with a remote. Either I wrote too well or not well enough. What's he writing to you?

I'm making almost frightening progress with the book now that I can work as much as I want. I leave the film books, VCR, and computer only to eat some yogurt or cereal, and I rarely leave my apartment.

I'm wildly excited about this idea: women go on the rampage when men tell them they can't feel desire. Generally, we're only allowed to react to male desire or, at most, to channel it. In each chapter, I'm dissecting a book and a movie—the way female rage looks on the page and on the screen. I'm calling it *R(amp)age: Reflections of Female Desire.*

Josh is motivating me to write it in ways he's never imagined. When he writes to you, what does he ask? What does he say? How does his "forcefulness" manifest itself?

7:45, 24 JUNE 1997
FROM: REBECCA FASS
TO: LEE ANN DOWNING

SOUNDS LIKE WE'RE ON THE SAME WORK SCHEDULE. EVERY minute counts here, and I have to make the most of my time. But, yeah, I am still writing to Josh. He's really smart, asks great questions. It's like you said. He's doing the paternal thing, very free with the advice. And major chutzpah, as you also said. It's impossible not to like him; I just don't think I'd want him in my lab. Marcia reports a disturbance. Has she told you anything about what's going on?

18:00, 24 JUNE 1997
FROM: LEE ANN DOWNING
TO: JOSH GOLDEN
SUBJECT: NO MORE GUMDROPS?

No more candy till you're back, you mean it? Not a Reese's Piece, not a Tic Tac, not a Rolo, not a Life Saver, not a Raisinet, not an M&M, not a gummy bear, sweet and firm in my mouth? For real? No more sugar to the Holy Land?

10:16, 25 JUNE 1997
FROM: JOSH GOLDEN
TO: LEE ANN DOWNING
SUBJECT: NO MORE GUMDROPS

I mean it, Leo, no more candy, not a Snicker(s), not a jelly bean, not a Jujyfruit, not a truffle, not a bonbon, no more cyber licking, sucking, chewing of any kind, no sweet little particles of female desire accelerated my way—collisions too disruptive.

You don't get it, Leo. Kids—they're the greatest, depend on you, have to come first. You screw around, you screw them.

Wanting and doing, two different things. River Jordan, deep and wide, can't cross over.

Voice says warning, warning, danger, Will Robinson.

Love candy, you know, Leo, could lick it, suck it, crunch it till I die, just don't want the sugar rush right now. Got a book to write, two kids to keep outa trouble.

Trouble is you, darlin, you are trouble, you are tref, très fine, trop fine, your fine little particles bounce all over my brain.

I demand a chapter, a full chapter of female desire, to be delivered on August 7 when I get home. Will be satisfied only with that. Now do us both a favor and write your book.

21:20, 27 JUNE 1997
FROM: MARCIA PINTO
TO: LEE ANN DOWNING

SOME CLAUSE IN MURPHY'S LAW SAYS THAT CRISES ONLY HAPPEN when there's no one around to handle them. I've been sending Becky daily updates on this one, and I thought you might also be interested for your book.

Dawn's ex-husband has turned up, this Salvadoreño guy. She's never wanted to talk about it, but they used to be married until the guy went nuts and turned paranoid on her. She's always been politically active, and she was trying to get word out about how we were training the death squads and what was going on down there. She used to try to help Salvadoreño refugees get started in this country. I think that's how she met him. It wasn't a green card marriage, at least not on her side. She really loved him. He might have been using her, but it doesn't look like it, not the way he's acting now.

Oh, yeah, you don't know. He's found her again, and he's been stalking her. If he comes into the lab, we can call security, but since this complex contains a hospital, it's a public building, and he has a right to be here. He seems to know just how much he can get away with. He's very smart for a caveman.

Dawn finally told us about him yesterday, because he'd followed her through the lobby telling her what a bitch she was. She was shaken, completely rattled. I've never seen her like that.

Usually she's so quiet and controlled. She had to explain so that we'd know to watch for him—little guy, black hair, nice-looking. His name is Pablo.

When they got married, she was still a grad student, and the trouble started when he wanted to have a baby right away. She wanted to finish her degree first and get a job. It was a culture thing. Where he's from, you plan your work around the baby, not the baby around your work. I think he was also under pressure from his family, like you're a loser if you don't have a baby right away to prove you can. He turned on Dawn when she wouldn't do it, kept throwing her pills away, then tried to keep her from working, sabotaging her work, and finally hitting her. He told her that her work was meaningless, that she was a selfish bitch, and that her values were fucked up. He knew how to control her, and he played the political guilt card. She valued work more than family because she'd been brainwashed by social institutions promoting capitalist egotism to maintain a world full of artificially motivated worker-slaves.

So she did a Lysistrata, a sex strike, and that's when he lost it, because he was sure if she wasn't doing it with him, she must be doing it with someone else. All she wanted to do was take electron micrographs of synapses, and she had to go home every night to this hell. She could never work past six, a terrible disadvantage in this business, because he would scream that she was allowing herself to be exploited, that she didn't love him, that she was fucking every guy here, or all three. Once when she went to a party and came home at eight, he beat her up.

After that she went to a women's center for help. I don't know why she waited so long. I bet it was that he kept pushing the guilt button. She was promoting third world oppression by not doing everything his way. Somehow they brought her back to reality. When they found her a lawyer, she divorced him.

Well, except that it wasn't so easy. Pablo was furious because he stood to lose his green card, and he did everything he could to slow the process, plus harass and demoralize her as much as the law allowed. She got an order of protection, but even then, he hung around and called her and stole her mail, trying to see who had replaced him. There was no guy, of course. She just kept slicing, fixing, and taking pictures—nerves like nobody's business, that woman.

This was still happening when she got her degree, but she thought she'd ditched him when she started her postdoc here. She's devastated, because if he's after her again now, he may keep it up for life. She's afraid for the lab, because once in the past he came in and tried to trash her work. I always wondered why she was so paranoid, making copies of everything, locking everything up. She lost three months of work that time. They couldn't do anything, because they couldn't prove it was him.

Becky told us to notify security right away, and we have. It's hard, though. People work here all night, and anyone can walk in and out. Tony or some guy walks Dawn to her car, but imagine how she must feel, getting out at her apartment, running for the door with her key in her hand, wondering if he'll be there waiting. I always wished I could be like Dawn, so organized, so much in control—and now this.

I wrote to you because I'm feeling female rage and immediately thought of your book. This seems to be the other side. Either they fuck you and dump you, or they "love" you so hard they turn into mondo-sado-control freaks. You get screwed either way. I don't know if I'm more scared or angry. I wish Becky were here. She would know what to do.

17:32, 29 JUNE 1997
FROM: LEE ANN DOWNING
TO: REBECCA FASS

You'll have to be my satellite now. He's declaring a blackout until he comes home. Apparently, I distract him from his book, and he wants me to write mine so I can be famous like he is. I write much better when I'm in contact with him. I get all sorts of ideas. It's depressing. I'd like to think I give him ideas too, but I guess they're the wrong kind. Is he still writing to you? Please tell me what he says. I'm generally self-entertaining, but sometimes I feel as if the whole world has gone off to some exotic place and left me here on Long Island.

For comfort, I went and got another one of his books. This one he wrote before he ever met me, so no mirroring, just some river-rafting though his sexy mind. I find I like this one best, his first one, the one he based on his dissertation. It's called *Learning Letters*. It's a play on the word "letter," comparing what letters (like *A, B, C, D*) and letters (the kind we send to each other) do. It's highly theoretical, about how meaning is created.

He says that letters aren't self-sufficient, that both kinds are meaningless out of context and make sense only in relation to other letters. If you read a letter that's addressed to someone else, you never know what's happening, because it's more a cue than an information packet. Letters don't carry meaning; they invite it. He claims a letter is a false contract that's never fulfilled, promising to deliver meaning that's supplied by the reader. A letter is the soul's portrait—but of whose soul?

He digs through letters from Victorian literature, then advances to his favorite topic, misreading. His best examples come from *Great Expectations*, where Pip's letters to Joe really ARE letters, badly arranged. And of course, the whole title, *Great*

Laura Otis

Expectations, tells about what we bring to letters. Hey, he wrote about the same book twice. Are you allowed to do that?

I'm more convinced than ever that his books are about misreading. I'm waiting to see how his new web book will veer toward misinterpretation. If it's about communications, I see major potential. I am so in love with his writing that I get turned on moving through his sentences—simple, clear, direct, funny, no matter how deep he goes. I'm about to go back now and read another chapter—level 3 rapids, this one on Hardy ("The Letter Killeth").

Hey, what's happening in the lab? Marcia told me some pretty scary stuff.

11:10, 11 JULY 1997
FROM: JOSH GOLDEN
TO: REBECCA FASS
SUBJECT: WHEW

THANKS FOR EDELMAN. LIBRARY HERE HAD HIM. AM DEEP INTO sugar and loving it.

Other pressures slacking off now, no more explosions, thank God.

Hey, listen, are there many vestigial connections in the brain? Are there a lot of connections sitting there unused that could be used, or if they're not used, do they just go away?

Hey, guess what? MIT wants this writer to lead its new interdisciplinary humanities and communications program. They've been courting me for a while now but have just come through with an offer. What do you think?

16:30, 15 JULY 1997
FROM: OWEN BAUER
TO: REBECCA FASS

THIS SENTENCE BELONGS ONLY ON TV SHOWS, BUT HER LAWYER called my lawyer. My lawyer says it's a good offer. She's surprised how good—every other weekend, plus every other Thanksgiving and birthday. She wants to keep Christmas but says I can have Easter. She's asking for child support only as a percentage of what I make, which is kind of her. For a while it may be nothing.

I had no idea it could get this detailed. I asked, does it say what I'm supposed to feed her for breakfast? She told me that I hadn't seen anything, that I'd be amazed. Anything not clearly written into the contract can become the object of power games later on.

Should I fight for Christmas? This is so absurd. Some guy is born and dies 2,000 years ago, and this becomes a way of defining when I can see my daughter. Easter! Pagan eggs and rabbits rewritten as Christian resurrection—pure insanity. Sanity is the spark of intelligence in her eyes when she spots an egg, and her squeal as she runs to grab it.

How do you slice up a year, write a contract about when two people can be together? I guess that's what time is, the boundaries, not the intervals between them. The whole idea of time is bizarre, our way of naming, controlling, marking, splitting. It's a violence we commit against experience, the revenge of culture against nature.

Space is the real concern here. Trish has found a good job in New Jersey, her mother is there, and Jeannie will be starting school this fall. The colony of women, three generations of them, is anchored in the East, and if I want to see my daughter, I should go there. But you're way the hell down on the other side. What a graceless way to say this. What do you see in me anyway?

What I'm trying to say is, I want to see you. And be with you, if I can. But Jeannie is too little to shuttle back and forth on a plane, even if we could afford it. I don't know what to do. I guess if I want to be with Jeannie, I'm going to have to look for work in the East. And if I want to be with you—do you want me to be with you? There's too much at stake to be presumptuous.

I seem to be battling space and time now, and the conclusion is foregone. How can we fight the parameters we invented to bind and squeeze our lives until they make sense? Maybe this is the physics version of your scientific-guilt nightmare. You talked about the biology version: you get to the gates, and God is a cat, and St. Peter is a lab rat, and you're in big trouble. I'm living the nightmare of the physicist in hell, tormented by the time and space he invented. Looks like the only weapon against these Goliaths (look at me, making myself the good guy) is telecommunications, but that makes things worse, reminding me of limitless possibilities in a world where my actions are so limited. You and your words fly over my head, possible to perceive but out of reach.

When can I see you, Becky? I have a little money saved. I think I'll use it to move East—New York, probably, I have some friends there—and look for a job, any job. Any chance of your stopping here on your way back before I go? I'll have to stay until my lease runs out at the end of August—more time and space contracts. I'd be happy to see you at the airport, like in *Casablanca*. I know you have to get back to your lab.

18:56, 15 JULY 1997
FROM: LEE ANN DOWNING
TO: MARCIA PINTO

I SAY YOU PUT THIS PABLO GUY UNDER, SPREAD HIM OUT ON A table, and stick needles in his brain. Then his life might have some value. Can't you have this guy arrested?

You're right about the polarization. This is *Sleeping with the Enemy*. Either they think you're after them, or they're after you. Maybe when they think you're after them, the ravenous obsession they're sure you're feeling is what they'd be feeling if they were after you. You're the satellite, reflecting their controlling lust back in their faces, so they try to shoot down the satellite. Maybe paranoia is possessive rage turned inside out, and *Fatal Attraction* is the lining of *Sleeping with the Enemy*.

It's amazing to think what women could accomplish if there weren't guys like Pablo, considering what we accomplish when there are. All power to Dawn! I have to write this new theory into my book somehow. Someone has ordered a copy and will be disappointed if it isn't ready by the end of this summer. Keep me posted. This is exciting.

9:33, 16 JULY 1997
FROM: OWEN BAUER
TO: REBECCA FASS

HOW ARE YOU? I THINK OF YOU ALL THE TIME NOW, INSIDE YOUR cells. What are they saying? You should go out and take a look at the city. I'd love to hear what it's like these days, our *Fußgängerzone*.

Well, I've decided to accept Trish's offer. Mainly it's impatience. If I can't hear Jeannie's voice again soon, I'm going to die, and the only way to reopen the line of communication is to flush out the parasites. Lawyer time costs 200 bucks an hour, and to have to go through two of them! But more than the cost, with two of them, how do you know they're conveying the right message? I want to know what my daughter's been saying, and I don't trust these two. The fastest way to get back in touch seems to be a quick surrender. I wouldn't know how to fight anyway. What would I do, claim innocence, swear that Trish is a lousy mother? She's completely in the right. I just wish she wouldn't take my daughter away. I wouldn't even know what to demand if I did fight. More time, I guess. How can you claim time, though? How can you own time? I just want to sign whatever I have to sign so I can be with Jeannie again.

I'd also like to see you if I could. How much longer do you have over there before you come home?

19:07, 16 JULY 1997
FROM: REBECCA FASS
TO: OWEN BAUER

I'VE BEEN THINKING ABOUT YOUR *CASABLANCA* IDEA, AND I HAD an inspiration. I'm going to have to fly right back to the lab when I finish here, because as usual, there's a crisis. This one is a human crisis, one that I couldn't have prevented. I'm dying to see you too, and your choice of the East Coast is motivating me to do something, anything, to see you before you're even further away.

So I have a plan. I can change my flight so that I have a layover in Chicago. Since the German government is paying, it's the kind of flight you can change without spending hundreds of dollars, so I can do this. On the way here they flew me over the pole, a 12-hour flight. Any ideas you may have gotten of my presence in the air over your head were figments of your imagination. But this time we could really see each other, no imagination needed.

Do you like to hang around airports? I hope so. I have to see you, and I think this could work.

I have two weeks left here, and I'm working nonstop. I don't go out anymore, even though I love it here, because of what my own neurons do when they see everything. Every sensory input labeled "Germany" is routed through the Owen associative pathway, and I can't stand your absence.

Only in the lab am I free. I have it down now, just ease the 'trode in, and I'm there. I can listen as long as I want, and the cell doesn't die. I feel strangely guilty, as though I'm getting away with something without paying the price—except that it's only the cells that paid anyway.

Yes, I want to be with you. But we should talk about this face-to-face. Email doesn't cut it for something this intense. I don't think even the phone would work. This is level 3 stuff, as my friend Lee Ann would say. (One is physical presence, public; two is email, private but remote; three is physical presence, private, intimate, and close.) I think you can only talk about being together when you are together. Otherwise, how do you know what you're talking about?

This would be August 3, about three in the afternoon. I've looked into it already. You could meet me at the gate. No one ever meets me at the gate. What do you think?

19:35, 16 JULY 1997
FROM: REBECCA FASS
TO: JOSH GOLDEN

Hey, congrats on MIT! Do you know yet if you're going to take it? Sorry to have taken so long to respond about unused connections. I'm in a rush to the finish here, plus some idiot is stalking my postdoc, the kind of idiot who could trash a lab. Is this the kind of thing a father has to deal with?

Is it hard to work when you're a dad? I would never work, just want to play with my kids all day. I imagine being a parent as me in my office trying to get an idea with someone coming in every five minutes with a new problem for me to solve. How can you write good books and be a dad at the same time?

Anyway, unused connections: you have a talent for picking the questions everyone wants to know the answers to and no one does. You could be a scientist if you wanted, so I'll assume you want the truth: no one knows. It looks as though unused connections cease to be connections if nothing ever gets routed through them. The key is plasticity: all of it can change at any time, not just at the early stages. You can form new links, and even established connections can disengage at any point. There may be some determination as to what connections can be formed, but we know almost nothing about this. As far as I'm concerned, in the brain, anything comes, and anything goes, never say never. I'm sorry not to be able to give a more definite answer. Try reading Alan Berg's 1986 *Brain Research* paper on changes in monkeys' mental maps.

10:07, 17 JULY 1997
FROM: JOSH GOLDEN
TO: REBECCA FASS
SUBJECT: MANAGEMENT

THIS SOUNDS BAD, BIGFOOT. HAVE YOU NOTIFIED SECURITY? CAN they post someone near your lab? Shit, can't they just get the guy? Be sure she takes out an order of protection.

Yeah, this is dad stuff. I find that a frontal attack on the attacker is the quickest and least painful policy. Step on 'im, bigfoot, stomp the lowlife out.

You got me in one of these moods again—love reading you on the brain, excites me 'cause you always say what I wanna hear. Victorian novels are all about trying to hide unwanted connections—déclassé relatives, income from sweatshops, shady ex-lovers—and failing. Am in the middle of a chapter on this right now.

Don't know if I'm a good dad or write good books, just try to. Secret is to be a fascist: block out a few hours a day when absolutely no one, absolutely nothing can get to you; a few in which you're semipermeable, do some work, nothing too crucial, and are semiaccessible; and some in which you deal with the little guys and are impermeable to work. It only collapses if you're semipermeable all the time.

So unused connections just fade away? This would be the Victorians' dream. I'm encouraged. Now I have to find out what they knew about this, if anything.

I'm here till mid-August, mercifully far from all the dendrites reaching out to me, tingling with suggestions about things for me to do.

20:49, 17 JULY 1997
FROM: MARCIA PINTO
TO: LEE ANN DOWNING

THIS IS GETTING SCARY. I'VE SEEN THE GUY NOW, BECAUSE WE never let Dawn go out alone, and we take turns walking with her if she goes across the street to the union. He generally hangs out in the hospital lobby, waiting to glare at her and taunt her, because he knows he can stay there and it's the main way in and out. He follows us across the street, then goes back to the neutral zone.

I've never seen such rage, hatred, disgust in anyone's eyes. It's so frightening. I get her to translate what he's saying, even though she doesn't want to: "Why won't you talk to me? Who are these people with you? You don't need protection against me," he says. "You need protection against your own conscience. You know what kind of woman you are. You pledge your life to a man, and you throw him away. You spend your time killing baby cats, and you think you're too good to make a baby." She won't translate the last word, but she doesn't have to. "Puta."

God, why can't we just kill the guy? We call security each day, and they say that as long as he stays in the public areas, there's nothing they can do. I remember this *Star Trek* episode where in an alternate universe Kirk had this alien machine that could make his enemies disappear with the touch of a button. I wish we had one of those.

For the first time, I understand how Killington may feel, going through life haunted by cast-off lovers. I don't glare at him, though, and I haven't shorted out his fish yet. I wonder if there's a double standard here, like it's forgivable for a woman to ditch a guy, but not for a man to ditch a woman. Nah. I think the woman gets screwed whether she's the dumper or the dumpee.

How are we going to get rid of this guy? Unbeknownst to Dawn, I've been thinking of sponsoring a contest, the best way to get rid of Pablo. We could put a hit on him for less than the price of a good centrifuge. I would feel a lot safer if Becky were back. It's hard to concentrate on work with this happening, and she's going to be pissed if I don't have the figures ready for this article.

17:15, 18 JULY 1997
FROM: LEE ANN DOWNING
TO: REBECCA FASS

HOW SOON WILL YOU BE BACK? FROM WHAT MARCIA IS SAYING, you need to be back in a big way. Me, I'm reading and writing like a maniac. The *Fatal Attraction* chapter, the guts of the book, is close to being done. You can do this in the humanities, write the conclusion first and then go back and trace the roots. You always end up changing the conclusion, though.

My quandary is this: What do I show to Josh? I can't show him the *Fatal Attraction* chapter, for God's sake. It's napalm, guaranteed to send any man with a liaison and an iota of guilt running for cover, except it will exfoliate the cover and turn the air to fire. I'm not sure whether I can show him any of this book. The *Crucible* chapter will be no better, nor will the *Liaisons* chapter. The safest bet would be the theory chapter, the introduction on what desire and anger ARE, but he's so smart, he'll know from the first sentence what I mean.

I'm finally writing a mirror-book, one as good as his, and of course his reflection is all over it. How is he doing? What is he writing you? I want him so badly, I can hardly think about anything at all. Funny how desire keeps you from analyzing desire. I guess you can either have a thing, or talk and write and think about it, but not both. Please tell me what's happening with him, anything he says.

12:30, 18 JULY 1997
FROM: OWEN BAUER
TO: REBECCA FASS

I LOVE YOUR PLAN. I WOULD LOVE ANY PLAN THAT WOULD LET me see you. It's a date. August 3rd, 3:00 p.m., O'Hare, just send me the coordinates. God, to see you, to touch you! You're right that there's something about being there that's incontrovertible. We can be together and drink coffee for $1.75 a cup, and I can hold your hand for a little while.

I go to the lab just to use the computer and try to ignore the looks of pity and contempt. I'm assembling a bunch of résumés, each of which presents a different identity: physics teacher, programmer, accelerator technician. I wonder how many different identities I could invent on the screen without abandoning reality altogether.

Trish has been silent, or rather my lawyer has told me firmly to communicate with her only through the double buffer of the two lawyers. I don't know whether I'd be committing some violation by calling her up or whether they're parasites who make their living by intervening in people's communications. I guess if we could really communicate, we wouldn't have ended up like this in the first place. I don't even know what I might have communicated that I haven't and didn't. Probably I'm getting divorced because I communicated too much. That must be what lawyers are for, to keep you from communicating too much.

19:46, 19 JULY 1997
FROM: REBECCA FASS
TO: OWEN BAUER

Okay, it's a date! Gee, I haven't been on a date in 15 years. Lufthansa, flight 703, arrives at O'Hare at 2:50 p.m., August 3rd. See you at the gate!

19:03, 24 JULY 1997
FROM: REBECCA FASS
TO: LEE ANN DOWNING

I found a spare minute and thought I'd do the satellite thing. This is fun—should I charge for this?

Your man (in German that would make him your husband) is in work mode. I know it because I'm so often in work mode myself. He just wants everyone to go away. You shouldn't take it personally. He would tell anyone to go away right now. I think he's onto something hot. When the biochemists get this way, they go at it all night, come in at noon, start work at two, and work until four or five in the morning. If you say hi to them in the hall, they don't answer. Same thing with Josh. He's spacing out in cyberspace. I am becoming rather fond of him. Manic, isn't he? Just leave him alone, let him write his book, and jump on him when he gets back. But be careful; he spooks easily. He won't be part of anyone's plan but his own.

21:08, 31 JULY 1997
FROM: MARCIA PINTO
TO: LEE ANN DOWNING

HERE'S A BRIEF REPORT ON SOME OF THE ENTRIES TO THE WASTE Pablo Sweepstakes. Tony says to call La Migra. Lily, his quiet girlfriend, surprised us all by saying forget La Migra, man, call ARENA, call the death squads. Everyone is into it, the whole department. Alan Berg has offered to organize a Neuro Death Squad. Tim Brady's group wants his cerebellum, and Nakamura's wants his liver. So far, the winner is this Australian postdoc in Killington's lab, who says put him in a T-shirt that says "Tootsie" and parachute him into Rwanda. This is the suggestion to beat.

Seriously, though, it is getting worse. He comes to the door of the lab and stares in at us. He yells that he wants to ask us questions about our research. We call security every time, but he never stays more than a few seconds, and he's gone when they get here. They say they're too shorthanded to post someone here permanently, given that he's not dangerous, only annoying, and they don't have the right to hunt him down systematically. They're starting to get pissed off at us, calling them every day to chase away a phantom. Well, Becky's due back tomorrow. She'll get rid of him somehow.

1:32, 4 AUGUST 1997
FROM: OWEN BAUER
TO: REBECCA FASS

AGONY, BECKY. I DON'T KNOW ANY OTHER WORD FOR IT. I'VE been through a lot lately, but nothing like this. Life is a long series of kicks in the face. I waited eight hours, staring at screens most of the time. After a while the letters and numbers dissolved and danced. I had no idea whether I could believe what my eyes were telling me. The place was in chaos. You had to wait in a line of angry, yelling, elbowing people to get that $1.75 cup of coffee, or worse, some of their noninformation.

Every now and then I did a reality check, looking through a glass panel that showed the world outside, wet, black, and wild. Tornado watch! How the hell could there be a tornado in Chicago today? I did what they tell the pilots to do, trust only your instruments, and I fixed myself like a pillar before one of those screens. 703 was delayed, first 30 minutes, then an hour, then two. Then that terrifying word started springing up all over the screen like shoots from a rhizoid: canceled, canceled, canceled. I accelerated in a circuit of hopelessness from the black, rain-beaten window, to the madhouse Lufthansa counter, to that terrible screen, and none of them told me anything.

Finally, around six, they said you'd been rerouted to St. Louis. I stayed at my post. Maybe they would fly you back here somehow. I mean, what about all the people who really had to go to Chicago and weren't just changing planes? I guess they were out of luck. Christ, a tornado! At midnight they kicked me out. No more flights till six tomorrow morning, they said, everybody out.

So I went to my terminal, the closest I could get to you. You'll find this when you get home, I guess. That's the best I can do for now. Where did they take you? What did they do with you? Are you in St. Louis, in the air, or back home by now? This was a whole new kind of torture, pain I never knew existed. Well, I shouldn't complain. It happened to you too. Maybe tomorrow I'll have you back on my screen.

6:37, 4 AUGUST 1997
FROM: REBECCA FASS
TO: OWEN BAUER

Oh, Owen! I am so sorry! It's my fault, isn't it—it was my idea. It just never occurred to me that they could shut down O'Hare. I mean, that's like canceling life—how could they do that?

For a long time, they held us prisoner in New York while they waited to hear what the weather was doing and decided whether to risk taking off. In the end they did, after holding us for two hours, but just as the juice and peanuts were going around, they announced that we were being rerouted to St. Louis, the nearest airport with no tornado watch.

There was nothing I could do. I tried calling you, first from the in-flight phone and then from St. Louis to page you, but they told me they could do it only in an emergency. I thought of lying. I mean, I could have said I was having your baby, but that seemed too sleazy.

I fought a screaming mob to reach the counter. Apparently, everyone who'd been headed anywhere in the Midwest had been kidnapped and taken to St. Louis. When I finally made it to the front, a harried woman told me she could either put me on a flight to San Diego right then or a flight to Chicago tomorrow morning. It was the Captain Kirk thing, the split-second decision. You know what I had to do. I've got a new postdoc who needs help and an angry stalker who needs the Terminator. I couldn't listen to my own desires. Well, okay, so both flights expressed my desires, but different kinds. I took the flight back to the lab.

Inside I was dying, and this morning I feel dead. This nine-hour time difference does a number on your body and mind. All through that flight I was tormented by visions of you doing what you said you were doing—that terrible circuit of pain and futility, with nobody working the controls. Even half-dead, though, I retain hope. You're alive. I'm alive. We couldn't come together yesterday, but maybe we can in a month, a year. I have to get to work now. I didn't go to bed. I have to check the rest of my mail before everyone gets here.

7:44, 4 AUGUST 1997
FROM: REBECCA FASS
TO: LEE ANN DOWNING

I'M BACK, AND ALARMED. NO REST FOR THE JET-LAGGED. IN MY semiconscious state, I forgot that Owen had asked me to delete the messages he'd sent when I was gone, and I fell through everything that had accumulated like a skydiver through clouds. I scanned the junk and the good stuff with the same attention. Selectivity shuts down when your body doesn't know what time it is.

When I hit the bottom of the box, there was Owen, the day I took off. He was going to kill himself, and he'd sent the word out to nobody, into nothingness, into an account with no one to read it. Why? I am devastated. Guilt and horror work just fine, maybe better, when time is disrupted.

I almost lost him. I can't believe anyone could do that, not see anything to live for. But then I never had a daughter, never had a wife, never lost my kid and my career at once. And I can't help thinking that it was me, that he lost his kid because of me. He almost lost his life because of me.

I have to do something. I have to help him get his life back. Did he want me to find out this way, the day I returned? Was he trying to torture me? In one sweep of the keyboard, he tells me how wonderful I am and that he's going to kill himself—that I'd be better off without him. How could he think that? He's the reason I want to live. What happened to make him change his mind? Who or what do I have to thank? I missed him at O'Hare. Did I tell you we were going to meet? I can't remember.

How can I ever face the parade? That's what today will be, a parade of people into this office, sort of like my email, an endless array of outdated bulletins, descriptions of crises breaking and resolved, polite requests, pleas for help, deferred complaints, wants, needs, proposals, questions. I'll hear them all. What else can I do? But all I have room for in my brain is one message: I'm going to kill myself, I just wanted to let you know.

12:16, 4 AUGUST 1997
FROM: LEE ANN DOWNING
TO: REBECCA FASS

WELCOME BACK! I'M WRITING TO YOU RIGHT AWAY, AND I HOPE you get this in time. You've helped me a lot in my various states of mental impairment, and I have to do the same for you. I know what you want to do right now, and hopefully the parade is passing between you and the phone. DO NOT do it! Do not pick up that phone in this guilt-logged, jet-lagged state and invite your poor, forlorn, love-starved, suicidal physicist to move in with you. I know you're reaching for that phone right now. STOP! Stay in level 2 until your brain decompresses! I saw the tornadoes on TV. I think you lucked out there, bypassing that level 3 contact. You might have bought him a ticket then and there. A guilt-motivated adoption won't be good for him or for you. Just wait, chill, think, unfold, and become yourself again.

He pulled out of his tailspin on his own that day, so he can probably rescue himself now, and that will make him feel best in the long run. He changed his mind so much that he asked you to delete the message. I would tell him you did, will it out of existence, and declare it was never read. He wrote it in a mental state that's gone, and the him that exists now doesn't want you to know that state. I would sit back, relax, enjoy the parade, then sleep 18 hours and write him that you deleted it.

Now a sample of my own impairment: How is my Lusty Language God in the Holy Land? Has he written you anything in the past week? He won't send me anything, and I'm writing a lot but suffering more. Only three days until he comes back!

20:11, 5 AUGUST 1997
FROM: REBECCA FASS
TO: LEE ANN DOWNING

WELL, I DIDN'T PUT IT OFF FOR LONG, THE MOTHER OF ALL problems. I wanted to feel like a human being again before I faced it—faced him, I should say. That seems to be the whole issue, whether a human being can be a problem.

I talked to Dawn first to get an idea of why he was hanging around her and what she thought he wanted. It made no sense. What did he think he was going to accomplish? What was he after? She told me he wanted her back—home making dinner at six each night, home making babies, his babies. Somehow all this was supposed to overthrow the establishment and fight third world oppression.

Dawn laughed a tight, bitter laugh. She told me over and over how sorry she was that something like this was wasting my time. I told her that she took the best pictures of synapses ever, and it was worth my while to keep her safe. I looked at her, this quiet, grim little person trying to save the world one monster at a time. I could imagine why she had married him—a way to make things right somehow, to compensate for injustice. As if there were such a thing in the world as equilibrium, a zero balance. Life is owing, and selling yourself into slavery doesn't pay the debt.

Would it help, I asked, if we went down together to talk to him? She shrugged. Chicken soup approach, we decided, it couldn't hurt. Kreplach soup, actually—it was Josh's idea.

We found him in one of the black chairs in the hospital lobby, staring out at the traffic going by. When he saw us, he smiled. Apparently, this was the response he'd been trying to evoke all along. He was short, dark, good-looking, as Marcia said, and there was a tension to him, an air of barely contained rage. I took comfort in the fact that he was several inches shorter than I was. Little Dawn is even smaller.

He started speaking to her in Spanish, an angry beating like heavy rain on a metal roof. She spat something back at him, and suddenly I got mad. I spread my arms and stepped in like a referee. This talk was going to be in English. "All right," he said, "if you can't speak Spanish." You could feel the intelligence under the anger. This was a warped but thinking creature. "Who is this woman?" he asked Dawn. "Why you bring her with you? You no have to be afraid of me." I told him I was her professor, and I wanted to know what he wanted from my postdoc. "I want to talk to my wife," he said. She answered that she wasn't his wife, that they were legally divorced, that he'd given up the right to be her husband when he'd started mistreating her. He looked at me disgustedly, realized I wasn't going anywhere, and decided to talk now that he had the chance. "You believe the lies you tell just like everyone here," he said. "You are my wife. You will always be my wife. You give yourself to me." Dawn said she had never given herself to anyone, just made a mistake and corrected it.

I could see his rage rising though the twitches in his fingers. "You think you get married, you use me to make you feel better, you fuck me like your country fucks my country. When you done, you throw me away like garbage. You do an experiment on me like a dog, like in your lab. I know what you do there. You torture animals, you kill them, you throw them away, you call it science. I am a person, not a dog. You can't throw me away. I will show you, you will learn, I will never go away." He was half crying by this point, and I could see he meant it, really believed he was in the right.

Dawn was doing better than I was, I guess because she was used to him. I found him so amazing I could barely think of what to say. She told him the marriage was between two individuals, not two countries. They wanted different things in life, and they should not be together. He should move on with his life and find someone more like him. He looked at her cynically, smiling at what she was saying. "You think it so easy," he jeered. "You find words to escape your obligations, you believe your own shit. You use me, then throw me away. Your country is shit. Your culture of individual is culture of selfishness. Family, husband, children, it is nothing to you. You are selfish just like your country, no morality. Your culture will die because you have no morality. You have no strength, thinking only of yourselves."

Finally I thought of something to say. I asked him if our culture was going to die anyway, why he needed to set things right by chasing Dawn. What good was he doing? Life was short. She obviously didn't want to be with him. Couldn't he find something better to do with his time? "Because, PROFESSOR"—he hit that word with provocative scorn that made me angry myself—"I am a man." I think he meant a moral man rather than a passionate man. He was there more to expose her hypocrisy, as he perceived it, than to reclaim a lost lover.

I tried to make myself as tall and professorial as possible, and I looked down at him. "Dawn does not want to see you or talk to you," I said. "What you're doing here is a crime, stalking, harassment. We will have the police make you go away if you don't have the sense to move on."

He just leered at me. "You are lying, PROFESSOR," he said. "You can't make the truth go away. I will make her remember. I am breaking no law. You tell me what law I break. You wish I break a law just being here, but I break no law." I told him he was wasting his time, and he was going to get himself in trouble. Dawn fired the parting shot, but it was in Spanish. Then we turned and went back up to the lab.

How did she live with this guy for two years? I'm in awe of her. What must she be made of to have stood up to constant provocation, constant insults, constant guilt, and still get up, come to the lab, and run the electron microscope? I wonder how many people go home to this at night and how many survive it. I don't think we accomplished anything.

20:28, 5 AUGUST 1997
FROM: REBECCA FASS
TO: JOSH GOLDEN

WELL, I TRIED THE FRONTAL ATTACK (FRONTAL DEFENSE?). No luck. He won't go away. What I really want to do is get on with my work. My student Tony is in the middle of something incredible, and my other student Marcia has an article almost ready to send off that I need to go over with her one more time. This guy is making me really mad. Any suggestions? Marcia is running a Waste Pablo Sweepstakes for the best suggestion on how to get rid of the guy.

11:26, 6 AUGUST 1997
FROM: JOSH GOLDEN
TO: REBECCA FASS
SUBJECT: SUGGESTIONS

SOUNDS LIKE AN ISRAELI. YOU'VE HEARD ABOUT ISRAELI FOREIGN policy, right? Draw me a line, and I'll cross it.

No threats or reasons will make him go away—wrong strategy. He'll dig in.

Instead implant an idea of new territory to invade. Draw him a line, and nuke him when he crosses it.

You can do it, bigfoot.

9:21, 7 AUGUST 1997
FROM: LEE ANN DOWNING
TO: JOSH GOLDEN
SUBJECT: BACK?

ARE YOU HOME, BACK IN THE GARDEN STATE, GARDEN OF MY Earthly Delights?

Have you strung your net, spun your web, mapped your neurons, tapped out your book, a million insectivorous impressions?

I have had my fingers all over female desire all summer, thinking of you, waiting to be read by your eyes.

Desire awaits you, Mirror Prince. Just tell me how to transmit it.

11:15, 9 AUGUST 1997
FROM: JOSH GOLDEN
TO: LEE ANN DOWNING
SUBJECT: SHOW ME

LEO, YOU CYBERSLUT.

Good to hear your voice, good to feel your lips, your langue on my screen.

Yeah, I'm back, myopic, aging gazelle at the water hole, all atremble to sense my favorite feline lying in wait.

Your desire inspires, had just hoped that in these sultry months it would have found a worthier object.

Fingers all over, hmm.

Okay, let's trade, let's mingle: my web for your desire, your lust for my links.

I'll show you mine, you show me yours.

Love to feel my language on those luscious, lustful lion lips.

19:16, 9 AUGUST 1997
FROM: LEE ANN DOWNING
TO: REBECCA FASS

HE'S BACK! AT LAST THE MOMENT I'VE LUSTED AFTER IS IN MY hands, and I don't know what to do. He wants to see what I've been writing, and I have to send him something. These are my choices: the *Fatal Attraction* chapter or the introduction, my theory of female desire and female rage. The movie chapter is better, because there from the beginning I had no doubt what I wanted to say.

Female rage, desire, and madness have to be shown as inseparable in pop culture because female desire alone, odorless, colorless, without the dye stain of destructive wrath, would be too frightening. Not only do women go on the rampage because men deny they can want; they do it because they can never get what they want the way society is structured. Men have to identify what women want as something impossible to have, because to preserve our culture as it is, women must appear unreasonable for wanting. Hence Alex, who desires with her great big knife.

Of course, I'm deferring the real question, the Freud question: What does a woman want? Honestly? I'd say the same thing as men: intimacy without enslavement, passion without bondage. We're not really that different. I don't think Alex knew what she wanted (that's part of the representation: women never know what they want). What drove her crazy was not so much being denied what she wanted as being blown off, not being taken seriously.

In the theory chapter I go for it, try to answer all the questions. The big one is what desire IS. It's negative energy that exists only when there's absence. It thrives on absence, depends on absence, yet seeks to end that absence. That means desire seeks to destroy itself, since its goal is to eliminate its food supply.

Language does exactly the same thing: it comes into being because of what's not there, and it tries to summon what's missing. If it succeeded, it would render itself obsolete. They're both the same self-defeating, negative energy, yet oddly persistent, so often better than what's absent. I guess what's there always has an advantage over what isn't.

The other question is whether female desire differs from male desire. I say no. I don't think there is male desire and female desire, only desire that's listened to and taken seriously, and desire that's told to shut up because it has no right to exist—or worse than that, treated as if it didn't exist.

It's all in how and why they tell you to go away. "Okay, I've had enough, you can go now!" Any guy who heard that enough times would turn into Alex. It's just that the guys so rarely hear it. It took Marcia to make me understand, since Killington articulated it so beautifully. What was it? "Don't hold on to this." They think that if we continue to love them, we're holding on to their cocks.

How and when does a connection become bondage? For some people, right away. Josh suffers from big-time ligophobia, and I know I do except with him. Women, men—we're not different in the ways we desire, just in the ways we're treated.

How is Josh going to read this book? I fear he'll look into my mirror and see a gingerbread castle of guilt, an Egyptian tomb booby-trapped with threats hand-carved for his benefit. He could be right. Who can separate what she is from what she writes? His absence tortured this silkworm to spin out this language-lust. Now I have my silk, and I want it to whisper against his skin. What should I send him?

19:03, 14 AUGUST 1997
FROM: REBECCA FASS
TO: OWEN BAUER

I PURPOSELY DIDN'T WRITE TO MY FRIEND LEE ANN THIS TIME before writing to you. Last time she told me to get some sleep, and when I woke up, I found that the message I had wanted to send had been deleted from my brain. This time I won't lose it. I have been wanting to write to you for hours, but there have been about a hundred people in here, the police—I'll explain soon. What happened today is catalyzing this message, not creating it. In my mind, it's been waiting to be sent for years, glowing silently on my hard drive.

Well, enough suspense. This is it: if you want to, I want you to come and live with me. Today I realized how fragile my life is and how short it's going to be. I've wasted so much time with guilt, convincing myself I have no right to enjoy anything. When I think back on everything I've done in my life, the worst and the best has been to turn and reach out and hug you back, breaking every rule about how people are supposed to bond.

I want you to stay connected to your daughter, because she's you, and for both your sakes, you mustn't be torn apart. But I want to be with you. If you would live with me, I would pay for you to fly out and see her. I'm in the lab so much I never know what to do with my money anyway. San Diego is a high-tech city. I'm sure you could find a job here in one of your capacities, maybe even as your real self.

Have you ever looked into the dark cylinder of a gun pointed at your face by a man angry enough to blow your head into a pulpy mass? Maybe you have—there's still a lot I don't know about you. Me, all I could think was "What a waste." Nights, days, months I might have been with you, and I was too ashamed, too guilty, too good. Keep us both, do it all, hook up with both of us. I'll make it happen. To be with you, laugh with you, rub you all over, that's what I want to do with my life—when I'm not in a cell. But I'll try to be in them less and in you more, if you will only come live with me.

If I had that gun in my face and my brain was going to explode in 10 minutes, I would want to spend those minutes with you, talking about anything and looking into your eyes. Please Owen, come be with me.

20:37, 14 AUGUST 1997
FROM: REBECCA FASS
TO: LEE ANN DOWNING

YOU'RE NEVER GOING TO BELIEVE WHAT HAPPENED HERE TODAY. I didn't believe it while it was happening, and I don't believe it now. My lab was in the news! Me, Marcia, Killington even, we were all in the news, but unfortunately not for anything we've discovered. Well, maybe for something Marcia discovered. She walked into the lab this morning and discovered Pablo pointing a gun at me, Dawn, and Jacobsen, the new postdoc who's been here two weeks.

Pablo took us completely by surprise. I'd actually gotten used to him sitting down there in the lobby. He's been by the lab a couple of times quickly, they say, yelling things in the door, but I was in my office and didn't see him. I'd assumed he'd reached some sort of equilibrium, and I'd moved him down the list as a problem that didn't need solving this week.

When he walked in today, I was in the lab, because Dawn and I were helping Jacobsen set up. Marcia had gone down to the coffee machine. He pulled out the gun and pointed it at Dawn. For a few seconds there was total silence. Jacobsen put his hands up, and his mouth dropped open. I had been extending mine, reaching out to him. I froze.

Pablo yelled at Dawn in Spanish. I signaled her with my eyes to be quiet, but it didn't work. When has anyone ever read in someone else's eyes the feelings that are there and not the ones she wanted to see? Dawn screamed right back at him, things that sounded really bad. Either she wasn't afraid and didn't think he meant it, or she figured that as long as she was going to die, she might as well tell him what she thought of him.

His hand was shaking as he pointed the gun, and he aimed it at her face like an accusing metallic finger. It occurred to me that maybe it was a toy gun—you know how you hear about cops accidentally shooting kids with toy guns—but it sure looked real to me. I wished a cop would come in and accidentally shoot him.

When Marcia walked in behind him, he didn't hear her. She was wearing sneakers, and Dawn was still telling him what she thought of his politics. Marcia was carrying her cup of coffee. "Puta!" he yelled. "Puta! NOW you no forget me!" He raised his arm a little, and it stopped trembling. The flicker that ran across our faces must have told him of the intruder behind him, and instinctively he turned his head just as Marcia flung the coffee.

She did it in two quick jerks—hurled the coffee against his neck, then slammed the mug down on his head as hard as she could. He fired. The shot caught Dawn on her lower face, the blood spurted, and she fell. Marcia had him down by then and was raising her arm again and again to bring what was left of the cup down on his sticky red-and-black head.

We moved. Jacobsen grabbed the gun, and I tried to pull Marcia off of Pablo. "Stop it!" I was screaming. "Stop it! It's not self-defense!" How crazy. I was hoping he was dead or at least brain-damaged, but I was scared they'd send Marcia to jail. Jacobsen called security, the gun still in his hand.

People came pounding in from all directions, having heard the noise, and someone grabbed Jacobsen, thinking he'd shot her. Dawn's whole desk was red and wet. A phrase came into my head from a first aid course long ago, three words about what to do for bleeding: "Apply direct pressure." I grabbed a lab coat hanging near her desk, wadded it up, and rammed it against the side of her head. It turned purple. I yelled at Marcia to check Pablo, who was also out cold. "Is he bleeding?" Alan Berg, who's an MD, took over for me, and then security and medical teams arrived, for once ready to take us seriously. The crowd just stayed, clogging the doorways.

In one bizarre moment Killington rushed in, throwing people aside, his face wild. He'd heard it was Marcia who'd been shot. I wondered for a moment whether he really cared or whether it was wishful thinking. We shoot people to make them remember us and to make them go away.

Laura Otis

We wanted to run down to the ER with Dawn, but the police told us we had to talk to them up here. "I'm in charge," I kept thinking. "This is my lab." I held it together all day, telling and retelling the story, doing memory gymnastics as they picked at inconsistencies between our accounts. The hospital people took Dawn and Pablo, and the police took the gun, but we cleaned up the blood ourselves, me, Jacobsen, and Marcia. I think I'm going to like this guy. I'm more in love with Marcia than ever.

Thank God for the phone. We've been on the line with the hospital most of the day. Pablo is fine, apart from a concussion and some mondo lacerations and a probable sentence of 30 years to life. Dawn is in critical condition, but they're optimistic. She lost a lot of blood, and some of her left jaw was blown off, but her cord and major arteries are intact. How evil we are to design machines that send balls of metal crashing into a beautiful thing like a human head.

No one knows where Pablo got the gun, but security is in deep shit for not having made him go away sooner. Everyone is congratulating Marcia. In the end she won the Waste Pablo Sweepstakes. When we were cleaning up, I found the pieces of her coffee cup. It had a fuzzy beast on it baring its teeth, saying, "Don't mess with me before I've had my coffee."

21:18, 14 AUGUST 1997
FROM: MARCIA PINTO
TO: LEE ANN DOWNING

LONG LIVE FEMALE RAGE! AFTER ALL THIS TIME, I FINALLY DID something with mine. I always knew the little creep was going to do something, but nobody believed me. Today I walk in, and he's pointing this gun at Dawn and Becky. Actually I never saw the gun, just their faces. They were scared to death—Dawn angry,

Becky pleading—you know that earnest look she gets when she's reaching out trying to make contact—but scared shitless.

I couldn't take it anymore. They abandon you or they terrorize you, nothing in between. Either way they end up wanting you dead. "I wonder how hot this coffee is," I thought. "Let's find out." I knew that I could take him if I got him by surprise.

I hope it wasn't my fault that the gun went off. Everyone tells me it wasn't, that he probably would have killed her if I hadn't done it. I'll never know. When I brought the mug down on his head, that organic crunch was the best feeling in the world—until I jumped on him and threw him on the floor and heard his head hit, which was better. They tell me I kept hitting him even after he was out cold. I don't remember that, only Becky grabbing my arms and trying to drag me off him. I never knew how strong she was.

Jacobsen, the new postdoc, grabbed the gun, called the cops, even helped us to clean the place. All these people came running in—Killington, even Killington came. I've never seen him look like that. Maybe he cares about me in spite of everything. Maybe someone has to point a gun at you for you to find out who gives a shit whether you live or die.

They tell me I won the contest, and already there are all kinds of caffeine jokes going around: "Now, honey, THAT'S great coffee!" Pablo has been wasted. The Caffeine Queen has made him go away permanently. Can you put that in your book?

Laura Otis

00:54, 15 AUGUST 1997
FROM: LEE ANN DOWNING
TO: JOSH GOLDEN
SUBJECT: FEMALE DESIRE
ATTACHMENTS: DESIREINTHEORY;
BOILINGTHERABBIT

HERE YOU GO, CYBERLOVER, TAKE EVERYTHING I'VE GOT. LET MY langue linger over you on this hot tempestuous night.

8:48, 15 AUGUST 1997
FROM: REBECCA FASS
TO: LEE ANN DOWNING

YOU CAN YELL AT ME NOW, BUT IT'S TOO LATE. I'VE DONE IT. THIS time I wrote to him first. You know what yesterday was like. I know you'll tell me I should have waited, but the urge was too strong. I invited him to come live with me. With maybe one second to live, I knew the life I wanted. He was in it. I want to keep doing what I'm doing, but our reasons for being apart are so insignificant. If he doesn't want to, if he chooses to be with his daughter, that's a good reason. But to stay apart because of money or time—what is money worth, what is time worth? I want to be with him at any price, so I made the offer. God, I sound like a university recruiting some professor. Okay, you can yell at me now.

YEAH, I THINK YOU'RE CRAZY. YOU'VE KIND OF DEFLATED ME with the anticipation. I know if it were me, I'd start to resent the drain on my time and money. Have you ever lived with anyone before? This is a high-maintenance animal you've picked, and you're a cat person. You won't be able just to put food out and then go back to the lab. Suppose you did it on a trial basis like in those magazines, free trial offer, your money back in full if you're not satisfied after 30 days. I mean, I want mine as badly as you want yours, but it's a whole nother thing if he's in your living room. And if he's there, what about email? You'll never be online, only on Owen—sorry, couldn't resist. Well, it's done. I hope it works out. What's he saying? Does he want to do it?

I AM OVERWHELMED. I HAVE ALWAYS KNOWN WHAT I FELT FOR you and known that you cared for me somewhat. I have tried not to think about it, because then I would have had to think that I don't deserve it. Flattered isn't the word. That's what you say when you want someone to leave: "I'm flattered, but ..." And I don't ever want you to go away. I don't deserve these feelings—but I want them anyway. And I return them a hundred times over.

I am very, very grateful for what you're offering to do, but I still have to think for a while. I'm not sure it's good to be that far from Jeannie, whatever the circumstances. And you—I don't want to be a burden to you, and I could be, at least at first. I know you too well ever to try to come between you and your work.

My impulse is to buy the ticket right now. Let's see: I could be there in four hours if I got on a flight right away. But I have to think. I don't know if it will help. Just look at my performance in the past six months, and I've been thinking out of control. But I have to try. I have to catch my breath. I'm so afraid of hurting you, the person I respect most in the world. I'm not sure if I'm good enough to do this.

9:32, 18 AUGUST 1997
FROM: JOSH GOLDEN
TO: LEE ANN DOWNING
SUBJECT: HOT STUFF

Leo, this is hot.

You've done it this time, babe, oh, it aches, this is so good.

Love your rage, love your desire, love to read you on the ram-page.

You write like a goddess, just needed direction, proud to have put you up to it.

Could always feel it in you, so hot it hurts.

Will tell Harvard to look at it when it's done if you want, they are publishing my web book.

Whatcha think?

9:33, 18 AUGUST 1997
FROM: LEE ANN DOWNING
TO: JOSH GOLDEN
SUBJECT: I THINK

You online? Gotcha at the water hole! You wanna know what I think, you get your ectomorphic ass up here. I'll give you thoughts, all the langue you can handle. Come on, I dare ya!

9:34, 18 AUGUST 1997
FROM: JOSH GOLDEN
TO: LEE ANN DOWNING
SUBJECT: TRUTH OR DARE

Okay, you vixen, you temptress, I'll play with you. Truth or dare?

9:35, 18 AUGUST 1997
FROM: LEE ANN DOWNING
TO: JOSH GOLDEN

Dare. You lose, you're here. I lose?

9:36, 18 AUGUST 1997
FROM: JOSH GOLDEN
TO: LEE ANN DOWNING

You lose, you place a cyber personal ad, I write the text. Look out your window, babe. Next plane outa LaGuardia, blue tail fins, I win, red fins, you win. I'll trust ya.

9:40, 18 AUGUST 1997
FROM: LEE ANN DOWNING
TO: JOSH GOLDEN
SUBJECT: TWA

RED, CYBERLOVER, RED, READ, READY, REDDI-WIP, RED BARON, Red Ball, Red bird, red wing, Masque of the Red Death, red, red, red!

9:42, 18 AUGUST 1997
FROM: JOSH GOLDEN
TO: LEE ANN DOWNING
SUBJECT: PLEASE

OH BABE, DON'T KNOW IF I CAN DO THIS. THIS ISN'T A GAME. Kids, please, Leo, my kids.

9:44, 18 AUGUST 1997
FROM: LEE ANN DOWNING
TO: JOSH GOLDEN
SUBJECT: CHICKEN, LIAR, CHEATER, WIMP!

YOU LOST, LOVER, C'MON, DARLING, YOU CAN DO IT, IN AND OUT, who will know, dontcha want it, hot, wet, deep, lips, langue, limbo? C'mon, Josh, I dare ya. You want directions?

9:45, 18 AUGUST 1997
FROM: JOSH GOLDEN
TO: LEE ANN DOWNING
SUBJECT: NO DIRECTIONS

No need, babe. Have had the way to 29 Blackwell, to your black hole bed, memorized for four years. Fuck everything. I'll be there in an hour.

17:32, 18 AUGUST 1997
FROM: LEE ANN DOWNING
TO: REBECCA FASS

Level 3. Mainlining, the hard stuff. I am shorted out, don't know how I'm even writing you. But I have to. If I don't tell someone, it's like it didn't happen. I have to baptize it, legitimize it. Hopefully you'll have an interest. You've recorded from him, after all.

He actually made it here in an hour. Even with no traffic at 10 in the morning, that's quite a feat. I could picture him streaking over the Verrazano, dodging potholes on the Belt Parkway. During that hour I flitted between the window and the phone, unwilling to believe he was coming, waiting for the call saying he'd changed his mind. I didn't believe it until I saw him on my front steps.

This was a new dose. It's one thing when you come together in a plushy hotel, a non-locus, all soft lights and mirrors with reality suspended, but it's different when he comes to you where you live. And there he was, the brown frizz, the sinewy arms, the silly sunglasses, the cocky grin, laughing at himself.

His grin faded as soon as the door swung shut. He grabbed me with a force that frightened me and slammed my back against it. "Leo," he said, "God damn it, Leo, you're fuckin' up my life," and he kissed me so hard it hurt. I clung to him any way I could, like a baby opossum to its mother, a reflex, and he kept saying my name, not so angry now, Leo, Leo, Leo, Leo.

I don't know how we released each other, but I know the first time was on the stairs. You have to go up a long, steep staircase to get to my apartment, and I'd gone up maybe three or four steps, my silk miniskirt flapping in his face, when he grabbed me from behind. I've never known anything like it, and I don't think he has either, the way he cried out. It hurt, and I didn't care. Somebody could have heard us, and I didn't care. My cheek was mashed against the edge of a stair, my nose and mouth were nuzzling the carpet, one of those whiplash arms had me around the waist, and all I cared about was that he was back inside of me at last, as deep as he could go. It was violent, rough, ugly. He cursed me, called me every name he could think of, Leo you bitch, Leo you vixen, Leo you witch. Why do all the bad words for women have "itch" in them, like we're an itch they have to scratch? Well, he scratched me good this time, the curses blurring into sobs and then a long red streak of human voice.

We did make it to the top of the stairs—to the bedroom, the first room you come to. He was tearing at my skirt, whipped off my panties one-handed. "Leo," he said, "you asked for it, oh, you asked for this, and now you're gonna get it." I dove into the bed before he could throw me there, and I tensed on my back, waiting for him to spring.

When he did, I was ready, and we wrestled. We have the same strength, the same impulses, the same reflexes, and we were evenly matched. Sometimes I was on top, sometimes he was, and I wriggled out. I fought dirty, and he alternated between laughter and anger. I butted and dug and kicked and jerked, and he grappled and grabbed and dodged and swore until at last he had me pinned. "Now I've got you, Leo, you little cat," he said.

"This is gonna be the last time, but oh, God, I needed this." He came inside me again. I didn't know a person could go that deep inside another person, seemed like he was somewhere near my kidneys, maybe near my rib cage, but I'd lost all sense of direction. He kept flipping me, trying to see what would let him go deepest. In the end he had me standing up, and he found the hall mirror where I've stood and looked at myself for four years, fantasizing about doing what we did today. This time my back was plastered against my own mirror, the world came and went in thumps and gasps. I closed my eyes, but he made me open them. He wanted to see them, he said, when it happened, watch them go black. I don't know how he talked. I couldn't talk, only cry.

I lost count after the second time. There weren't times, really, just one long bout, one long embrace and one long interruption. When I used my lips, his rage that had scared me softened to despair. He could never resist that, his favorite. I gave him a real licking, and he went incoherent, loved me, hated me, Leo, oh God, you're killin' me, Leo, more, Leo, more ...

He was finally inside, really inside, seeing where I lived, how I lived. He peed in my toilet in a bountiful gush and turned on my faucet so hard that the water sprayed all over. He tossed my stuffed animals in the air and fingered the perfume bottles on my dresser. But mostly we clung together in my bed, and he told me jokes, talked about work, people, books, politics. I couldn't tell him about desire or rage. They were gone, foreign, alien. I just wanted to BE as hard as I could, concentrate on every word and every sensation, store it up because I knew I would need it. He was pouring out, and I was drinking in. Probably we broke some kind of record. Who knows? People never tell the truth about this sort of thing.

It ended badly, with a thud, when he saw the pulsing blue figures on my clock radio. Stupid—why didn't I put it away? "Oh,

SHIT!" he yelled and jumped up, panicked. The traffic. Life here is shaped by traffic: 6:00–9:00 a.m. you'd better not go west, and 3:00–7:00 p.m. you'd better not go east—or over any bridge in either direction. As far as his wife knew, he'd been at school all day. Now it was 4:16, he'd never make it home for dinner, and he had no cover story.

I've never seen anyone dress so fast. He was fully clothed in the time it took me to get most of my hair going the same direction. His goodbye kiss was a slam on the mouth, and I heard his car starting below my front window before I realized he was gone.

I never got to say anything. I never got to tell him how I feel. I don't know how I feel. I've been wandering, dazed, around my apartment. There are crusty splotches of his pee on my toilet, and my bed is full of his smell and his hairs, long wiry ones and little curly ones. He sheds like a dog. I walk from the window to the mirror to the bed to the stairs and back, not believing, like the people you see on the news whose homes have been smashed by a tornado.

So I sat down to write to you, a chronicle, a tale, to prove that it really happened. I think it did. My poor, stinging, battered vagina knows it did. If I were a cartoon, I'd be lying with my tongue hanging out, *x*'s for eyes, and a halo of stars spinning over my head. I hope he's not feeling like this. He must be on the New Jersey Turnpike by now. I can't think of anything really. It happened. I think it happened. I had to tell someone.

20:42, 18 AUGUST 1997
FROM: OWEN BAUER
TO: REBECCA FASS

I HEARD JEANNIE'S VOICE TODAY! I CAN'T TELL YOU WHAT IT means. It's like hearing your own voice, but filtered, purified, all the bad stuff taken out and only the good stuff left, intelligence, perceptiveness, honesty, wonder. "Daddy!" she said. "When are you coming? It's no fun here without you. I want to play bear." I wish you could see that sometime. I'm the bear, and she tames me in various ways. She hides blueberries (blue marbles) for me to find, and I crawl all over the living room, poking things with my nose and snuffling.

No more living room now. It's disappearing in gulps as I sell it to grad students—Trish told me to. When she left, she took only what would fit in her car and one of those U-Haul trailers. I can't tell you how weird it is to live in an 80% dissembled apartment, especially when you have no idea where you'll be in a month. It's rented, says the landlord, to the couple who came through with the measuring tape. I'll be glad to get out of here. Every shadow reminds me of Jeannie.

I avoid home, and I avoid the lab now too, although I was there yesterday because Rhonda asked me to come and read the article. It's so good, it's unrecognizable. Dave always did write better than I do. I'm honored to be second author.

I spend a lot of time these days just thinking, walking around. Funny how wonderful it felt to talk to Trish, in spite of everything. She's accepted my acceptance, and the deal is cut, so we can talk now. She actually called me. She's back on autopilot, which for her means trying to help. I think it's guilt, retro-guilt about her easy victory. She keeps urging me to get out of here and move East. She doesn't want me back, but she still wants to take care of me—that's Trish.

I don't know what I want, except to see Jeannie and to see you again. I am thinking as hard as I can about your offer. I am truly moved by it, and I want to come, I do. But I have a responsibility to Jeannie. I am trying to decide what to do.

20:03, 21 AUGUST 1997
FROM: LEE ANN DOWNING
TO: JOSH GOLDEN
SUBJECT: COME OUT, COME OUT, WHEREVER
YOU ARE

STILL SLEEPING IT OFF?

Want a little bit more?

Say something, darling.

I am stretching, writhing, twisting, turning, sleek in the sun, waking up, ready for more.

Ooh, aah, a little bit more.

How about it?

17:59, 22 AUGUST 1997
FROM: LEE ANN DOWNING
TO: REBECCA FASS

HAVE YOU HEARD FROM JOSH? IT'S BEEN FOUR DAYS. HAS HE SAID anything to you? I am losing it here. The worst thing is the wondering. What is he thinking? Is he thinking about the mirror? Is he about to go into another renunciation cycle?

Then there's my body. A guy once told me, "You women, you have all these plumbing problems." Although I wanted to kill him, he was right. I have the most searing, stinging, burning, excruciating vaginal–urinary tract infection ever known to womankind. It's reached the point where you don't care about anything; all you want is for the pain to stop. I mean, it feels like there's a blowtorch in there, and it's cauterizing my memory of Josh.

Feeling the bubble, bubble, toil and trouble between my legs, I can't recall ever having had any good association with anything being in there. My mother would call this a punishment from God. She was always gleeful when I hurt myself, especially if it was linked to enjoying something. She never punished me, but she loved seeing me get hurt. I can still hear her laughing, "It's a punishment from God." The hangover principle seems omnipresent in the universe. Is there any sort of delight you can enjoy without paying in pain a hundredfold? And how can you judge the scale, since the pain comes only when the joy has ended?

It's an unfair match, a memory of joy against present agony. With your back plastered against the mirror, you laugh at pain; you're sure what you're doing is worth anything. And slumped on the toilet, staring down at your feet, gasping from the burn that comes with each spurt, you curse your lover, curse life, curse yourself, curse the principle of conservation of pleasure whose sum is less than zero. I don't see any way to judge intelligently whether it's worth doing something unless you have access to the pain and pleasure at once. My cyberlover and his virtual self in my memory are now equally inaccessible. Where, oh where is my imaginary friend?

19:30, 23 AUGUST 1997
FROM: LEE ANN DOWNING
TO: REBECCA FASS

IT'S STARTING TO LOOK LIKE A RENUNCIATION CYCLE. I MUST have blown something, shorted him out. Shit. If only he'd say SOMETHING, anything at all. If he just said, "Hi, I need some time to recover, don't write for a while," I could live with that. If he said, "Leo, ecsta— Looking forward to further interactions," that would be heaven. But nothing could mean anything. Maybe he's floating in an enkephalin bubble bath, and maybe he's saying "Nevuh again." This is torture.

Finally I gave up trying to tough it out and went to see my gynecologist. I had to tell him the truth: "It burns." He smiled. "Okay, let's take a look in there and see what you did." I lay down and spread my legs, feeling like a smashed-up Chevy. The hangover principle can be so humiliating. Do guys go through this? If sex is smashup derby, how come we're the ones who end up at the body shop?

Listen, can you help me out here? Could you prod him with a stick to see if he's alive? Tell him you made some big discovery about neuronal connections that you have to tell him about. Please, I'm dying here.

8:32, 25 AUGUST 1997
FROM: REBECCA FASS
TO: LEE ANN DOWNING

WELL, OKAY. IT'S AGAINST MY BETTER JUDGMENT, BUT WATCHING Marcia get treated like the invisible woman for months has shown me what you're going through. I'll think of something.

20:03, 25 AUGUST 1997
FROM: REBECCA FASS
TO: JOSH GOLDEN
SUBJECT: SYNAPSES

HI, HOW ARE YOU? I HAVEN'T HEARD FROM YOU IN A WHILE. I figured you were working through Edelman and our thoughts about neuronal connections, and you'd form your connections best if left undisturbed.

I had to tell you this, though: my student Tony made this amazing discovery. He's been collaborating with a postdoc from another lab who studies a gene for a receptor, and they're finding that a kitten blindfolded for just 10 days almost stops making one subunit of the receptor. They're really excited. It looks as though the connections are still physically present, but they lose the ability to function with no signals coming in. The gene itself seems to be affected, at least temporarily. Shut down the flow of information, and you shut down the ability to hear it. It's logical, just sad.

How is your book going? I'd like to read it when you get done.

7:12, 26 AUGUST 1997
FROM: OWEN BAUER
TO: REBECCA FASS

THIS HAS BEEN THE STRANGEST DAY OF MY LIFE. FIRST THIS NEW Swiss postdoc called up unexpectedly. He said Rhonda told him I had furniture to sell, and could he please come over and see it? When he got here, he looked appalled at the condition of the place—stacks of books and papers along the walls (the grad students bought the bookcases first thing), piles of clothes, only a sleeping bag, no bed. Then he bought everything that was left: the TV stand, the table and chairs, my desk, two beat-up armchairs, and most of the dishes. He said he'd come over later with some of the grad students in his group to pick it all up. They had a van.

His appearance jolted me, and I felt ashamed of the place. So I gathered up all the garbage (interesting concept, distinguishing the garbage from the good stuff—I hear dirt has been defined as matter out of place) and took it out, and I went to buy boxes. When I got back, there was a message from Trish: United had kicked off a fare war, and I could get a ticket at a great price if I bought it by midnight tonight. This was what I needed. She's always been great at that, giving me what I needed: this time a deadline. God knows, I have to conserve what little money I have left.

I packed things into boxes—book boxes, paper boxes, clothes boxes. It felt good, finally packing for real. For about five hours, until the Swiss postdoc came back, I didn't think about anything except what to put with what and what would fit where. The grad students carried everything out in minutes. They laughed and joked, filling the Swiss guy in on Rhonda, and they asked me what I was going to do. I told them I didn't know, and they laughed some more to cover their uneasiness. When they left, I could hear them in the stairway, filling the Swiss guy in on me. "Poor guy," I heard. "Wife ... Rhonda ... not renewed." I was their example of the worst that could happen, of what not to become. They would go to bed tonight and swear never to end up like me.

The travel agencies were closing at seven. I went on packing my boxes. As it got later, I was tempted to classify more and more as matter out of place. I let the agencies close and decided to call United myself. All these articles, other people's articles. Why did I need them? The iron. I can't remember the last time I ironed anything. Trish must have done that, but I never saw her do it. Maybe the Swiss postdoc could use it.

I thought of New Jersey, of Jeannie playing in the snow. Once she lost all her blue marbles playing polar bear. And I thought of you, walking with you and letting the Pacific wash over our feet. That California smell—eucalyptus, dust, and crazy Star Trek flowers that never stop blooming.

At 11:30 p.m. I saw all my possessions arranged in brown caramel cubes distributed randomly around the apartment. Then I killed 20 minutes throwing away the last few things that hadn't made it into a box. I would have to seal the boxes and address them—to Trish, to hold for me until I found a place there, or to you.

At 11:54 p.m. when I called the airline, I still hadn't decided. Would you believe it, they put me on hold for three minutes, even then? Maybe a whole bunch of people like me were bifurcating at the last minute. Then the music broke, and a human voice cut in. I told the voice I wanted to buy a ticket. She asked me when I'd be traveling before she asked me where I'd be traveling, and I said in a week—the deal is a seven-day advance purchase. "And where will you be traveling, sir?" In my head the coin was spinning, the Janus face. Newark or San Diego? Newark or San Diego? I was waiting for it to fall. "Where will you be traveling, sir?" Newark. San Diego.

In the end my mouth made the choice for me. I can't say I decided, just spoke. I'm not surprised, really. It talks. It eats. It kisses. It must know what I want. There was no "I" speaking or deciding. I just heard the words: San Diego. San Diego and warmth and water and your voice and your arms in the night. San Diego, the future, real time, and time that's yet to come.

As I gave her my credit card number, I was wondering how soon I could buy enough tape to seal the boxes. I could have walked down to the 24-hour pharmacy, but I didn't want to get killed, not now. For some reason, I couldn't call you either. I wanted to imagine you reading this on your screen. You have no idea what happens to your face when you smile. I wanted to picture you there in your office one last time reading me, but smiling for once instead of groaning. So I crashed among the caramels and waited in the dark.

This is the earliest I've ever gotten to the lab without pulling an all-nighter. It's tomorrow now, isn't it? I can go buy my tape. Call me when you get this. Now I feel ready to talk to you in real time. Want to meet a little girl who likes bears?

9:16, 26 AUGUST 1997
FROM: JOSH GOLDEN
TO: REBECCA FASS
SUBJECT: BY A THREAD

Bigfoot, beauty, good to hear your voice.

I crashed, every sense.

Big smashup, car totaled, broke my back, body cast, cord still transmitting, don't know how.

I screwed up real bad.

Talk to me, Neuro-Queen.

Tell me 'bout my cells, plastic, dynamic, encourage me.

Have accepted MIT—used injuries to win sympathy in negotiating process.

Wouldn't you?

19:07, 26 AUGUST 1997
FROM: REBECCA FASS
TO: JOSH GOLDEN

I am so sorry! What can I do? Good for you! You always seemed like you have a tough cord. Just DON'T MOVE. Your bones will grow back together, and your neurons seem to have escaped the worst of it. Tracts can take a surprising amount of abuse. I would guess your hardest job will be lying still for three months until you mesh. I bet you hooked up the computer the first day and extended the reach of your nervous system to compensate for the immobility of the meat, like Case in *Neuromancer*.

Can I send you any articles to read? Can I put you in touch with any neurologists, anyone who could answer more questions for your book? That's terrific news about MIT. I know a whole bunch of neuro people there. I can send you their addresses. How many people know about this? Can I tell Lee Ann? Or would you rather tell people yourself?

9:22, 27 AUGUST 1997
FROM: JOSH GOLDEN
TO: REBECCA FASS

SEND ANYTHING, SEND EVERYTHING. EDELMAN, GIVE ME MONDO Edelman, love Edelman.

I'll tell Lee Ann, don't worry.

You don't tell, do you, bigfoot? Like that about you, a semipermeable membrane.

9:38, 27 AUGUST 1997
FROM: JOSH GOLDEN
TO: LEE ANN DOWNING
SUBJECT: OVER

WIPED OUT ON BELT PARKWAY, ENDORPHIN-DRUNK, ADRENALINE-buzzed. Car totaled.

Broke one wrist, two ribs, three vertebrae—spinal cord, lifeline, mercifully, miraculously intact.

Beth hysterical. Am trapped at home, body cast, please don't write.

Somebody's trying to tell me something.

No more, Leo. It's over. This has been one big long mistake.

Find a nice guy. I'm staying with my nice wife and kids.

9:48, 27 AUGUST 1997
FROM: LEE ANN DOWNING
TO: JOSH GOLDEN

Oh, God, Josh! I'm so sorry! I'm so happy you're all right! I had no idea. I'm so, so glad you're okay, Josh, I love you so much. Please, can I still write? If God were trying to send a personal message to everyone who wiped out on the Belt Parkway, we'd be overrun with latter-day saints. I love you, Josh. All that matters is that you're still alive.

11:09, 28 AUGUST 1997
FROM: JOSH GOLDEN
TO: LEE ANN DOWNING
SUBJECT: INTELLIGENCE

Lee Ann, I am appealing to you as an intelligent woman. I do not want to continue this relationship. You are bright, beautiful, powerful, irresistible. You can have any guy you want, but not me. I do not love you. I have never loved you. Be fair. When have I ever said or done anything to make you think that? I love my kids, my home, my job, my life. For the sake of all concerned, I do not want any further contact with you. Surely you must see the logic behind this request. Please do not write to me again.

11:50, 28 AUGUST 1997
FROM: LEE ANN DOWNING
TO: REBECCA FASS

I am so furious. I am so sick. He's telling me he never wants to hear from me again. I know he's in a body cast, I know he almost died, and I know he was on his way home from my place. But to blame me—to use this as an excuse—as if this all happened because of me. It's like he thinks if he can get rid of me, everything in his life will be okay. He's going to load me up with every thought he's ever been ashamed of and shoot me out into deep space. He is so full of shit. You can't smite the hand that offends you without smiting your own hand. We did it together. I am completely devastated. If only I could see him. Can't he see how I feel about him? He almost died! She can see him whenever she wants, and he tells me to go away—permanently. I can't believe he feels nothing for me. I want to tell him the truth.

9:27, 29 AUGUST 1997
FROM: LEE ANN DOWNING
TO: JOSH GOLDEN
SUBJECT: LOGOS

WELL, THERE'S AN INTERESTING VERSION OF THE TRUTH. WHO the hell started this anyway? I was minding my own business, giving a talk, when you came to ME and stuck your tongue in my mouth. Do you actually believe this shit you're typing: "never said or done anything"? Every look, every word, every move you've ever made in my direction has been a thread in the text you claim you never wove. I don't care if you are in a fucking body cast, I know bullshit when I hear it.

20:45, 29 AUGUST 1997
FROM: REBECCA FASS
TO: LEE ANN DOWNING

LEO, BE CAREFUL. I THINK YOU'RE ONE OF THESE PEOPLE WHO should count to 10 when they're in front of a keyboard. You're so brilliant, but you're always shooting things out. Can't you force yourself not to write to him, maybe for just a week? Even with his cord hanging by a shred, he could still hurt you. He would too, I can feel it. He's invincible as long as he's connected.

We've never been in a body cast, and we've never been married and had two boys and made a recreational trip to Long Island, and we can't know what he's going through. I bet the immobility is driving him nuts. Hyper, isn't he? I could feel it in cyberspace, his twitchy energy. Maybe this is just another renunciation cycle. You pulled him out of it last time, and probably you can again. Let him heal. Let him feel clean and righteous while his conscience and bones knit. He'll be ready for you again in time. The libido is at the bottom of Scotty's repair list. Leave him alone at the starbase for a while.

Hey, big news from the hospital! Dawn is awake! They had to rebuild her jaw, so she won't be able to say anything for weeks, but she's going to be all right. Her face looks like hell. I didn't tell her.

14:00, 30 AUGUST 1997
FROM: JOSH GOLDEN
TO: LEE ANN DOWNING
SUBJECT: GROW UP

LEE ANN, YOU ARE BEING CHILDISH. WHAT DO YOU, THINK sticking a tongue into something is love? Shit, I stick it into mashed potatoes. You were minding your own business—"giving a talk" about lips and female desire, wearing a tight black suit, high heels, your hair loose down to your waist, and black stockings with seams up the back. What does female desire want, what is it there for? We both got what we wanted, now let's move on. Do not write to me again.

14:17, 30 AUGUST 1997
FROM: LEE ANN DOWNING
TO: JOSH GOLDEN
SUBJECT: MAKE MY DAY

YOU KNOW NOTHING ABOUT FEMALE DESIRE AND NOT MUCH about language. You're pathetic, retreating into formulas when you're scared. What do you, think I'll show up, think I'll send her a letter? Your definition of maturity: get fucked and shut up. That is not what female desire wants. I may not get fucked again, not by you, but I will never shut up, you can't make me. Just try it, I dare you.

9:20, 1 SEPTEMBER 1997
FROM: JOSH GOLDEN
TO: LEE ANN DOWNING

IF YOU WRITE TO ME AGAIN, I WILL NOTIFY YOUR DIRECTOR OF Academic Computing that you are using a university-sponsored account for sexual harassment. That is what this is. You continue to write to me when I have repeatedly asked you not to.

9:26, 1 SEPTEMBER 1997
FROM: LEE ANN DOWNING
TO: JOSH GOLDEN

KISS MY ASS, YOU HORNY, HYPOCRITICAL, PATRIARCHAL, hyperaggressive, self-righteous hack.

11:27, 1 SEPTEMBER 1997
FROM: OWEN BAUER
TO: REBECCA FASS

THIS IS THE LAST MESSAGE I'LL BE SENDING YOU (WHO KNOWS, once we're together, there may never be a need for email again), and it's about something you have a right to know, something I was going to do the day you flew to Germany. It's the day I was going to die. I have felt so ashamed of it ever since that I tried to cover myself. I asked you to delete it, as I presume you did. If only we could delete memories. This one is ugly, but you have to see it. If you're going to be with me, you need to see all of me.

Now that I've changed my mind, it's hard to explain why I was going to do it. I can tell you the words for it, but I can't convey a feeling I don't have anymore. I wanted to die because I was superfluous. I had no connection to anyone, wasn't an integral part of any structure. I was an inert element, forming no bonds. No one needed me, and I did no one any good—only harm, a whole lot of harm. Free particles are like that—when unconnected, they crash into things, cause damage. I needed to be removed for the good of humankind, so that I wouldn't hurt anyone anymore, or mooch emotionally off of other people.

How should I do it? Guns occurred to me first—after all, this is Chicago. But I couldn't imagine myself buying a gun, playing macho, admiring the specimens some guy laid out in front of me.

I would have burst out laughing, even though I was so depressed. I considered going for a walk on the South Side, but I had a feeling they don't shoot you there on demand, only when you want to live, when you least expect it.

Drugs. I looked around. Neither Trish nor I take any medications to speak of, and I could find nothing I thought would kill me, even if I took the whole bottle. Buy drugs? I wouldn't know how or where. I doubt if anybody would sell me any, I look so innocent.

I decided to take the train into the city. I thought I could jump off something, but there are no bridges high enough, and the skyscrapers are sealed at the tops. Not like San Francisco—there they practically dare you to do it. No, I would need to jump in front of something. I could jump off an overpass onto a highway. That could kill innocent people, though, if they swerved to avoid me and crashed into each other.

Then I knew—a train. A train could crush me without derailing, and no one would get hurt. I only needed to pick the place, someplace where there weren't a lot of people, so no little kid could see me do it and get upset. I walked for hours, thinking, picking my spot.

It was Memorial Day weekend, a spectacular day. There was a bicycle race, and I found myself in a crowd of people, herded along with the others. Loud whistles blew when a group of racers approached, and they shot by making a grinding insect sound. I found myself applauding. One racer caught my attention, a woman I spied just in a split second. She had a fluffy brown ponytail, but other than that, every inch of her was taut, sheer force. I caught a glimpse of her in a kaleidoscope of color, but I couldn't stop thinking about her—who she was and why she wanted to win so badly.

Kids were everywhere, yelling, "Lookit, lookit," little girls on their fathers' shoulders who made me think of Jeannie. More whistles, more racers, another wave of applause. Food was everywhere: Italian ices, hot dogs, pretzels, and I realized I was hungry. A woman thrust a free soda in my hand, icy and dripping, and I looked at her, surprised. Other than that, it was as if I weren't there. No one noticed me, and no one spoke to me. It was as if I didn't exist, and I was reminded of what I had come to do.

When I saw the 'L' tracks, I followed them south, away from the crowd. I found a spot that was perfect: well between stations, so that the train would be going too fast to stop, and out of sight from the street because of a long billboard. I walked there from a station platform. A few people looked up at me when I jumped off the end onto the tracks, but no one seemed to care. I could still hear the bicycle race in the distance, the cheering, the whistles, the sirens.

Then I heard the train. It clattered as it approached the station, screeched as it stopped, and paused while it was loading. I looked up at the sky. It was clear, deep blue, and the moon hung bleached and uncertain overhead. The tracks smelled of urine and tar. Someone had been here before me, and it bothered me. The train started up. I had to time it right. Spring, or fall? It was growing on the left, square, ribbed, and silver. Jump, or fall? The urine smell disturbed me. The sky was so blue. The train was a hundred yards off, and I bent my knees to throw myself forward.

An image hit me. We were at the Christmas market. I was behind you with my hand on your shoulder. You had stopped, enchanted, at a booth of painted wooden animals, and you had picked up a rabbit pushing a wheelbarrow full of eggs, a lost Easter rabbit at Christmas. The air was damp and icy, and they'd flooded the place with light to make us feel warmer. You were turning to face me, your hand reaching up to show me the rabbit, your mouth full of laughter, your eyes full of a question you were going to ask. That was all, just a simple living moment, and I wondered, why wasn't I seeing Jeannie? Shouldn't I be seeing Trish and Jeannie at a time like this?

I was flattening myself against the billboard, straining back as hard as I could as the train slammed past. I stayed that way, just breathing, for a long time after it was gone. I knew then that I couldn't do it and I wanted to live in spite of everything. When I found the strength, I made my way out of there, three, four ties at a time. I hauled myself back onto the platform, and when the people there looked at me with amazed disgust, I rejoiced inside.

I didn't care. I knew only what a fool I'd been. Integrated into a structure, what a thought. Life IS superfluous. Life comes into being and persists without anyone wanting it. Life doesn't care. Life is excess and collisions and bonding and releasing. Whatever life is, it isn't structure. What could be more stupid than destroying a life when you discover it doesn't fall into the pattern you thought it did?

I have been so ashamed, Becky. I felt so cut off, so alone that day. I wouldn't ever do that again, not even if you told me we shouldn't be together, not even if Trish told me I'd never see Jeannie again. The smallest sensation, the humblest thought on the most ordinary day makes it worth being alive. You at the market, your eyes in the night, Jeannie on my shoulders, that blip that showed my top quark was there for the briefest instant—I knew I could ask nothing of life, just be thankful for what I have lived and will live.

I thought again of that woman racer straining in the sun. A blue jersey. I think she was wearing a blue jersey. I realized I had five bucks in my pocket, and I bought a hotdog. When I'd finished it, I clapped loudly for the stragglers who were struggling by, and other people joined me.

I am leaving for the airport now, just as soon as I say goodbye to some people here. I think I'll even say goodbye to Rhonda, what the hell. Five hours, and I'll have the real you under my fingers, and I'll be living in real time, no more flickers on the screen.

All my love,
Owen

TRANSLATION OF LEE ANN'S FRENCH MESSAGE TO JOSH

An Arrow

When they write, prostitutes affect style and fine sentiments; well, the great ladies, who affect style and grand sentiments all day long, write as the prostitutes act. … Woman is an inferior being, she obeys her organs too much.

—Honoré de Balzac, *The Splendors and Miseries of Courtesans*

It's almost carnival, and at carnival, one speaks a new language. With you, I've discovered a new space: cyberspace. I am Alice in Wonderland; I have followed you down the hole. Here there are two levels of liberty: a new space; a new language.

They say that cyberspace is a utopia. I read that just the other night. How funny, this idea. They say that in cyberspace, one can satisfy all the desires of the flesh without sinning. But it's a joke of a utopia; it's a shitty utopia. It's a utopia where one can do everything but touch. Imagine, but not have. Play. It's the space of Tantalus, always the same story. One plays, but is there ever fulfillment?

Here is a new scientific poem. Take it. It's yours, it's a gift.

Tantalus

Desire, the force that drives all,
Seeks its own end.

We live as a capacitor,
Two plates aglow with charge,
Forever split by that purposeful,
Maddening sliver of space.

No distance, no energy;
No wanting, no being.
And the flash-flow
For which nature screams
Is the death of the circuit.

Oh, for that end,
The leap of charges, the collapse of fields,
The touch that blasts potential
Into nothingness!

But being, we bear the charge of the world,
And as with the demigod
Straining toward the sweet fruit,
Our sin is wanting.

"We," I've said. But I speak only for myself. All right, fine, I wanted to write about the "human condition." But I presume nothing. I can speak only for myself.

My virtual dream, it's simple. One dances slowly. One wears a dress of blue velvet, blue as midnight. One caresses the blue velvet everywhere, at last down below. This dream was born four years ago.

Don't be afraid that I'm crazy. A dream is a dream, and truth is truth. The dream: one dances, one touches. The truth: one is taken, one is happy, one is far away; one was already taken, and happy, and far away four years ago. I am a professor; I respect the truth. Tonight, I'm declaring carnival, but I won't write like this again.

Between the dream and the truth, a new space, a new language. There remains a space where one dances, where one wears a blue velvet dress. There remains a space where one sleeps, in absolute peace, in strong arms.

From my neurons, to my lips—no, that's another circuit, a parallel circuit. From my neurons, to my fingers, to your eyes. I embrace you.

Happy Valentine's Day.

ACKNOWLEDGMENTS

I wrote *The Tantalus Letters* in 1997, and in the twenty-three years since, many friends and colleagues have devoted time to making it a better book. I thank my colleague at Hofstra University, Julia Markus, who encouraged me as a writer and introduced me to her literary agent, Harriet Wasserman. In 1998, Wasserman showed the manuscript to editors at several publishing houses. At the time, an email novel was a new concept, but despite strong interest, no traditional publisher could commit to *Tantalus*.

In 2007, an earlier draft of *The Tantalus Letters* was serialized on the website LabLit, dedicated to the publication and review of realistic fiction about science, scientists, and their lives and work: https://www.lablit.com/. I am grateful to LabLit's creator, cell biologist Jennifer Rohn, for suggesting valuable revisions and for organizing the serialization: https://www.lablit.com/series/2.

I would like to thank the friends and colleagues who, in reading *Tantalus*, have kept me thinking about the characters and their exchanges. I am indebted to Michael P. Stryker for his scientific curiosity, his fine teaching and mentoring, and his frank and helpful writing advice. I am thankful to historian of science Peter Galison for his ideas about topics in particle physics research in the 1990s. I thank my colleagues at Emory University, fiction writers Jim Grimsley and Lynna Williams, for their thoughts not just on the novel's characters but on the writing. I am grateful to my friends Victor Anaya, Neil Bockian, Sarah Braun, Sander Gilman, Jim Goldenring, Herman and Anne Gordon, Jesse Moskowitz, Lynn Nyhart, Serena Reswick, Francesca Sawaya, Stephanie Schaertel, and Kathy Zahs for their input on logistics, scientific practice, and human emotions.

I am thankful to the iUniverse editorial, design, production, and marketing teams who helped bring this novel to life, including Check-In Coordinators Samantha Anderson and Jeremy Carey, Editorial Services Associate Courtney Wallace, Line Editor Kelsey Adams, Production Services Associate Reed Samuel, and Marketing Services Associate Nolan Estes.

The Tantalus Letters refers to or informally quotes brief excerpts from the following books, films, television series, and songs. These excerpts are not all enclosed by quotation marks and do not all exactly match the original texts:

Allen, Irwin, creator. *Lost in Space.* Irwin Allen and Jodi Productions. Twentieth Century Fox Television, 1965–68.

Beresford, Bruce, director. *Tender Mercies.* Produced by Philip S. Hobel. EMI Films and Antron Media Production, 1983.

Bainbridge, Merril. "Mouth." Gotham, Arista, and Universal Labels, 1994.

Balzac, Honoré de. *Splendeurs et misères des courtisanes.* Librairie Générale Française, 1988 [1838–47].

Bellotte, Pete, Harold Faltermeyer, and Keith Forsey. "Hot Stuff." Performed by Donna Summer. *Bad Girls.* Casablanca Label, 1979.

Bradbury, Ray. "Kaleidoscope." *The Illustrated Man.* Bantam Books, 1976 [1951].

Columbus, Chris, director. *Mrs. Doubtfire.* Twentieth Century Fox and Blue Wolf Productions, 1993.

Cronenberg, David, director. *Dead Ringers.* Morgan Creek Productions and Telefilm Canada, 1988.

DeFoe, Daniel. *Moll Flanders.* Norton Critical Editions, 2003 [1722].

Dickens, Charles. *Great Expectations.* Oxford University Press, 1998 [1860–61].

Douglas, Mary. *Purity and Danger: An Analysis of Concepts of Pollution and Taboo.* Routledge, 2002 [1966].

Edelman, Gerald M. *Neural Darwinism: The Theory of Neuronal Group Selection.* Basic Books, 1987.

Eliot, George. *Middlemarch.* Norton Critical Edition, 1999 [1871–72].

Euripides. *The Bacchae.* Translated by William Arrowsmith. In *Euripides V: Electra, The Phoenician Women, and The Bacchae,* edited by David Grene and Richard Lattimore. University of Chicago Press, 1968 [405 BCE].

Fleming, Victor, director. *Gone with the Wind.* Produced by David O. Selznick. Selznick International Pictures, Metro-Goldwyn-Mayer. Loew's Inc., 1939.

Freud, Sigmund. *The Interpretation of Dreams.* Edited and translated by James Strachey. Avon Books, 1965 [1899].

Gibson, William. *Neuromancer.* Ace Books, 1984.

Gore, Michael, and Dean Pitchford. "Fame." Performed by Irene Cara. RSO Label, 1980.

Hardy, Thomas. *Tess of the d'Urbervilles.* Oxford University Press, 2008 [1891].

Hytner, Nicholas, director. *The Crucible.* Produced by Robert A. Miller and David V. Picker. Twentieth Century Fox, 1996.

Joyce, James. "The Dead." *Dubliners.* Penguin Books, 1993 [1914].

Laclos, Choderlos de. *Les Liaisons dangereuses.* Librairie Générale Française, 1987 [1782].

Lyne, Adrian, director. *Fatal Attraction.* Produced by Stanley R. Jaffey and Sherry Lansing. Jaffe/Lansing Productions. Paramount Pictures, 1987.

Melville, Herman. "Bartleby, the Scrivener: A Story of Wall Street." *Billy Budd, Sailor, and Other Stories.* Penguin Books, 1986 [1853].

Miller, Arthur. *The Crucible.* Penguin Books, 1981 [1953].

Minghella, Anthony, director. *The English Patient.* Produced by Saul Zaentz. Tiger Moth Productions. Miramax Films, 1996.

Piper, Watty. *The Little Engine That Could.* Platt and Munk, 1930.

Pollack, Sydney, director. *Tootsie.* Produced by Charles Evans, Sydney Pollack, Dick Richards, and Ronald L. Schwary. Mirage Enterprises. Columbia Pictures, 1982.

Richardson, Tony, director. *Tom Jones.* Woodfall Film Productions. United Artists, 1963.

Roddenberry, Gene, creator. *Star Trek.* Desilu Productions. Paramount Television, 1966–69.

Rose, Bernard, director. *Anna Karenina.* Produced by Bruce Davey. Icon Productions. Warner Bros., 1997.

Ruben, Joseph, director. *Sleeping with the Enemy.* Produced by Leonard Goldberg. Twentieth Century Fox, 1991.

Shakespeare, William. *Romeo and Juliet.* Folger Shakespeare Library. Washington Square Press, 1992 [1597].

Shakespeare, William. *MacBeth.* Signet Classics, 1963 [1606].

Sharman, Jim, director. *The Rocky Horror Picture Show.* Produced by Lou Adler and Michael White. Michael White Productions. Twentieth Century Fox, 1975.

Stendhal. *The Red and the Black.* Translated by Catherine Slater. Oxford University Press, 1998 [1830].

Tauber, Simon, and Steve Rodway. "Ooh Aah … Just a Little Bit." Performed by Gina G. Eternal and Warner Bros. Labels, 1996.

Wind, Juergen, Frank "Quickmix" Hassas, and Olaf Jeglitza. "Another Night." The Real McCoy. *Another Night*. Hansa Records, BMG, and Arista Labels, 1993.

Wrye, Donald, director. *Born Innocent*. Produced by Bruce Cohn Curtis. Tomorrow Entertainment. Sony Pictures Television, 1974.

Wyler, William, director. *Wuthering Heights*. Produced by Samuel Goldwyn. United Artists, 1939.

Yeats, William Butler. "Sailing to Byzantium." The Poetry Foundation. https://www.poetryfoundation.org/poems/43291/sailing-to-byzantium. [1928].

Printed in the United States
By Bookmasters